Becky h...
she'd li...
touched...

She'd felt the warmth of his fingers, and she'd felt safe—until she'd realized she was playing with fire.

It was all so confusing. She shouldn't want to be near him, yet she did. She shouldn't want to care about him, but she couldn't help it. The truth was, he was a part of the fabric of her life, and that would never change. He was the only man she'd ever loved. That was why it hurt so very much.

She stood and looked at her son's face, with the dark eyes and dark hair he got from his father. She wished she could promise him that everything would be all right. But how could she, when she didn't believe it herself?

Dear Reader,

Welcome once again to a month of excitingly romantic reading from Silhouette Intimate Moments. We have all sorts of goodies for you, including the final installment of one miniseries and the first book of another. That final installment is *MacDougall's Darling,* the story of the last of The Men of Midnight, Emilie Richards's latest trilogy. The promised first installment is Alicia Scott's *At the Midnight Hour,* beginning her family-themed miniseries, The Guiness Gang. And don't forget *The Cowboy and the Cossack,* the second book of Merline Lovelace's Code Name: Danger miniseries.

There's another special treat this month, too: *The Bachelor Party,* by Paula Detmer Riggs. For those of you who have been following the Always a Bridesmaid! continuity series from line to line, here is the awaited Intimate Moments chapter. And next month, check out Silhouette Shadows!

Finish off the month with new books by Jo Leigh and Ingrid Weaver. And then come back next month and every month for more romance, Intimate Moments style.

Enjoy!

Yours,

Leslie Wainger
Senior Editor and Editorial Coordinator

Please address questions and book requests to:
Silhouette Reader Service
U.S.: 3010 Walden Ave., P.O. Box 1325, Buffalo, NY 14269
Canadian: P.O. Box 609, Fort Erie, Ont. L2A 5X3

HUNTED

JO LEIGH

Published by Silhouette Books

America's Publisher of Contemporary Romance

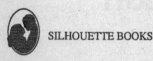 SILHOUETTE BOOKS

ISBN 0-373-07659-2

HUNTED

Copyright © 1995 by Jolie Kramer

Books by Jo Leigh

Silhouette Intimate Moments

Suspect #569
Hunted #659

JO LEIGH

is a relocated Texan who began her professional career in the motion-picture industry. After years of collaborative film efforts, she decided to strike out on the solitary road of novel writing. Much to her delight, she's found enduring friendships, generous mentors and a thriving community of romance writers. She loves to hear from readers. You can write to her at: P.O. Box 720361, Houston, TX 77272-0361.

This book is dedicated to my dear friends Venita, Peter and Vicki, for years of love and kindness.
And to Susan, Terry, Stephanie, Barbara and Debbi for their support, insight, input and, of course, laughter.

Prologue

The wrong man was dying.

Mike McCullough watched his partner from behind the washing machine crates. Gordon was lying on the concrete floor, not more than ten feet away, a dark pool of blood growing beneath his left ear.

It should have been me, Mike thought. *I should have taken that bullet. It would have been better for everyone.*

The warehouse was as dark and quiet as a crypt. The only sound Mike heard was his own labored breathing. Mojo had been silent ever since he'd delivered the last barrage, but that didn't mean he wasn't moving. The shots had come from across the cavernous room, the report echoing like thunder in a canyon. Mike had yelled when Gordon hit the floor. Yelled until he was sure Gordon couldn't answer him. Mojo could have run then. He could be right behind this pallet.

Mike reached inside his pants pocket and pulled out his wallet. He tossed it underhanded so it landed with a skid about fifteen feet from Gordon. Instantly, a shower of gunfire lifted the wallet and sent it skittering across the floor. By the time it came to a halt just inches from his hiding place, it was in shreds. It had served its purpose though. Mojo was behind the refrigerators across the way, deep in shadow. Mike knew there was no way to move from his position. He would be cut down in seconds.

He leaned back, rested his head on the stacked crates and tried to slow his rapid pulse. His .45 was in his right hand, the safety off, a full clip engaged, another in his shirt pocket. He flexed his thigh muscles, trying to ease the tension from standing so still. He glanced again at Gordon—no need to watch him dying any more. That part was over. All Mike had to do now was get his revenge.

The sound of a shoe squeaking on the concrete caught Mike's attention. He should wait. Backup was on the way. Gordon had called in their position before they'd entered the warehouse. Mojo was alone, with a limited supply of ammunition.

Seconds ticked by in absolute silence. Mike breathed through his mouth while he studied the black shadows that hid the enemy. It was cold, maybe fifteen degrees. Where was that son of a bitch?

He switched his gun to his left hand and swiped his right on his pant leg. When it was dry, he took the weapon back, curling his finger around the trigger. Damn it. Why didn't Mojo move?

Morris Jones, alias Mojo. Bank robber. Kidnapper. Killer. He'd torn up Boulder like a tornado, leaving pain and destruction in his wake. Two weeks ago he'd broken into the home of Colorado Federal Bank president Jim Greer. He'd held Greer's wife and child hostage while Greer took three-hundred-thousand dollars worth of cash and bearer bonds from the safe. The FBI had taken charge. By the time it was all over, Greer, his wife and their son were all dead, tossed on the side of a farm-to-market road like garbage. Mojo had his money, and the FBI had excuses.

Then Mike had picked up his trail. Gordon had tried to tell him to wait for the rest of the team, but Mike hadn't listened. Now Gordon was dead.

Mike leaned to the left, until he could peek around the edge of the crates. Nothing. His eyes hurt from the strain of staring into the shadows.

At first, he thought he'd imagined the sirens. But no, they were coming closer. Then the red spit of gunfire lit up the night, and he felt the impact of bullets smash into the heavy crates behind his shoulder. Ducking down, he waited as the volley of automatic weapon fire slammed all around him. He had just enough time to send his wife and son a silent goodbye. Then he hit the floor, rolling away from his cover, squeezing the trigger as he spun. He heard a scream, but he kept firing, aiming straight at the mouth of the gunfire. His arm jerked with the recoil as he used his left hand to push himself to his feet. He ran straight, the gun an extension of his body.

"Come on, you bastard!" Mike yelled, not able to hear his own words as the roar of gunfire filled the warehouse. "Come and get me!"

He nearly fell over Mojo. In the seconds it took to get his bearings, his mind registered the sirens just outside. He saw the Uzi machine gun near Mojo's outstretched hand and he kicked it hard. It slid across the floor, but Mike didn't bother noticing where it landed. He planted his feet wide apart and pointed the muzzle of his gun at Mojo's head.

"FBI! Mike, where are you?" The voice carried from across the huge room.

"Over here, Tommy," Mike yelled. "I've got him. Get an ambulance. Gordon is down."

Mike ignored the activity at the door. He focused on one thing only. That Morris Jones didn't move a muscle. The overhead lights came on, blinding him momentarily. When he could see, he wished for the darkness.

Mojo wasn't dead. He was smiling. Staring right into his eyes and grinning. Mike shivered involuntarily and straightened his aim.

"You better pull that trigger, McCullough." His voice was sharp and high, like a scrape on a chalkboard.

"Shut up."

"Pull it now. Do it."

Mike didn't respond.

Mojo's eyes narrowed, and the smile left his lips. "I'll find you. No matter where you run. You're a dead man."

It was dawn when he pulled into his driveway. All he wanted was a hot shower. He was bone cold. The heater in his Dodge had only managed to make him sleepy. His fingers were so stiff, he had a hard time gripping the door handle. When he stepped out of the car, he noticed the newspaper boy had already been there. Ice formed a diaphanous blanket over the lawn, made visible by the strip of orange sunlight at the edge of the horizon. It looked like it might snow.

The house was dark, but Mike didn't flip on the hall light. Walking softly, he shrugged out of his coat as he crossed the living room. When he reached the dining room, he listened for a minute. It was as quiet in his home as it had been at the warehouse. But there was a safety in this silence. His wife and child were in their beds, blissfull[y] unaware of how close they'd come to losing him. Beck[y] would figure it out when he told her about Gordon. Sh[e] would look at him with wounded, frightened eyes. Sh[e] would ask him again to quit the bureau. He would want t[o] say yes, want to please her. But he wouldn't.

He reached for the light switch. The first thing he sa[w] was the birthday cake on the table. God, he'd forgotte[n]. He hadn't even picked up a card for her. One piece ha[d] been sliced out—the *B* of her name and half a flower gone. The candles were still imbedded in frosting. Becky had baked her own cake.

On the walls, he saw pictures of cakes and party hats. All drawn with the fierce crayon of his seven-year-old. Bold black lines filled in with improbable colors. Happy misspelled. Then there were the photographs. All of happier times. There was Sam at his first birthday. Amy on a tricycle, before she'd gotten sick. Becky with a backpack in Estes Park. Him smiling.

He put his coat over a chair and cut off a slab of cake. Then he saw the envelope. His name, in Becky's handwriting, was written across the front. He sat. For a moment, he just looked at his plate and felt his stomach tighten.

He picked up the envelope and ripped away the edge. There was a single sheet of paper inside.

Mike, I can't take it anymore. Sam and I have gone to stay with my father. It's not that you missed my birthday. That didn't even surprise me. But I can't stay here and wait for you to get yourself killed. I can't go another night waiting for that phone call. I'm sorry. I tried.

She'd signed it Becky. As if he wouldn't know who'd just ripped his heart out.

Chapter 1

Two years later...

The second she heard the knock on the door, Becky knew something was wrong. She checked her watch as she hurried down the stairs. Her stomach tightened in a sickening, familiar way. Good news never came after midnight.

"Who is it?" she asked, standing on her toes to look through the tiny peephole. Mike's distorted features filled her gaze.

"It's me."

Mike? What was he doing here? He never came by without calling. In fact, he rarely came by at all. Becky's hand shook as she unlocked the door and pulled it open. The icy night air followed him in, giving her a chill that matched her apprehension at his late night appearance.

"What's wrong?"

He didn't answer. He took off his heavy parka and fur-lined gloves and hung them on the coatrack. His flannel shirt stuck to his back, and when he turned she saw a sheen of sweat on his brow.

"Mike, what's going on?"

He closed his dark eyes briefly, and in that split second she knew she didn't want to hear the answer.

"There's a problem," he said, his voice low and strained. He reached for her, then let his arm drop. He nodded toward the living room. "Let's go sit down."

She tightened the belt on her robe as she walked to the sofa, then sat facing the fireplace. Her mind raced with possible scenarios. Her father, her son—no Sam was upstairs in bed. Mike stood in front of her. She wanted to scream at him to tell her, but she didn't. It wouldn't make him talk any faster. She just stared straight ahead at the faded creases in his jeans. The foreboding in her chest swelled with each breath. It was just like when they'd been married. The terror of those late night phone calls. The dread that swallowed her each time he put his gun in his holster.

"Do you remember two years ago, the man who killed Gordon? Morris Jones?" he asked.

The name was so out of left field she felt off-balance for a moment. "You mean Mojo?"

"Yes."

Remember? How could she ever forget? That was the night she'd left with Sam. She nodded.

"He's escaped from prison."

She looked up. Mike towered over her. His tall, muscled body blocked out the light behind him and all she could see were the shadows of the man. Except for his eyes. She could see the dark pupils clearly. Black, penetrating, worried. He was frightened. Mike was never frightened.

Her hands started shaking, and her stomach clenched tighter. She didn't like this. Not one bit. "What does that mean?" she asked.

"It means I'm getting you out of here. I want you to go upstairs and wake Sam. I'll bring in a suitcase from the garage. Take enough clothes for a week."

"Wait a minute. What does this have to do with us?"

Mike moved to her side and sat down. She could see his face now. The worry there creased his forehead and she could see his jaw muscle tense. His eyes were the most troublesome thing, though. They seemed darker, some-how clouded.

"I don't want you in Boulder while Mojo is loose."

"I thought he'd been sent to Leavenworth. That's in Kansas."

"That's right."

"So, why do we have to leave?"

"Because he knows we're in Colorado." Mike's gaze shifted briefly to the V of her robe.

She wished she'd put on some sweats. It didn't seem to matter that they'd been divorced for nearly a year. When he looked at her like that, she still felt something, and it made her uncomfortable.

"Mike, I don't understand. What does he want from us?"

He said nothing. His gaze moved slowly over her face. He studied her so intently she felt her cheeks flush. She wondered if he could see the dread mounting inside her.

His thoughts were unreadable. That didn't surprise her. She'd loved this man once. She'd shared her bed, her life, her children with him, and even then, as now, she'd never really known what he was thinking or feeling. Even when she'd felt closest to him, there had been secrets.

"It's possible that he'll be coming this way. Not likely, but possible. He's a sick bastard, and I'm not willing to take any risks. You need to trust me on this, Becky. Don't ask any more questions. Just wake up Sam, and get your-self packed."

There was more he wasn't telling her. She would probably never know the whole truth. But it was very clear he thought they were in enough danger to warrant this incredible request. The one thing she knew above all else was that Mike was a good agent. His instincts had saved his life more times than she cared to remember. If he said they had to leave town, she wouldn't argue. She stood. "We'll be ready in fifteen minutes."

Mike felt the tension in his shoulders ease the moment Becky said the words. She wrapped her arms around her waist in a gesture he found familiar and sad. She seemed so alone when she did that. Hugging herself, seeking solace the only place she had left. It made him feel like hell.

He was grateful Becky didn't argue. That she accepted his reasons without too many questions. Now he could get her and his son out of there. Far away from the man who'd sworn to kill them. If he needed to, he would take them to the ends of the earth.

The letters had started a few months after Mojo had entered the federal penitentiary. At first they'd been about Mike. Personal letters about his job, his divorce, his life. In each one, Mojo reiterated his promise—he would track down Mike and kill him, no matter what.

It was the most recent letter that had brought him here tonight. He'd gotten it this afternoon, at the office.

This one had been about Becky and Sam.

Accurate, detailed and filled with the promise of revenge. Mike had no idea how Mojo had gotten his information. All he knew was that if Morris Jones said he was going after Becky and Sam, Mike believed him.

"Bring in all three suitcases," Becky said. "They're in the garage. We'll need them for the heavy sweaters and boots." With that, she moved toward the stairs.

He looked after her, at the long, lean body he knew so well. What had he gotten her into? She'd left him because she hadn't been able to stand the unknown quantity of his life on the streets. She'd run here to escape from the killers and the death. Now he had brought it right to her doorstep.

He got up and went to the kitchen. There was the clock they'd gotten as a wedding present, the silver set his mother had given her, the clay bowl Sam had made in first grade. They were relics of a past life, with no connection to him now.

After opening the garage door, Mike flipped on the light. Behind the Volvo, he saw his jigsaw and bench. She'd asked him to take that with him, but he had no room and no time for hobbies. The suitcases were stacked on shelves he'd built for the old house. She'd hired a handyman to put them up. Sam had asked the man if he was going to be his new daddy.

He grabbed the cases and went back through the house without looking at anything. When he got upstairs, Sam's door was open, but his light wasn't on. Mike walked in, and saw Becky standing just inside his room. She was still hugging herself, staring at her son as he slept.

She was a beautiful woman, that hadn't changed at all. No, that wasn't true—she'd gotten more beautiful after they'd split up. She'd thrown herself into school and work and the PTA, and it had been good for her. She looked years younger. Her hair was shorter than when he'd seen her six months earlier. He liked it like this, just below her shoulders, smooth and straight. She turned to look at him, her brow furrowed and her eyes full of fear.

It was like old times. Standing in the bedroom, afraid for their child. But this time it was Sam she was worried about, not Amy.

Mike put the cases down, and looked at his son. Sam looked tiny underneath the big comforter. He was on his side, with his fist curled under his chin. His dark hair was smooth, like his mother's, and so shiny it caught the trace of moonlight filtering in through the window. If Mojo tried to touch him, Mike would kill him with his bare hands.

"There's no other way." Becky whispered.

It wasn't a question. He crossed behind her and walked to the bed. Sitting softly, he put his hand on his son's shoulder. "Sam. Wake up, son."

Sam's eyes flickered, then he kind of snorted and moved his shoulder. Mike gently shook him. "Wake up."

This time his eyes made it open. "Dad?"

"You need to get up, son. We're going on a little trip."

Sam's big brown eyes widened, and his gaze moved from Mike over to Becky.

"What's going on?"

"Do what your father says, Sam. Get up and get dressed. Wear a sweater and put on long johns under your jeans."

The boy pushed himself up. He looked back at Mike, and his face formed a question, but he didn't ask it. He just got out of bed.

Mike turned to Becky. "You'd better get dressed. I want to be out of here in ten minutes."

She nodded distractedly. She looked at her little boy, then back at him. "Make sure he packs enough underwear and socks. And talk to him." Then she left, flipping on the light as she passed through the door.

Sam walked slowly to the bathroom, without saying anything. He was a quiet kid, although that hadn't always been the case. The older he got, the more serious he became. Mike understood that. He'd been a loner, too.

He looked around the room. It was comfortable and a little too neat for a nine-year-old. His desk was the only exception. It was filled with the odd treasures of boyhood—rocks and shells and plastic replicas of his favorite TV characters. On the bulletin board above the desk was a newspaper article about Mike from about two years ago.

His picture looked faded, and the bottom of the paper was curled.

The posters in the room hadn't changed since his last visit. A Tyrannosaurus rex still growled down from above his bed.

"Dad?"

He turned. Sam stood by the bathroom door wearing his long johns. He looked thin but sturdy.

"Are you coming back to stay?"

He'd prepared for every question but that. "No, son."

"Oh. I just thought..." He looked down and stared at his bare feet.

"We're just going up to the mountains for a little vacation. That's all."

Sam nodded. "Okay. Can you put my clothes in the suitcase? I've got to load up my laptop. I've got a game going, and I want to copy it to disk just in case."

Mike went to the hall and got the smallest suitcase. By the time he got back, Sam was busy at his desk, quickly typing commands into the machine. He was a whiz at that thing. Mike had come into the computer age so he could keep up with his kid.

He learned the details of his son's life through the electronic mail. He would turn on his old computer and go to the bulletin board. There, he could not only read the private messages just meant for him, but the posts Sam left for his computer buddies. The kids talked about school and games and baseball. Sometimes about their folks. It was a new world, this electronic community. It left Mike bewildered at times. But he was grateful for this window into Sam's life. Now, they talked to each other every couple of days.

The sound of breaking glass came from Becky's room. Mike shot down the hall and was at her door in seconds. She seemed to be okay. A picture had fallen, the glass of the frame splintered, that's all. He let go of his breath.

Becky leaned over slowly and picked up the broken picture. She turned it, and he saw it was of Amy.

"I didn't want to leave without her," she whispered, as she carefully slid the photograph from behind the shattered glass. "Now look what I've done."

He walked over to her and took the frame from her hands. "Don't cut yourself," he said.

She took the sleeve of her robe and ran it over the picture. Amy smiled from a swing set, her tiny hands gripped tightly on the chains, her feet dangling above the sand. Mike remembered the day he'd taken that. They hadn't known, then, that she had cancer. They wouldn't find out for months. "It's just a frame," he said. "It can be replaced."

Becky looked at him as if he'd said something wrong. "Did you talk to Sam? Did you tell him not to be scared?"

"What do you mean?"

"You're taking us away in the middle of the night, Mike. There's an escaped killer out there. Don't you think your son might be frightened?" The photograph in her hand trembled.

"Sam doesn't know about Mojo," he said. "He just thinks we're going on a trip."

"He's not stupid. He has to wonder what's going on."

"I'll talk to him."

"What are you going to say?"

"The truth."

She shook her head. "No."

"I'll make sure he knows there's nothing to be scared about. There's no way Mojo can find us where we're going."

"He has nightmares."

"We'll be with him."

She walked over to the bed and put the photograph inside her suitcase, between two sweaters. "Is he packed?"

"No."

"Go on, then."

He looked at the room as he walked out. There wasn't much familiar in here. She'd sold their old bedroom furniture and gotten this oak set. The comforter was full of flowers. There were flowers everywhere, even the wallpaper. He didn't know she liked them that much. He did recognize her needlework pillows, though. She liked to keep busy. That hadn't changed.

She had gone into the bathroom, and he could see her collecting her cosmetics, and he wondered why she cared so much about a broken picture frame.

He got back to Sam's room and opened the suitcase on the bed. Then he pulled out everything from the dresser—socks, underwear, pajamas, T-shirts. Becky probably would have been more selective, but if he took some of everything, it ought to be all right.

"Mike?"

Becky stood at the door. She'd gotten dressed in jeans and a large beige sweater. Her hair was pulled back with a scarf. She was flipping the pages of her day runner. "I'm going to have to stop at a bank. I have almost no cash. And I have to cancel my appointments at the hotel. I'm supposed to lead a PTA meeting tomorrow night, and Sam has his piano lesson. Are we going to be near a phone in the morning?"

"I've got money. We'll take care of the rest when we're out of town. You almost ready? Need my help?"

She walked over and stopped when she saw inside the suitcase. "I thought you said to pack for a week. There's enough stuff inside there for a world cruise." She didn't wait for an explanation, she just got busy.

Mike watched her move with grace and purpose, folding clothes in one fluid motion, packing so neatly it was nearly an art. He shook his head. It had to be a female thing. Women just saw things that men didn't. That's all.

"Help Sam get his schoolbooks together and take them to the car."

Sam was still busy with his computer, so Mike picked up the brown paper bag covered books from the desk, and the MTV three-ring binder. Sam finally finished and put the laptop into the carrier, along with an extra battery pack and a package of blank disks.

"Honey, go brush your teeth, then bring me your toothbrush," Becky said. "Then put on your boots. It's freezing in here, and you're walking around barefoot."

Sam gave Mike the universal eye-roll, then went back to the bathroom. Mike smiled, then turned to Becky. "Are you almost ready with that suitcase?" he asked.

"Just a few more sweaters. Why don't you take that stuff down to the car? We'll be ready by the time you get back."

Mike nodded, but he didn't move. He didn't want to leave his son's room just yet. He looked back at his picture, stuck up on the bulletin board next to an A+ geography test and an advertisement for a 9600 baud modem.

Then he remembered Mojo. The man was headed here. If he'd left straight from the Leavenworth, and didn't stop, he could be in Colorado in a day. Mike intended to be miles away by then.

The road was empty, Boulder was asleep. Marquee lights glowed over barred shops and traffic lights swayed with the heavy wind. A sheen of snow covered the street. Mike had the heater of the Bronco on high.

He looked at Becky. She sat very stiffly, facing straight ahead. He'd scared her. But there was nothing he could do about that now. He pressed the gas pedal down farther as they headed west. Checking the rearview mirror, he saw Sam's eyes were at half-mast. It was late, and he would be asleep soon. Good. Let him get some rest. It was going to be a long drive. Maybe Becky could sleep, too.

"We have to stop the newspaper delivery," she said, her voice hushed to go with the quiet of the night.

"There's plenty of time for that when we get where we're going."

"Where are we going?"

"Past Steamboat Springs, by the Utah border. I've got us a cabin in the mountains. It hasn't been used in a while, but it has heat and it's secluded."

"Aren't all the roads closed?"

He nodded. "I've mapped out a route that's safe. We'll be going on some maintenance roads once we get up there. It isn't going to snow tonight, so we'll be okay."

"What about when we get there? What are we going to do?"

"Wait till he's caught."

"How long will that take?"

"It shouldn't be long. This is precautionary. We've called in all agencies in four states. The local police are on the lookout in every town and truck stop. He's probably headed north, to Canada. That's why we're going west. They'll catch him."

"And in the meantime, we're going to be holed up in some cabin in the woods. Mike, I don't like this."

He turned to look at her. She was staring at him. Her parka rose and fell with her deep breaths. "I don't like it either, but we have no choice." He looked at the road. They were almost at the edge of town.

She glanced in the back seat, while Mike checked out Sam in the mirror again. He was asleep, his head leaning on the window.

"He's going to be confused," she said.

"He's a smart kid. He'll understand."

"He's going to wonder why we're together again." She sighed heavily. "I just don't want him hurt. He's been through enough."

They were climbing now, heading into the Rocky Mountains. Mike flipped on the brights and watched the curving road for deer. He listened to the sound of the tires on the pavement. He knew the kid had been through a lot. But he was tough. He wasn't so sure about Becky. "How about you? How are you doing?"

She didn't answer, and the seconds of silence turned to minutes. He heard her shift in her seat. Finally, she said, "I keep myself busy. The hotel takes up a lot of my time."

"That's good."

"I wish you saw him more often, Mike. He misses you."

"We talk."

"Typing to each other on the computer isn't enough. He needs to see you."

"I'm with him now."

"Is that what it takes to get you to see your own son? An escaped killer?" She'd whispered, but she looked back at Sam to make sure he was still asleep.

"I don't want to discuss this."

"The problem is you never want to discuss it. I don't know who you are anymore. All I do know is that Sam loves you so much it hurts. And you don't seem to give a damn."

He stared at the lines on the road. "You'd better get some rest. It's going to be a long drive."

Chapter 2

No one had said a word for twelve minutes. Becky had sipped her tea, Sam had torn open two packets of sugar, and Mike had downed a cup of coffee. But they hadn't spoken, except to the waitress.

The sparsely filled boxcar diner echoed with music from the tabletop jukebox. Mike didn't recognize the song or the singer. He shifted and put his arm across the back of the leatherette booth. Becky's gaze followed his movement. She touched the handle of her teacup, but didn't bring it to her lips.

"How's the hotel job coming along?" he asked. His voice seemed loud and intrusive.

"Fine," she said. "It's nearly done. I was supposed to meet with the florist today. The artwork goes up next week."

He nodded. "That's great. I bet your father's pleased."

"He is."

Her gaze met his, but only for a second. She studied her hand as the silence returned.

Becky had been the one person in the world he'd been able to talk to. She'd always known what questions to ask, and when to say nothing at all. He'd listened to her, too, and he'd known when to tease her and when to be serious. They'd lost that rhythm in doctors' offices and hospital rooms. There had never been the right words when Amy had been dying. But Mike remembered when Becky had been his best friend. He'd never found anyone to take her place.

"How's the bureau treating you these days?" Becky's voice was light and only a little forced.

"Same old, same old," Mike said. "Too much paperwork, not enough time."

She nodded, but didn't comment. She turned to look for the waitress.

"Becky."

She turned quickly back to face him.

"I didn't mean to scare you."

"You didn't."

But he had. Her smile didn't fool him. "Look, we're going to be together for a while. It will be a lot easier if we can talk to each other."

Her smile faded and she glanced at Sam. He'd stopped playing with the loose sugar and was staring up at her. "Don't play with the food, honey," she said, then she looked back at Mike. "Can't we discuss this later?"

Mike shook his head. "I'm not saying anything that Sam doesn't already know."

"I'm sure that's true, but I'd still like to discuss it later." Her green eyes flashed a warning, and her tight-lipped smile was anything but friendly.

"Fine. We'll just sit here then."

"Why don't we talk about school? Sam's working on a big history project, aren't you honey?"

Mike took a slow, deep breath. He studied Becky as she turned her attention to their son. She asked him questions, laughed at a silly joke, stroked his hair. It was so clear that she loved him.

It wasn't right to be jealous of his own kid.

Moose Lake Summer Resort

Mike read the sign and slowed down the car. This is where his new partner, Cliff, spent his summer vacation with his wife and kids. Their lakeside cabin would make a perfect refuge. The whole resort was closed for the winter, nearly impossible to get to, and the only person in the park was a caretaker named Witherspoon.

It was almost two in the afternoon, and he felt as though they'd been on the road forever. After lunch, they'd found a market and stocked up on supplies. Then they'd made the dangerous ride up the mountain. The roads were all closed to the public, and he'd had to take it slow and easy. He'd worked out the route using maintenance roads so the snow never became impassible. But he still had to stop a dozen times to remove chains and roadblocks, then drive through and put them back up again. It had taken a lot longer than he figured to make it to the resort.

Mike turned in the driveway and headed toward the lake. The sky was gray and the wind made the snow-laden trees tremble. He passed long, low public buildings and one- and two-story houses. He thought of hibernating bears, closed-eyed and silent for the winter. Their cabin was number fourteen.

"Is this where we're going to stay?"

Mike looked at Sam in the rearview mirror. "Yep."

"It's empty."

"It's a summer resort. No one's here."

"So what are we going to do?"

"I got the puzzles and the board games at the store," Becky said. "Remember?"

He didn't say anything. He just stared out the window.

The cabin was a two-story A-frame, like most of the others they'd passed, with a large deck that ran all around the structure. The windows were dark and draped; the white paint looked dull and chipped; it was singularly unwelcoming. But it was safe. That's what mattered.

He pulled the car around to the back and stilled the engine. Sam flung open his door and jumped out into the snow. Becky looked at Mike, her frustration at the situation, at him, quite clear. Then she climbed out, too.

Mike joined her, immediately aware of the quiet of the place. There was an almost unnatural stillness. No birds, no cars, no airplanes overhead. The only sounds were the crunch of boots on snow and gravel and the wind in the pines. He shut his door and a patch of snow from an overhanging branch fell on the roof with a splat. It did feel good to be out of the damn car. He stretched, trying to ease the kinks, but it was useless. Everything felt stiff and all he wanted was a hot shower and bed. Unfortunately, he wouldn't get either for a while. He saw a large woodpile at the side of the house. At least they could have a fire.

Becky walked with him to the back door, and when he unlocked it, she started to go in. He grabbed her arm and pulled her back. "Let me check it out first."

She looked over at Sam, who was packing some snow into a ball. "I thought you said this place was safe."

"Doesn't mean there won't be a spider or two around. I'll just be a minute."

Becky watched him move into the house. The long trip and the awkward lunch had made it clear that this "vacation" was going to be difficult. All alone, away from the rest of the world, she and Mike would be forced to talk. To share the cooking and the cleaning. She shook her head. Share? If this turned out to be anything like the last few years of their marriage, Mike would find some perfectly reasonable excuse for being late for dinner. He would be too tired to help with the dishes. He would go to bed early, and then the phone would ring and he would leave and she would worry the rest of the night away.

Sam was on the deck now, walking toward the boat dock. She followed him. The lake came right up to the rear of the house. In the summer it must be beautiful, but now the frozen water just looked forbidding. A chill shot through her, a cold shiver of terror. Someone was out there, somewhere, looking to hurt her and her child. Mike didn't have to say the words; his actions had told her the truth. He wouldn't have brought them to this isolated mountain unless they were in real danger. Would they be safe here?

Becky looked around the desolate grounds, and knew she shouldn't count on it. If Mojo wanted to track them down, he would. There wasn't a fortress strong enough to stop him. No heroes on white chargers would save the day. If she thought it would do any good to pray, she would have. Instead, she gave her word to the sky and to the trees that she would do whatever she had to, to keep her son safe. No matter what.

"Becky? Sam?"

"Over here, Mike," Becky called. She heard his boots on the deck as he came toward them.

"The house is fine. I've turned on the gas, so it should warm up soon. Let's get the bags inside, then I'll get a fire started."

"Look over there, Dad." Sam pointed to a treeless bank. "That's perfect for sledding. You think we could get a sled or an inner tube or something?"

"I don't know, Sam. Let's just get inside and we'll talk about that later."

Sam didn't put up a fight. He walked toward the car, his shoulders hunched forward, and kicked a fallen branch.

Becky waited until he was out of earshot before she turned to Mike. "Don't keep chasing him back to that

damn computer of his. Can't you see that he's too quiet?"
She sighed. "Look who I'm telling. He's just like you."

He stared at her, his cheeks ruddy in the cold wind. He
looked tired and thin, but he was still Mike. Still dangerous. The man used to steal her breath with a glance. His
brown hair was a mess and needed a trim. It was below his
collar and ragged. He hadn't shaved in almost two days—
she could tell by the length of his whiskers. She knew just
how those whiskers would feel on her cheeks. They would
be sharp and prickly, and he would rub her skin on purpose until she laughed and made him go shave.

She had to look away.

Mike went to get the suitcases from the car while she
moved inside. The kitchen was cold and it smelled from the
unused gas heater being cranked up for the first time in
ages. The room itself seemed familiar in a cheesy sort of
way. That same Formica dining table, the same torn plastic chairs she'd seen in a hundred guest cabins in the area.
There was nothing lovely at all about the room. It was
function over form, decorated in the fifties to be strictly
utilitarian. She wasn't the least bit surprised that the fridge
and the stove were that awful salmon color. Or that the
curtains over the window were so faded, they seemed almost white. But, she thought, as long as it all worked,
what difference did it make?

Becky heard Sam in the other room and she followed his
voice. He was in the living room, at the base of the stairs.

"There's a bedroom up there," Mike said.

Becky turned to see him in the kitchen, a suitcase in each
hand.

"That's where you'll be sleeping. My room is down
here," he said.

Sam raced upstairs, and Mike followed him.

Becky turned her attention to the downstairs. The furniture in the living room had been covered with sheets. The
whole place looked dark and spooky, like something out

of an old horror movie. She turned to look upstairs. In a moment, Mike came out empty-handed.

"Is there a washing machine in this place?" she asked.

"In the basement," Mike said. "The stairs are in the kitchen."

Becky flipped back the sheet on the couch. Beneath it, the sofa was nicer than she'd expected. A big pattern, white with large red flowers, good for a summer cottage, but wrong in the dead of winter. She gathered the sheet up in her arms, then plucked the others from the two fake-leather wing chairs. She ran a finger over the coffee table, and it came up brown. Once she put the food away, she would clean the house.

At least there was a big fireplace to warm up the place. The hardwood floors would probably work well in summer, but not in this weather. She wished they'd put in wall-to-wall carpeting instead of just the one long carpet runner.

She moved over to the large windows and found the cords to open the floor-to-ceiling beige drapes. The meager light from outside helped brighten the room a little. Not enough. It still felt stuffy.

"What the hell are you thinking?"

Mike's voice scared her and she dropped the sheets on the ground. He walked behind her and pulled the drapery cord so hard she thought he might break it. The drapes trembled as if they, too, had been startled. The room grew dark again.

"We're in hiding here. It's bad enough there's going to be smoke from the chimney. I don't want you making yourself an easy target."

"Don't scare me like that."

He lifted the edge of the curtains and studied the front yard. "We've got to be on our toes, Becky," he said, his voice strained and weary. "That's all."

"He's going to find us, isn't he?"

Mike dropped the edge of the drape. "No."

He'd taken off his jacket. His flannel shirt was open, and the white T-shirt underneath wasn't so white anymore. Over it all, strapped on his body like a prosthesis, was his shoulder holster with his precious .45 ready for action.

"I hate this." She kicked the sheets, but they just billowed a bit and sank to the floor again. "How did he escape? He was in Leavenworth, for God's sake. No one gets out of there. Weren't there guards and dogs and guns? Why didn't they just kill him?"

Mike took a step toward her, but she backed away from him. "Don't touch me. And don't you dare say everything's going to be all right."

"I won't let him hurt you or Sam."

She looked at the couch. In the dark room, the red looked like blood. "You shouldn't tell lies, Mike. They only make *you* feel better."

"Dammit, Becky. Stop it. You think it's my fault the bastard broke out of prison?"

"Nothing's anybody's fault," she said. She looked up at him, fighting the anger that was churning inside her. "It's no one's fault, but people keep dying, don't they? Well, not my son. So help me God, I won't let him take my son."

"I'll keep him safe."

He stood straight and tall, his hands loose and open by his sides, ready to fight. His warrior stance. Once upon a time, she'd found it the most reassuring sight in the world. But she'd learned how dangerous it was to believe he could fight every battle and beat every foe. "I know you'll try," she said, unable to hide the sadness from her voice.

"I'll do more than try."

She took a deep breath and let it out slowly. She studied his tall, fierce body, the determination on his face, the hard cut of his jaw, and she wanted to run to him. To fold herself inside his arms. To have him stroke her hair and tell her everything was going to be all right. But she knew she wasn't welcome in those arms. She never would be again.

"I just want this over," she said. "I want to go back to my life. I have to meet with the florist and the carpet man. Sam's got a geography test."

"I understand."

"Do you?" She bent down to pick up the sheets. "I'll go put these in the wash. Then we'll put the groceries away."

Mike was next to her then, grabbing for the linens, too. He touched her, his fingertips brushing lightly across the back of her hand, and the shock of it ran up her arm. She pulled back, but it was too late, the damage was done.

It had been a long time. It used to be that she needed the feel of his skin like she needed water to drink or air to breathe. It had taken her a year to stop needing him. To stop waking up in the middle of the night, alone and frightened. To stop longing for his touch.

She risked a glance at him. He'd felt the shock, too. He was still, like an animal is still when it smells danger. She wished she could tell him there was no danger here. But there was. It wasn't just about the madman out there, either. No one had ever had the power to hurt her like Mike had. And she knew she had that same power over him. That's why they needed to be apart. So no more damage would be done.

She gathered up the laundry as he straightened up. Then she walked away.

Mike watched Becky head to the basement door. She'd made her feelings clear—she hated him for this. Which wasn't a surprise. He was no good for her. They both knew that. The best thing was for him to keep his distance, for his sake as well as hers. Hadn't he just proved that? He'd touched her and she couldn't get away fast enough. It didn't matter. It hadn't mattered for a long time.

He stilled. Something had caught his attention, but he wasn't sure what. He looked around. Nothing had moved. Then he heard it. A high-pitched engine, getting louder as it approached the cabin.

He moved quickly to the window and pushed aside the curtains just a hair while he reached for his gun.

He saw the snowmobile coming up the road. The driver was taking his time. There was no way to make out a face behind the fur-lined hood of the parka. He eased the gun's safety off with his thumb. Logic told him there was no way Mojo could be here this soon, but with Mojo, there was no logic. He waited as the driver stopped the snowmobile and cut the engine. In the silence, he could hear the sound of water going through the pipes downstairs.

The man walked up the front steps. Mike tensed, lifting his gun shoulder high. Then the driver pushed back the hood of his coat. It was Witherspoon.

Cliff's description of the caretaker had been right on the money. Tall, whippet thin, a shock of white sparse hair. There was no one behind him. The scene from the window couldn't look more innocuous.

Mike breathed again, and cursed himself for letting his feelings about Becky get in the way of the job he had to do. It wouldn't happen again. He slipped his gun into the holster, then opened the door.

"McCullough?"

Mike nodded.

"Witherspoon's my name. Cliff said you were going to be here. Thought I'd come by and make you welcome."

Mike stood aside to let the old man in. "Thanks."

Witherspoon walked past Mike into the house. He eyed the place as if he were looking to buy it. "Now, I'll come up if the pipes are broken, or if the heat doesn't work. I don't think you'll have any problems, but you never know. The cabins are for summer, so I kind of let them go until spring. But you've got a nice fireplace here, and plenty of wood outside, so you should be warm." Witherspoon walked over to the fireplace and bent low from the waist peering up and into the chimney.

In a minute, the old man finished his inspection and turned back to Mike. "I've got a couple of snowmobiles that you can rent. When the storms hit, you won't be taking that Bronco of yours anywhere. Take out the garbage on Tuesday. There are barrels under the porch. I'll pick it up from there. Be sure and put the lids on tight, so the raccoons don't make a mess. Any other questions?"

"Where's the TV?"

Mike turned at the sound of Sam's voice. His son had come down from upstairs and was standing near the door to the kitchen.

"Sorry to disappoint you, son, but we don't have TV here."

"What?" The alarm in Sam's voice would have been funny if it hadn't been so pathetic. "No TV? What kind of place is this?"

Mike coughed. "Sam, this is Mr. Witherspoon." He turned to the old man. "My son."

Witherspoon nodded at Sam. "Pleased to make your acquaintance, and I'll tell you what kind of place this is. Quiet. At least in the winter. Summertime, this place busts from the seams. People don't miss the TVs when they only stay up here for a week or two a year."

"What about you?" Sam asked as he moved to Mike's side. "Don't you have one?"

He shook his head. "Can't say as I do. I've never been much of a watcher myself."

"Then what do you do?"

"I've got myself a ham radio. And I sculpt."

"Sculpt?" Sam looked up at Mike.

"I work with metal. Scrap iron."

The look on Sam's face told him just what he thought about sculpting.

"You come on by my place sometime," Witherspoon said. "I'll show you what I mean."

Sam looked down at his shoes, obviously uncomfortable with the caretaker's invitation.

Mike stepped forward. "We'll only be here for a few days," he said. "But if we have time, we'd like that a lot."

"Just so's you know, I'm not proud. It's been a long, lonely winter, and I wouldn't turn down a dinner invitation from you, either. I'm pretty sick of my own cooking."

Mike smiled. "Sure," he said. "Maybe tomorrow. And by the way, I'd appreciate it if you didn't mention us being here to anyone on that radio of yours."

The old man nodded. "Cliff told me not to say a word. I won't. What we've got to do is fix you up with the snowmobiles. We can get one now."

"That would be great."

Witherspoon walked over to Sam and looked him over like he was a side of beef. "You want to come, half pint?"

Sam looked up at Mike. It was clear he didn't want to go fetch the snowmobile. "Sam, I think you'd better stay here with your mother. Why don't you go downstairs—" he pointed to the basement door in the kitchen "—and tell her I'm going with Mr. Witherspoon."

"Yes, sir." He was off like a shot.

Witherspoon watched him run to the stairs. "I had two sons," he said. "Good boys."

"Had?" Mike asked.

"Passed away now. Like the misses. I just lived too long, that's all."

Mike felt a knot in the pit of his stomach, but he shook it off. Now was no time to start feeling sorry for some old man. He had enough problems of his own. He grabbed his parka from the couch. "If you don't mind, I'd like to get a move on. We still haven't unpacked."

"Sure, sure. It will only take a minute." He pulled up the hood of his parka and his face disappeared behind fur. The old man left and Mike went to the kitchen. He heard footsteps on the stairs, and soon he saw Becky.

"What's this?"

"I'm going to get the snowmobile from the caretaker. I'll only be gone a little while."

Becky looked behind her to make sure Sam wasn't around. "I don't want to be here alone. What if—?"

"There's no way he could be here this soon, even if he did know where we were. Which he doesn't. I want to get this over with. We might need the mobility."

She didn't look happy about it. "Sam says the old man is creepy."

"Not creepy. Lonely. He was trying to be friendly."

"I don't like this, Mike. I don't like the idea of you leaving."

"I would never go if I thought you were in any danger. You know that." He zipped up his parka and put on his gloves. "I'll make this as quick as I can."

He had the urge to touch her, to make her look into his eyes to see she had no reason to be afraid. Not yet, at least. But he kept his hands to himself. "Just lock up behind me."

He walked to the door and went out.

Becky followed him and set the dead bolt. She leaned her head against the cold wood. She felt as if she were living in a nightmare. What was she doing here? She should be home. She should be cooking the turkey she'd taken out of the freezer. There were the drawings she wanted to do for the florist, and she was supposed to confirm Sam's field trip chaperons. There were a million things to do, none of which included hiding in a cabin with Mike. Damn him for dragging them into this. Damn his job and his guns and his madmen. He had no right.

"Geez, Mom. That guy was such a goober."

Becky spun around. She hadn't heard Sam come up the stairs. Her heart was racing and she took a deep breath to calm herself down. "Don't say things like that."

"I only said goober. I can't believe there's no TV. How long do we have to stay here, anyway?"

"I don't know."

Sam moved to the couch and sat down. "You think they'll catch that guy soon?"

Becky was only a little surprised that Sam knew. He was a bright kid, and they hadn't been completely discreet. She only hoped he didn't realize the depth of the danger they were all in. "I don't know that, either, Sam. But if you're worried about this, don't keep it to yourself. Talk to me or your dad."

He nodded. "I'm not worried about anything but dying of boredom."

Becky studied her son as she walked over to the sofa. She saw so much of Mike in the boy. Not just his looks, but in his quiet ways. He hardly had any friends, just those computer ghosts. Every time she tried to get Sam involved in activities with other kids, he resisted. When he did go, he hardly said two words. The last thing she needed was for him to be scared that some maniac was coming to get him.

"Have you set up your computer yet?"

"I can't find a phone plug for the modem." His eyes widened with horror. "They have phones here, don't they? I mean, come on. No TV, no phones. I'm in the middle of a game with Warren, and I haven't answered any of my e-mail."

Becky walked over to the staircase. "Let's go see what we can find before we panic, okay?"

Sam shot up from the couch and passed her on the stairs. Why couldn't he use some of that energy to play ball or ice skate?

The second floor wasn't large, just one room with two single beds and a tall dresser. Sam was looking at the baseboards for a phone jack. Becky thought about the layout of the room, and figured there were only a few places to wire for phones. She walked to the bed where Sam had piled his stuff and moved it aside.

"Hey, kiddo. Look what I found."

Sam was next to her in a flash. "Cool." He unzipped his computer case and pulled out a telephone wire. He handed one end to Becky and he plugged the other end into a slot on the side of his computer. Becky hooked him up, then moved some sweaters aside so she could sit next to him.

"Got it." Sam typed in his password. In a moment, he was in the bulletin board itself.

It was an incredible thing, really, this nationwide communication system. A user could talk "live" with one or a hundred other like-minded people either one-on-one, or in a "real-time conference."

Mike and Sam talked privately. Mike would log on to the computer and write to Sam to ask about school and his friends. Sam would get the message when he got home from school and write back. They'd repeat the process every couple of days.

She supposed it was better than nothing, but she wished Mike would use the real phone more often. Sam needed him. Not some disconnected words on a computer screen.

She looked over Sam's shoulder. A long letter was scrolling quickly by. "Who's that from?"

"Darrelyn."

"A new friend?"

Sam shook his head. "I've known her for a long time. She's not like most girls. She's into computers and science fiction. She lives in Denver."

"I see." Becky wasn't all that surprised to find Sam had connected with a girl. Most nine-year-old girls were more sensible than their male counterparts, and Sam was nothing if not sensible.

"Her parents are divorced," Sam said.

"That happens to a lot of people."

Sam's fingers stilled on the keyboard and he looked up at her. She thought he might say something about her divorce from Mike, but he didn't. Not out loud. Only his eyes asked "Why?"

"Come on, kiddo. You can talk to Darrelyn later. I want to play a game."

Sam frowned. "You never want to play my games."

"I do today. Come on. Teach me."

Sam sighed. He signed off from the bulletin board, then reached once more for his computer case. This time he got out two joysticks and handed one to Becky.

"How much you want to bet I can beat the pants off you?" she asked.

"Ha. No way."

She smiled. At least this would keep him busy, she thought. If he's busy, he won't think. He won't be scared. She turned her attention to the game.

Chapter 3

Sam had 124,000 points. Becky had 345. She tried to concentrate and shoot down the little triangles, but she kept thinking she heard the snowmobile. It was hard not to shush Sam, to keep smiling, to do anything but run downstairs and wait by the door. Every little noise made her jump. She was tense, and she could feel the beginning of a headache. If only Mike would come back.

"Mom, can't you move faster? You have to keep hitting the button all the time, that's why you keep getting zapped. Look." He held up his joystick so she could see his nimble fingers at work.

"Give me a break," she said. "I'm new at this."

He lowered his hand and concentrated on his battle. In seconds, he'd wiped out a whole battalion of space monsters. She kept hitting the buttons, but she turned her attention from the game to her son.

He chewed on his lower lip while he struggled against the forces of evil. His brown eyes skittered across the screen with absolute concentration. She envied him. She wished she could find something that would swallow her up so completely. God knows she tried. Despite her work at the hotel, the PTA, the city council and everything else she could fit into her life, she still managed to have too much time to think.

She heard another sound and listened as hard as she could. It wasn't an engine. It was the wind, and she sagged with disappointment. Her back started to hurt from sitting at an angle on the bed. She shifted a bit, then forced herself to look at the game again. Explosions filled the screen as Sam moved faster and faster. She stopped pressing her buttons and just watched him.

The need to protect him surged through her. He was her baby, her only living child, and she would do anything to keep him safe. The only problem was, her best might not be enough. It hadn't been for her daughter.

Night after night, she'd begged a silent God to give her the cancer and leave Amy alone. Her prayers had not been answered, and she'd been forced to sit by and watch as her little girl died. There was nothing on earth worse than that feeling of helplessness, and now it was back. The only thing she had learned from Amy's death was the uselessness of asking why. It had taken her far too long to learn it was an unanswerable question.

She remembered the hospital room, the single bed with the heavy guard rails on the side. The smell of disinfectant. The squeak of rubber shoes on the linoleum. Mostly she remembered how tiny Amy had looked. How every whimper had slashed through her like a knife.

She stood up, nearly knocking the computer from Sam's lap.

"Hey!"

"Sorry, honey. You're going to have to finish this game alone. Daddy's going to be back any second, and I haven't put away the groceries yet."

His hands stilled on the joystick as he stared up at her. "Can't you do that later?"

She reached out and touched his cheek, the skin so soft it nearly made her weep. "When your father comes back, I bet he'll play with you."

Sam nodded, and she thought she heard him sigh. He put the joystick down, and typed on the keyboard.

"You don't want to finish? You were doing great."

"It's no fun alone."

She felt terrible. She debated sitting down again, but she just couldn't. She had to move and do something or she would scream. Where the hell was Mike?

"You can come down and help me," she said.

Sam shook his head. He kept his eyes on the computer screen. "No, thanks."

"Okay. I'll call you as soon as your dad gets here."

Becky walked slowly down the stairs. She promised herself that she would spend time with him tonight. They wouldn't play on the computer, though. She hated it, and he loved it too much. She wouldn't forbid him to use the thing, but she would encourage other activities. If only he could go outside, she thought. He needed to be with Mike doing guy stuff in the snow.

Before going into the kitchen, she stole a quick look out the front window. Nothing but the branches moved outside. Everything looked clean and beautiful and peaceful. It should have been relaxing, but all she could think of were the hundreds of places Mojo could hide. The house across the street. Any of the houses. How hard would it be to break into a summer cabin?

She let go of the drape and hurried into the kitchen. The grocery bags were still on the countertops. She would put away the things that needed refrigeration, but that was all. It was getting dark out, and she needed to fix something for dinner. Why wasn't Mike back yet?

As she folded an empty bag, she remembered she hadn't finished the laundry. After she put the milk in the fridge, she went downstairs. It only took a few minutes to transfer the wet sheets to the dryer. She didn't like being in the basement. It was too far away from Sam. The single overhead light bulb wasn't bright enough, and shadows filled the room. She kept thinking she saw something move, but then she'd turn and nothing was there. She finished as quickly as she could and went back upstairs. As she shut the door, she heard the snowmobile. She froze, afraid she'd conjured the sound, but no. It really was Mike.

Relief flooded through her, and only then did she understand how frightened she'd been of being alone. How was she going to get through days of this? The second Mike was inside, she would insist that he call his office. Maybe they'd caught Mojo.

The engine noise got louder as she went to the staircase. "Sam," she called. "Daddy's back." She went to the kitchen and waited by the door. Mike parked the snowmobile by the Bronco. When he reached the porch, she unlocked the dead bolt.

A wave of déjà vu washed over her. She was in her old house, and Mike was coming home from yet another dangerous night in the field. Fear and anger roiled inside her, battling for dominance.

The memory slipped away, but the feelings didn't. She'd spent so much of her life worrying about him, thinking he'd been killed. The night she'd left him, she'd sworn never to go through that again.

She opened the door, and the freezing air entered before he did. Mike's parka was dotted with snow. He took off his heavy gear as she slipped the dead bolt closed.

When she turned around, he was peeling off his gloves as he headed for the living room.

"Everything okay?" he asked.

"No," she said, following him. She hated that he sounded so calm. "I thought you said it would only be a few minutes."

He tossed his gloves on the couch, alongside his parka and face mask. "I was as quick as I could be. Witherspoon's cabin is over a mile away."

She folded her arms across her chest. "You're not leaving us alone again. Not until Mojo is caught."

He walked closer to her. His hair was a mess from the snow gear. His skin should have been chapped from the cold, but it wasn't. Even with practically no sleep, and being out in the freezing weather, he looked rugged and sexy. It was absurd to think about that now, but when he was this close, it was hard to ignore.

"I'm going to have to go out one more time," he said. "But that's all. I promise."

"Tonight?" The panic started low in her stomach. "Why?"

He shook his head. "Tomorrow morning. I have to make sure I know the back way out of here. According to the old man, there's a fire access road that leads to the highway, but he hasn't been on it this winter. I have to make sure we can make it out of here if we have to."

"Take us with you."

"I can't. I'll be on the snowmobile."

"If only one of us can fit on it, what good is it? If Mojo gets here, we all have to leave."

"I know. Witherspoon has another one in his garage. I'll get that one, too. If it comes down to that, Sam will ride with me, and you'll take the second one."

"I've never driven one before."

"You'll do fine. There's nothing to it. If you want, you can practice on it in the morning."

"All I want is for this to be over. Can you call and find out if they've caught him yet?"

"Sure," he said, as he ran a hand through his hair. "Did you tell Sam I'm back?"

She nodded.

"Why don't you go check on him while I call Cliff?"

He probably didn't want her listening in. Well, she wasn't going to argue. All she needed to know was that Mojo was caught . . . or dead.

Mike swore into the phone. "What the hell happened?"

"We lost him in Limon. He ditched his car. We're pretty sure he had help from the outside."

"Do you have men covering Becky's house?"

"Two."

"Go there yourself, Cliff. That's where you'll find him."

His partner didn't say anything for a minute. "I don't think so, buddy."

"Why?"

"There was a map in the car. He's headed to Canada."

Mike stood up and walked to the bedroom door, checking the lock one more time. He didn't want Becky or Sam to come in now. "You can't believe he's stupid enough to leave a map? That's a plant. He wants you to think he's going to Canada."

"We're not eliminating that as a possibility, but I can't make the chief commit all the guys just on your hunch. They believe he's trying to get out of the country."

"Did you tell them about the last letter?"

"Yep. Don't get me wrong. They're taking his threats seriously. They just can't be sure he's headed toward Boulder."

"Then screw 'em. You go to Becky's place. I know he'll show up there. He has to."

Mike heard Cliff sigh. "You think you could keep me away? Buddy, you just tell me where, and I'm there."

Mike swallowed. "I know, Cliff."

"I'll talk to you." Cliff hung up.

Mike put down the phone. He hadn't realized how much he'd counted on them catching Mojo quickly. Somewhere in the back of his mind, he'd assumed this would all be over by now. Wishful thinking. Every moment Mojo was on the loose was dangerous. Thank God they were listening to him about the letter. He would feel better if the whole force was going to Becky's, but he trusted Cliff to make sure there would be enough men. If there ever could be enough men to stop Morris Jones.

He went over to his duffel bag and pushed his clothes out of the way until he found the stack of papers on the bottom. There were twenty-two letters, each one a window into a madman's mind. The way to catch Mojo was right here in his hand. He just had to be clever enough to figure it out.

He sat on the bed and listened to the wind outside. It sounded stronger than it had when he'd been on the snowmobile. Witherspoon had said a storm was coming.

Mike unfolded the top page. The first one. White paper, no lines. No watermark. Prison stock. The typewriter was old, and the *o*'s and *t*'s blurred, but it was legible.

Dear Mike,
I feel as if I know you well enough to call you Mike. I mean, shooting someone creates a bond, don't you think? And how is the wound, you ask? Not healing well, my friend. Not well at all.

But, this letter is not about me.

I've been hearing things about you, Mike. You have many friends, it seems. Most, sadly, behind bars, but then that is your specialty. I've been trying to understand what it is that makes you feel the need to hide behind your badge. I considered the small man complex, Napoleon's cross, but you're quite a big fellow, so that doesn't fit. Then, of course, there is the, how shall I say it, "inadequate" man's syndrome—the urge to substitute a long weapon for... Need I spell it out? If that's the case, there's really nothing I can do to help.

Regardless, friend, I do think about you. Your face is never far from my dreams, your death is my tonic. Why didn't you pull the trigger when you had the chance?

The knock on the door startled him and he dropped the letter. "Yeah?"

"Mom needs you in the kitchen, Dad."

"I'll be right out."

He picked up the paper and folded it in thirds, then put it with the others. He would read the rest tonight, after Becky and Sam were in bed. He was positive there was something in those words that would point the way to Mojo's capture.

For now, though, he would go out and be with his son. He would act as if there was nothing in the world to worry about. If he were lucky, Becky would buy it, too.

He made his way into the kitchen, and stopped when he saw her at the stove. Her back was to him, and she was pouring something into a pot. Her head tilted to the right, and he knew she had captured her lower lip in her teeth. She always did when she concentrated. He used to sit and watch her when she worked at the house. He'd memorized that move, the little bite on her bottom lip. He'd tried like hell to erase that image, that and a hundred others. But every time he looked at her, it all came back, pouring over him like floodwaters.

She turned, and studied his face. "What did they say?"

He looked around for Sam.

"He's upstairs."

Mike turned back to her. "They don't have him yet."

She leaned against the sink as if her legs couldn't hold her. He moved to help her, but she waved him away.

"Do they know where he is?"

He debated whether he should tell her everything, but looking at her, vulnerable, scared to death, he just couldn't. "Yeah. They'll have him soon."

She pushed her hair behind her ear. "I want to believe you," she said. Her gaze met his in a silent plea. But he had no reassurance, no promise that would make her feel better. After a long, quiet moment, she let her gaze drop. "Would you set the table please?" She pointed to a drawer by the sink. "Silverware is in there. Make sure they're clean."

He got busy, and they fell into silence. He was acutely aware of just how small the kitchen was. He stood right next to her, trying to reach for the glasses. He caught her soft scent, and everything else was forgotten. "You're wearing that rose perfume."

She didn't step away. She just kept stirring the pasta. "I had it on last night."

"Before I came over?" He tried to catch her gaze, but she wouldn't look at him.

"Yes," she whispered.

He didn't believe her. He touched her shoulder, and when she didn't back away, he moved his fingers to the back of her neck. The feel of her skin was familiar, like coming home. She wore the roses for him. She always had. The perfume had been a gift. Not for any special occasion. Just because.

If he moved closer, she would know what the smell of her and the touch of her were doing to him. He closed the distance between their bodies, moving his hand to her cheek.

"No." She stepped away, breaking the contact between them. "Don't."

Where he was and who he was crashed in on him with those two words. He backed off quickly, angry that he'd gotten so carried away. He fought to bring his body under control. He had no right to touch her. No right at all.

She turned to look at him. Her gaze was so filled with pain and confusion, it ripped at his insides.

"Is the guy that's after us the one on the news?"

Mike spun around. Sam was standing just inside the kitchen door.

"What?"

"Some people were talking about it on the bulletin board. They said some guy deluded capture. That he escaped from prison and he's real dangerous."

"Eluded," Mike said, trying hard to get his bearings. He glanced at Becky, but she'd already turned back to the stove.

"Is he?" Sam walked to the table and sat down.

Mike shoved his feelings aside and concentrated on his son. The last thing he wanted to do was scare him, but he needed Sam to be ready in case the worst should happen. "The man doesn't know where we are," he said, moving away from Becky and the roses. "No one does. He can't find us here."

"Why does he want to hurt us?"

Mike sat down next to Sam. It was all he could do not to steal another glance behind him. "He's sick, Sam."

Sam's eyebrows came together. "He's crazy, so he wants to hurt us?"

Becky walked over with the salad. When she put it on the table, she shot Mike a look. No words were needed; he got the message. Tread softly.

"Sam, we're going to be fine. I promise." What was one more lie? he thought. Who knows, maybe this one would turn out to be true. Even if it didn't, Sam would sleep well tonight. That had to count for something.

Mike kept his eyes on his son, waiting to see if he believed the words. Sam started eating, the worry gone from
his face. At least for now.

Becky put the rest of the food on the table. Before she
sat down, she got the glasses Mike had forgotten and
poured them each some milk. The kitchen table was so
small the plates and dishes covered it from one end to the
other. Mike was reasonably sure something would end up
on the floor before the meal was over.

Becky sat to his right. She didn't look upset anymore,
but she avoided his gaze. "How about after dinner, we
start on a puzzle, Sam?"

Sam shrugged. "I don't care." He continued eating
without looking up at his mom.

"Well I think it would be fun," Becky said. "We can
have a fire. I bought marshmallows. We can roast some for
dessert."

That caught his attention. He smiled. Mike realized it
was the first smile he'd seen since he'd showed up at
Becky's. A pang of guilt hit him in the chest. Had he done
one thing to make his kid smile?

He leaned forward to reach for the pasta, and his knee
touched Becky's leg. She pulled away from him as if he'd
burned her.

He didn't think it was possible to feel worse, but that did
it. He wanted to be back at his apartment, back in his life.
He'd let his guard down for one moment with Becky, and
look what happened. He should never have touched her,
dammit.

He served himself some food, and they all concentrated
on eating. Except for the sounds of a fork on a plate or a
glass put down on the table, the room was quiet. Mike
couldn't help remembering meals from the past, when
food had grown cold while they'd talked about everything
from work to politics to books. But that was a long time
ago, and he'd grown accustomed to the silence. He didn't

think he would know how to talk like that anymore. Or that he could make someone laugh, the way Becky had once laughed at his jokes.

He stared at his almost clean plate. They'd been stupid jokes. The only reason she'd thought they were funny was because she'd loved him. He could say the exact same things now, and she wouldn't even smile.

"After the puzzle, can we play Space Blaster, Dad?"

Mike nodded at Sam. "Sure."

"Fortress, too?"

"I don't know. One game is probably my limit. What about that puzzle?"

"I hate puzzles," he said, pouting. "Puzzles are for babies."

"Not this one," Becky said. "It's a really hard one. I'll need your help."

"No you won't. You're just saying that because you don't like my computer. I don't have to work on the puzzle, and you can't make me."

"You want to go straight upstairs to bed, mister?" Mike snapped. The minute the words were out of his mouth, he wanted to take them back.

Sam didn't give him a chance. He scooted his chair back and ran out of the room.

Becky whipped around to face Mike. Her elbow bumped into a half-full glass of milk and it crashed to the floor, spreading liquid and glass shards everywhere. Becky didn't even look at it. "For God's sake, Mike." She got up and went after Sam, but only after giving him a look that told him just where he could go.

Then he was alone. He lifted his napkin off his lap and tossed it on the table. "Damn."

"Honey, you okay?" Becky sat down next to Sam. He pulled his computer onto his lap, then reached across the bed and got his joystick.

"Sam?"

He didn't look at her. His lips were pressed tightly together and his cheeks flushed pink.

"Listen, Sam. Daddy didn't mean to make you feel bad."

"I don't."

He stared rigidly at the screen in front of him.

She scooted a little closer to him. "You know, Daddy and I both love you very much. He's just worried about us, that's all."

Sam grunted and jerked the joystick back and forth. She couldn't see the game screen, but she would bet he was killing off hundreds of little spacemen, or monsters or whatever evil creatures were in that make-believe world. What a powerful thing for a nine-year-old to do, she thought. It was no surprise to her that Sam preferred his computer friends to his schoolmates.

"I bet if you go downstairs and ask Daddy, he'll come up and play." She reached over and touched him, just under the chin, and lifted his head until he looked at her. His eyes were too old and sad. He was just a little kid. He shouldn't be hiding in a stranger's cabin, afraid for his life. Afraid of his father. He shouldn't have to pay because she and Mike had failed each other.

"He's mad at me," he said, shaking free with a toss of his head.

"No, he's not."

Sam didn't look at her again. He just played his game until his parents and the cabin and Mojo were far, far away. At least he had that. She wouldn't say any more. She would just sit with him for a while and let him know that she was here for him.

Her thoughts went back to Mike, but not to the dinner. Before that, when he'd come close to her by the sink. When he'd smelled her perfume.

She'd lied to him. She hadn't been wearing the rose perfume before. She wasn't even sure why she'd put it on. For old time's sake? Maybe she'd just wanted to see if he would still react to her in the old way. She hated to admit it, but she'd liked it when he'd touched her. She'd felt the warmth of his fingers and she'd felt safe. Until she'd realized that she was playing with fire.

It was all so confusing. She shouldn't want to be near him, yet she did. She shouldn't want to care about him, but she couldn't help it. The truth was, he was a part of the fabric of her life, and that would never change. He was the only man she'd ever loved. That's why it hurt so very much.

She stood, and looked at Sam's beautiful face, with the dark eyes and dark hair he got from his father. She wished she could promise him that everything would be all right. But how could she, when she didn't believe it herself?

She wrapped her arms around her waist. The branches of the pine tree outside hammered at the window. The storm had hit, and she hadn't even noticed. She looked back at Sam. Better to leave him to his world, for now. She'd give him some time alone, before she sent Mike up. Besides, the kitchen wasn't going to clean itself. "I'll be right downstairs if you need me."

He didn't even nod.

She saw Mike when she got halfway down the stairs. He was at the fireplace, lighting kindling with a long match. At least he was holding a lit match in the general area of the fireplace, but not near anything that could actually catch fire. He just sat on his haunches, his elbows on his knees, staring at the pile of wood and newspaper. It was clear he was deep in thought, and it startled her to realize she had no idea about what.

It wasn't such a long time ago that she would have known. He always accused her of having a sixth sense, but it hadn't been that. She'd just known Mike. What made him tick. What bothered him and what made him happy. Now she knew nothing about him. He'd closed himself off to her long ago. The only thing familiar about him was his touch, and that was too dangerous to contemplate.

She thought again of that moment in the kitchen. How her body had reacted before her mind could get a grip. How his touch made her melt. At least she knew, now, to be careful. To keep her distance from him. "You'll burn yourself," she said as she reached the landing.

He came out of his trance with a jerk, and dropped the match into the fireplace. He picked up another, lit it with a scratch on the bottom of the box, and brought the flame to the paper. This time he got the fire started. He pulled the mesh screen closed, then stood up to face her. "Is Sam okay?"

"He's hurt and frightened. You didn't have to talk to him like that. All he wants is to spend time with you." She hugged herself tighter, wishing the fire would hurry up and warm the room. She was freezing.

"I'm sorry I snapped at him," he said as he sat down on the wing chair nearest the fireplace. He looked exhausted. The lines in his face were deep, and he was having trouble keeping his eyes open.

"Go on up," she said. "Play with him for a while. I want him to go to bed soon. You both need some rest."

He nodded, but he didn't move.

She needed some sleep herself. Her bones ached with weariness and cold. She thought about the messy kitchen. "Who cares," she whispered. She sat down at the edge of the couch and curled her feet under her.

"What?"

She shook her head. "Nothing. I should go clean up in there."

"Don't worry about it. I picked up."

She stared at him. "Really?"

He nodded. "You cook, I clean. Remember?"

She did. She remembered the day they'd made that deal. It had been their second anniversary, and Mike had bought her a vacuum cleaner. She'd been so disappointed, she'd gone into the bathroom and cried. Mike had coaxed her out, telling her she didn't have her whole gift yet. When she'd opened the door, he'd handed her a card. It said that from now on, he would share in all the chores. She would cook, he would clean. She would dust, he would sweep. They would be a team. Forever. Then he'd given her gold heart earrings.

"We were quite a pair, weren't we?" she asked.

"A hell of a team." He stared at her, and she saw a wistfulness in his eyes that she understood completely.

But it was foolish to let the past trick her into believing things had changed. They weren't married anymore. They knew each other too well to simply forgive and forget.

A surge of sadness rose from deep inside her. She'd lost so much. Her whole world. And now she faced losing even more. "I'm scared," she said. She covered her face with her hands, trying hard to stop the tears. But there was too much fear and hurt to stem the tide, and she wept.

He touched her shoulder. She hadn't heard him get up, or felt him sit next to her, but when she took her hands away and opened her eyes, he was there. Right beside her. It was easy to lean back, to fall against his hard body. To take comfort in his strong arms. He lifted his hand to her face, and with a gentleness she'd forgotten he had, he wiped her tears.

"I'll keep you safe, Becky. I swear to God."

She sniffed. "I know you'll try."

He shook his head. "I'll do more than try."

She took his hand in hers, knowing she shouldn't, but needing to anyway. His long fingers, full of strength and dexterity, felt rough and masculine. She found the scar near his thumb that he'd gotten when he was seventeen, and traced it. "Why is he after us, Mike? What does he want?"

He became still and she looked up at him. The softness was leaving his face, his stony mask taking its place. "Vengeance," he said.

She squeezed his hand, urging him to come back. "Because you caught him?"

"Because I didn't kill him when I had the chance. Because I crippled him."

"But why would he want to hurt me? Or Sam?"

He pulled his hand from hers, and she felt a terrible chill.

"Because he knows I loved you," he said.

She made the mistake of looking at his eyes. He wasn't telling her everything. "There's something else," she said. Her mouth was so dry she could barely speak. "Oh, God, it's something terrible, isn't it?"

Mike leaned forward and put his elbows on his knees. "He wrote to me. From prison. I got the first letter about four months after he'd been locked up. It came to my apartment." Mike's head drooped so he was looking at this feet instead of at her. "The letters were about me, about my life and how he was going to come after me one day."

"And?"

He studied his hands for a moment, then brought his gaze back up to meet hers. "I got the last letter yesterday afternoon. It was about you."

She sat back. She hadn't even realized she'd been leaning forward, or that she'd been holding her breath, but now she took in a gasp of air. "Me? How does he even know I exist?"

He shrugged. "I don't know."

"Why didn't you tell me before?"

"I didn't want you to be scared."

She laughed, although not one damn thing was funny. "Too late. Dammit, Mike, don't try to protect me so much. You have to tell me what's going on. I deserve that."

"I'm sorry."

"Don't be sorry, just trust me. For once in your life, tell me the truth. You think I could watch my baby die and not be able to handle this?"

Mike stood up and walked over to the fireplace. He picked up the poker and knelt to stoke the fire. "It's my job to protect you."

"Says who?" She got up, too, and moved toward him. "I'm not your responsibility. We're not married anymore. Even if we were, it's not right for you to treat me like a child. All I ever wanted was to be your partner, don't you know that? To work through things together. But every time it got tough, you checked out. You disappeared inside yourself, and you never let me in."

He stood up straight, with his arms at his sides. There was no remorse on his face, no guilt. Nothing. As if he hadn't heard a word she'd said—or hadn't cared. "I better go check on Sam."

"Oh, don't. Don't leave now." She reached over and touched his cheek.

He turned away. "It's late. We both need to get some sleep."

She let her hand drop. "For a brave man, you are one hell of a coward."

He swallowed. That was all. He didn't blink, or frown or get angry. Then she realized the man in front of her was an imposter. He looked like the man she'd married, but that was all. This man was a stranger. There was nothing she could do about it. And it broke her heart.

Chapter 4

"I don't know what you want from me," Mike said, struggling to keep still, to not let her see how her words were tearing him in two. "I tried to apologize."

"You say you're sorry, but you still don't talk to me. You don't include me in the decisions. You came to my house in the middle of the night, and brought us to this godforsaken place. Did you discuss it with me? No. You said jump, and we jumped."

"It was for your own good."

"Since when are you an expert on what's good for me?"

"I'm trying to save your life."

Becky shook her head and walked over to the couch. She didn't sit down, though. He guessed she just didn't want to be so close to him.

He didn't blame her. For any of it. He'd failed at the only thing that mattered—keeping his family safe. He hadn't been able to save Amy; he hadn't been there for Becky. And now he'd delivered his family to a madman. His wife and son might die because he loved them.

The worst of it was that, dammit, he still wanted her. That when she touched him, he remembered the feel of her hands and the taste of her skin, and that he could never have her again.

Let her be angry. Let her despise him. It would be easier for both of them.

"I'm going to see Sam," he said.

Becky didn't try to stop him this time. Mike felt her angry gaze on his back as he walked past her to the stairs. It was better this way. If she hated him, she wouldn't let him touch her. One of them had to be strong.

He paused as he reached the door to Sam's room. His son was on the bed, sitting cross-legged with the computer on his lap. He looked so serious. Mike remembered that little smile from dinner.

He'd done some job tonight. First he'd chased Sam away, then he'd run from Becky. He tried to blame it on lack of sleep, but he knew better. He was a bastard, plain and simple.

The least he could do was try not to act like one.

"Hey," he said, as he walked toward the bed. "Why don't you put that thing away and come downstairs? We can give that puzzle a try."

Sam didn't look up. "No, thanks."

Mike walked over to the bed, and sat next to his son. Sam still didn't look at him.

"I'm sorry I snapped at you," Mike said. "I didn't mean to make you feel bad."

Sam shrugged. At least he stopped typing.

"You don't have to do the puzzle, but it would be nice if you would come downstairs."

"Why?"

"Your mom needs you. She's on edge, and she could sure use your company."

"You were downstairs."

Mike put his hand on Sam's shoulder. It always surprised him how small his son was. How fragile. "I'm pretty lousy company. You know that. But I think you could save the day."

Finally, Sam looked at him. He expected to see the hurt he'd put there at dinner, but Sam surprised him. His brown eyes were full of trust. The little guy didn't expect much. Just a father he could count on.

He squeezed Sam's shoulder and gave him the best smile he could. "Come on, sport. Let's go make your mom happy."

Sam nodded. "Will you do the puzzle, too?"

"You bet," Mike said, as he stood up. "I'll do whatever you want."

He watched his son put away his computer. He ached inside, as if he'd been punched in the gut. Sam was so young, and so innocent. He still wanted his dad to be a hero. But how long would that last? How long before he realized that his father was nothing but a fraud? That when things got really tough, Dad couldn't do one damn thing about it?

He'd made peace with losing them a long time ago. When this was all over, he would make peace with it again. In the meantime, he would try to make things tolerable for both of them. He would act as if everything was going to be fine. That Mojo couldn't touch them. He would spend time with Sam, and hope that his boy wouldn't hate him for it later.

Sam walked in front of him down the stairs. Becky was still sitting on the couch. She turned to look up at them.

"What's going on?" she asked.

"Sam and I thought we would take a whack at that puzzle," he said. He tried to make his voice sound cheerful.

Becky's smile told him he'd succeeded. It was a start.

* * * *

"You've got his eye in upside down." Sam lifted the puzzle piece and put it aside.

"Come on," Becky said with a laugh. "Where's your creative spirit? If you push hard enough, anything will fit."

Sam shook his head. "You are too weird. Dad, tell her."

Mike looked at Becky sitting at the opposite side of the dining room table. "You're too weird," he repeated.

"Thanks," she said. "Both of you." After a brief glance at him, she went back to studying her side of the picture.

She had spent most of the last hour talking to Sam. She'd been pleasant to Mike, but she hadn't looked at him. Not really. He'd tried to ignore her, too, but he hadn't been very successful. He kept stealing glances. Whenever their gazes met, she turned away.

Sam didn't seem to notice. He was sitting on his knees on the kitchen chair, leaning over the table. Although he'd groused about the puzzle, he was the one doing most of the work. He picked up a small piece, a corner of a mouth, and slipped it in place. "See?" he said. "If you're careful, you can make it work right."

Becky nodded. "Ah," she said. "A million apologies. I'll try to be more careful in the future, Professor."

Sam snorted. "Geez. Women."

Becky's mouth came open in a loud gasp. "What did you say?"

He giggled.

Becky stood up, her mouth still open in mock surprise. "What did you say, young man?"

Sam scrambled off his chair and backed away from his mother. Mike knew he wasn't scared, though. No, he was feeling that incredible mixture of delight and anticipation that precedes a major tickle. Mike recognized it with his own blend of pleasure and remorse. He hadn't tickled Sam in years.

The boy continued to back away. Becky wasn't even close to him, and he was already protecting his vulnerable parts by keeping his arms up tight against his chest. Mike couldn't hold back a smile as he listened to his son's laughter. Becky kept on moving toward him, wiggling her fingers to show him what was in store as she chased him into the living room.

Mike got up and followed them.

Sam had backed up all the way to the front door. Becky pounced. The squeal was loud and high, filled with anguish and glee.

"Dad, help me!" Sam struggled to get away from his mom. "Dad!" he said, but an octave higher.

Mike laughed. It felt strange and wonderful, like a long-lost friend had come to call. He moved toward the wriggling twosome. "Here I come," he said, in an awful imitation of Dudley Do Right. "I'll protect you."

He grabbed Becky around the waist. She yelped as he lifted her into the air. Sam broke free and ran across the room, then fell in a laughing heap on the couch.

Becky tried to get out of his grasp, but he didn't budge.

"Mike, put me down."

"Never!" He looked at Sam. But his boy wasn't smiling any more. He was staring at his mother's face. All the laughter had gone.

"Mike, put me down. Please."

He heard her this time. He did as she asked. The second her feet touched the floor, he let go and backed away.

"It's time for bed, Sam," she said.

Mike couldn't see her face, but her posture said enough. Her back was stiff and straight. Her arms were crossed, hugging her waist. She hated that he'd touched her.

Sam didn't argue with her. He looked from his mother to Mike with wide, sad eyes. He didn't even say goodnight. He just walked up the stairs.

Becky turned around slowly. Her cheeks were still flushed. "It's late," she said. "We all need some sleep."

He couldn't speak. He'd let down his guard for one split second, and look what had happened. She couldn't have hurt him worse if she'd picked up his gun and shot him.

Mike listened to the storm as he stretched his legs in front of him. It was late, after midnight, but he couldn't get up and put himself to bed. He stared at the dying embers of the fire and thought about the night.

She'd fooled him. She'd smiled and made jokes. Even laughed. For a while there, he'd thought she'd forgiven him. But it had all been a pretense for Sam's benefit. She deserved an Academy Award.

"Mike?"

He turned abruptly, startled by Becky's quiet voice. He figured she would have been sound asleep by now. "What are you doing up?"

"I can't sleep," she said, as she walked down the stairs. "I thought I would make myself some hot milk. Do you want some?"

"No, thank you." He stretched as he stood, trying to ease the stiffness in his back. Now seemed like a really good time to go to bed.

"Please?"

He almost said no. In fact, he wasn't really sure why he didn't walk right past her. But he didn't. Instead, he nodded.

Becky led him to the kitchen. She'd changed from her jeans and sweater into her bathrobe. Her hair was loose and tousled, falling below her shoulders. God, how he used to love to see her when she'd just gotten out of bed.

The kitchen seemed too bright and cold. He thought about getting his jacket, but he just sat down. He yawned and rubbed his face with his hands, the stubble of his chin scratchy and uncomfortable. When he looked up again,

Becky was standing over the stove, pouring milk into a pan.

The bathrobe was the one he'd given her for Mother's Day three years ago. It was pink terry cloth and it made her look soft. She wore socks, big thick white ones. Her feet were always cold. She used to warm them on his back. Or he would lift them on his lap and rub them until she was comfortable.

His gaze traveled up slowly, but instead of seeing the bulky robe, he pictured what was underneath. The length of her thighs and the swell of her hips. He was a fool for thinking about that. Especially now. Hadn't she made it perfectly clear she didn't want anything to do with him? That she couldn't even stand to have him touch her? It seemed to be an apt punishment, knowing what was under her robe, remembering how good it had been.

The moment before she raised her hand, he knew she was going to push a lock of hair behind her ear. Because she always did that. Even when there was no hair on her cheek. It was just her way.

He stared at her hands, the short oval fingernails unadorned and all the more beautiful for it. There was something intoxicating about her hands, even when they did something as mundane as pour milk. He'd always loved her hands. He could still remember the feel of them when she ran them over his body as they made love. When they finished, he always lifted her palm to his lips and kissed her.

She'd liked it, too. There had been a time when she'd begged him to touch her. To make love with her.

She brought the small pot and the glass to the table and sat next to him. She waited a minute or so, then poured the warm liquid so she could drink it.

He held himself still, afraid that if he moved, she would see what he was thinking. He watched her through half-open eyes and tried to ignore the ache between his thighs.

She put both hands around her glass, then brought the milk to her mouth. He watched her lips part, and her tongue touch the rim of the glass just before she drank. It seemed to take forever. His heartbeats grew farther apart, the seconds stretched. She placed the glass on the table, sighed, then turned to look into his eyes, all in slow motion.

"I shouldn't have reacted that way," she said. "I know you were just having some fun. I didn't mean to spoil everything."

"You don't have to apologize."

"Yes, I do. You really tried hard tonight with Sam. You were good with him. I haven't seen him laugh like that in a long time."

So it was all about Sam. He should have figured. "It was no big deal." He had to stop looking at her. He kept thinking about old times. About making up after fights.

"He loves you so much, Mike."

"I love him, too."

"You need to tell him that."

He stared at his hands, then his gaze slid across the table to hers. She rubbed one finger along the side of her glass.

"Okay," he whispered. "If you want me to tell him, I will."

She didn't respond. He heard the trees outside, whipping in the wind. Then she moved the hand that wasn't on the glass. She moved it closer to him. Just an inch. Before he could think, he leaned forward and slipped his open hand beneath hers. He knew she would pull away from him. It was obvious she hated his touch. But somehow, for some reason, her small fingers slipped between his. He didn't look at her. If he did, she would see what he wanted, she would realize what she was doing.

Still, she didn't pull away. She gripped him tightly, moving her thumb so it rubbed the back of his hand.

Something stirred inside him, something stronger than the physical need. It was an emptiness so deep he felt hollow inside. He'd tried to fill that hole, packing his days with work and exercise until he could barely move. Now, as he felt her beating pulse with his fingertips, he knew the emptiness had won a long time ago.

Slowly, he lifted his gaze.

She was exquisite. Her mouth opened slightly, showing the edges of her even, white teeth. Her breaths were deep and slow, her chest rising and falling beneath the pink robe. Her gaze met and held his. He saw something he'd thought he would never see again. She wanted him.

"I've missed you," he said.

She nodded. "I know."

"Do you?" He leaned forward, never letting go of the connection of her gaze. "Do you know what I think about most? Waking up next to you. Not sex, although that's there, too, but about feeling you next to me when I first open my eyes. Turning over in bed to see your hair on the pillow. Sometimes I would wake up and you would be in my arms. I wouldn't remember how you got there. I would just be grateful."

She sighed and looked down. "I think about you sometimes, too."

He squeezed her hand, wanting her to look at him again. "I know I can't have you back," he said. "I know that. I would never even ask."

She did look at him, then. He saw the tears in her eyes.

Then he was standing, and he pulled her up and into his arms. He stopped the trembling of her lips with his own.

The shock of his kiss took Becky's breath away. He breathed for her—filling her with memories she'd tried for two years to forget.

She knew his lips, soft and smooth even while his mouth was hard and demanding. She knew the velvet of his tongue as it touched the corner of her mouth in a wordless plea. She felt the bristle of his beard on her skin, and she didn't care. Mostly, she knew the smell of him, the combination of soap, sweat and skin that now, as always, aroused in her a primal yearning that had no name.

Without her willing it, her lips parted and she tasted him. Then, as if the kisses were not enough, he moved his arm around her back and brought her closer so that she was flush against him from chest to knee. His body was different, leaner, more muscled, yet still achingly familiar. She lifted her arms and brought her hands to the back of his neck, her fingers threading through his thick, dark hair.

He ran his hands over her back, touching her as if he'd never felt her before. Eager and insistent, his fingers explored through the fabric of her robe, then stilled at the base of her spine. He pulled his mouth away before she was ready, but then his lips were on her neck, just below her ear. His hot breath made her gasp.

His hands moved down and cupped her buttocks, holding her steady as he pressed himself against her stomach.

She knew that part of him, too. She'd dreamed of him too many nights to forget. No matter that she'd banished thoughts of him during the day, he always managed to sneak up on her in sleep.

He moved, and she moved with him. He sighed and kissed her, and she kissed him back. She was falling, slowly, sinking. Losing herself. Losing control.

Then she snapped, like a branch in the storm, awake and aware of who she was and where she was and why she was in his arms. She pulled away and turned her head away from his kiss. "No."

He released her quickly, as if she were fire and he'd been scorched. "Remembered who I was, huh?"

She stepped back until her heel touched the bottom of the cabinet. "No. It's not like that. I'm sorry. I should never had done that."

He stared at her, wounded and angry. More than that, he was lonely. She'd never guessed it was this bad. His eyes seemed black and empty. His cheeks hollow, his smile gone forever. There was no life to him at all. Her heart broke in a brand new place. "Mike," she said as she reached for him.

He winced, and turned his head, stepping back and away from her as quickly as he could. "Go to bed, Becky. It's late."

"But—"

"You were right. I should never have touched you. Now go on."

"It's just that I can't go back to the way it was when we were married, Mike. I can't live like that again."

"I'm not asking you to."

"My life is calm and peaceful, and I don't lie awake at night anymore wondering if you'll be alive in the morning. I don't worry every time I hear a siren. I've finally gotten control over things, don't you see? If I let go, it will all unravel. Don't ask me to give up what I've worked so hard for. I can't do it. I lose myself when I'm with you, and there's nothing left over. Not for me or for Sam, and he needs me so much. I can't invest everything in you, when I can't trust you to be there."

"I'm going to check the house and make sure it's locked up," he said calmly, as if she'd never spoken.

She moved to the door and blocked his way. "Were you listening? Did you hear me?"

He wouldn't look at her. His face was rigid, his mouth set in a thin line. "I won't touch you again," he said, his voice a low whisper, void of emotion. "I won't mess up your life. As soon as this is over, we'll go right back to the way we were. I give you my word."

She shouldn't let him go like this. She'd seen what was behind his eyes. He was dying inside, and he needed her. But how could she go to him when the price was so high?

She moved to the door, and when she was very close to him, she touched his face. He closed his eyes. He didn't move or shake her off, but it was clear her touch was painful. She dropped her hand. "I have to put the milk away," she whispered. "I'll go up in a minute."

He left without another word.

She went to the table and sat down again. Her milk was cold, but she didn't want it anyway. Lord, she was tired. Maybe if she got some sleep she could figure out what all this meant. Right now, all she felt was confused and sad. The only thing she had to hold on to was the life she'd built for herself and her son. That life did not include Mike.

She would bury the ache inside her. She'd done it before; she could do it again. If he just kept his word, and he didn't touch her again, she would be all right.

He would be all right, too. He would go back to his job and to talking to Sam on the computer. Mostly, he would go back to that island he'd lived on for so long. She couldn't let herself believe that what she'd seen tonight made any difference. It was a quirk, a mistake. She'd spent too much of her life trying to figure out who was behind Mike's mask to believe she'd seen the truth in an isolated cabin in the middle of the night so very far from home.

She pushed back her chair and stood up quickly, collecting her glass and putting it in the sink. It was time she went to sleep and stopped thinking. She turned off the light and went into the dark living room. There were still embers in the fire, but they would soon die. The unfamiliar shadows made her uneasy.

As she stepped on the stairs she saw a wide band of light from Mike's room. She wondered if he was going to come back out to the living room, but after a few moments it was clear he wasn't. She retied the belt on her robe, and walked over to his room. It wouldn't hurt to make sure he was okay. She'd been pretty brutal with him.

She reached his door and looked inside. At first, she didn't see him, but a movement from the closet caught her attention. Mike was pulling himself up on a chinning bar that had been mounted in the doorway. His shirt was off, and the body she saw shocked her. It wasn't his. Not her Mike. Every bit of softness was gone. He was muscled and hard. She could see his ribs as he pulled himself up, his biceps bulging and straining. Even from this distance she heard the rhythm of his deep breathing.

His jeans rode low on his waist; they didn't fit this new body. The only thing familiar about his chest was the dark, curly hair that tapered to a thin line at his waist and below. His legs were together, slightly angled in front. He wore no shoes, and even his feet showed tight lines of sinew and muscle. He let himself down again, him, not gravity. He controlled the move and made it slow and specific. She stared at his right arm, the swelling muscle, the cords of steel beneath the skin. He paused, and she looked up again. He caught her gaze.

His face was as finely chiseled as his chest. Hard lines and curves, as if he were made of granite instead of flesh and bone. His eyes were hardest of all. Unblinking, steady, unforgiving.

He lifted himself again, his chest expanding with his breath. His gaze never moved from her face. He went up slowly, inch by inch, with the control of a machine. *A machine.* That's what he'd become and why she couldn't love him. It had begun the night Amy died, bit by bit, piece by piece. He was the Tin Man. And everyone knew the Tin Man had no heart.

Chapter 5

Mike reached for his bag and took out the stack of letters. A drop of water from his still-wet hair fell onto the upper right corner of the page, and he wiped it away with his thumb.

It was nearly nine. He'd had a lousy night's sleep. He didn't remember his dreams; only the feelings of loss lingered. He'd gotten out of bed when he heard Becky and Sam in the kitchen.

He didn't want to see her. What he wanted was to be in the field, tracking down Mojo. Doing something he knew how to do. Instead, he would have to go through another day of watching Becky, remembering when she was his.

For his own sanity, he had to concentrate on finding Mojo, and all he had were the letters. As far as he knew, the bastard was still free and heading this way. Cliff would have called if they'd caught him. The letters would tell him something, reveal a weakness. Mike had no delusions about Mojo. He knew if he made it to the cabin, he would try to kill them all. So Mike had to stop him first.

He unfolded the top page. Same stationery. Same type-writer.

Dear Mike,

A priest came to me today. An old man with bad teeth. He asked me if I wanted to confess my sins. It's never too late to get God's forgiveness. At least that's what he said. I don't know about that. I don't believe that some things can be forgiven. But who knows, eh? What if all it takes is one good session on your knees to be absolved? Of course, I can't kneel, you took care of that, and what kind of a God would listen to a man who wasn't kneeling?

Have you been absolved, Mike? Did God forgive you for your sins? No, of course not. You know what I think? I think we're going to see each other in hell. Keep the light on for me, would you?

Ah, the dinner bell is about to ring. I wouldn't think of missing the world-class cuisine of the State Penitentiary system.

That son of a bitch had no business talking about ab-solution. He was the one who killed at random. Mike had been doing his job, that's all. Trying to stop Mojo from hurting more people. Gordon's death was an accident, dammit. Isn't that what everyone said?

Mike folded the paper and put it on the bottom of the stack. As he opened the next letter, he heard a high-pitched engine outside. He dropped the packet and grabbed his gun. A snowmobile. It was probably Witherspoon, but the old man had said he would phone. Mike had stressed the point. He wanted no surprises. Witherspoon wasn't the only one with access to a snowmobile.

He ran from his bedroom to the living room and pulled the drapes aside. Snow pelted the window, making it hard to see. The drifts against the house were knee-high now, and building. The engine was louder in here, coming from down the road. His breath fogged the window and he wiped it clean with the arm of his shirt. There it was. He couldn't make out who was riding it.

"Who's coming Dad?"

Mike whipped around and saw Sam standing by the couch. "Get upstairs. Now."

Sam took a step back. His eyes widened until they seemed to take over his face. But he didn't move.

"Go on, Sam. Get upstairs."

"Is it that guy?"

"Do what I tell you." Mike looked back outside. The snowmobile was nearly at the house. "Becky!" he yelled. "Get out here and take Sam upstairs."

He heard her come, but he didn't take his eyes off the man in the parka. It wasn't the jacket Witherspoon had worn yesterday. That one had been blue. This one was white.

Behind him, Becky told Sam to come with her, then Mike heard their footsteps on the stairs. He'd scared her, too.

It had to be Witherspoon. Mojo would be a fool to make such a blatant entrance. But Mike wasn't willing to take any risks. He eased the safety off as he lifted his .45 to his shoulder. The weight of the weapon was reassuring. He held his breath as the rider pulled up near the porch. When the engine cut off, Mike could hear the wind whip the trees. He stared at the man as he walked toward the door, but he couldn't see past the fur-lined hood that surrounded his face.

Two steps more, and he would be at the door. One.

It was Witherspoon.

The old man's weathered face looked red and cold. Mike released his breath, swore, then called up to Becky that everything was okay. He slipped the safety on, and tucked his gun into his waistband in the back.

He moved quickly to the door and opened it. The wind pushed him back. Snow came in first, then the old man, padded and covered from head to toe in an Arctic suit. Mike shoved the door closed while his guest stomped the snow off his boots.

"Morning," he said.

Mike nodded. "Morning."

"Came by to check the house, and to finish up with the snowmobiles like I promised. This storm is going to get a lot worse before it gets better."

"You were supposed to call."

"Couldn't. My phone's on the blink. Happens a lot, what with the weather in such a snit. Lines go down, no one up here to put 'em back up. Then there's the mice problem. They do get at the wires. That's why I came with this." He held up a coiled length of cable. "I thought it was more important for you folks to have phone service, so I saddled right up. I've got my ham radio, see, so I'm okay. But if it's the lines, the wire won't be of much use."

Mike walked to the end table and picked up the phone. He heard the reassuring hum of the dial tone. "It's working fine," he said.

Witherspoon nodded. "If you don't mind, I'll still take a look-see downstairs before we head out."

"Sure, no problem." Mike went to the base of the stairs. The old man's story about the wires bothered him. Not that the weather could knock out the phones, that made sense. But so selectively? If the wires went down, wouldn't the whole mountain be without service?

As soon as Witherspoon went downstairs, he intended to make a few phone calls. It wouldn't hurt to talk to the phone company and get some answers.

Becky and Sam hadn't come down, and he was concerned that they hadn't heard him before. "Becky. It's all right. Mr. Witherspoon is here."

He waited for her and Sam to appear. A moment later, they opened the door and started downstairs. Sam held Becky's hand tightly, and both of them seemed pale. After Mike's call to the phone company, he would call Cliff. This waiting and not knowing was torture. For all of them.

"Becky, this is Mr. Witherspoon."

"How do you do." Becky's voice was steady and casual, but Mike thought that was for Sam's benefit. So was her smile.

Witherspoon nodded. "Pleased to make your acquaintance."

Becky, still clutching Sam's hand, walked next to Mike. "This is crazy," she whispered. "Can't you do something? Call someone?"

He turned to Becky. Her eyes pleaded with him to go, now, to the phone. "Right away," he said. Then he looked down at Sam.

The poor kid was holding on to Becky for dear life. He'd really scared him. What could he do, though? Pretend nothing was wrong? He lowered himself down to eye-level with his son and placed his hands on Sam's small shoulders. He stared into his wide, frightened eyes. "How about we go upstairs and play a couple of games on the old computer after I get back? I still owe you from yesterday."

Sam nodded. "Sure," he said, but there was no enthusiasm in his voice. Not like there would have been before this whole mess had started.

"It's all right, kiddo. I was just being careful. Okay?" He smiled at his boy, hoping like hell he looked confident, because he sure didn't feel it.

Sam smiled. Not a great smile, but it was better than nothing.

Mike reached over and tousled his hair, then stood up, facing Becky. She seemed a little calmer now, too. He wanted to tell her he was sorry about last night. That he was sorry about so much. He reached out and touched her arm.

Her gaze followed his hand. She didn't flinch or move aside. She touched his arm, very lightly with her fingers. Such a little move, almost nothing. But the connection made him feel a hell of a lot better.

She nodded, almost imperceptibly, then gave him a small smile. "It's okay," she said, very softly, then turned to Witherspoon. "I've got hot coffee in the kitchen."

Mike was sorry to let her go.

Witherspoon had taken off his parka, revealing a red flannel shirt and a tool belt around his waist. "Don't mind if I do," he said. He dropped his gloves on top of his coat and headed for the kitchen.

Becky looked at her son. "Go on and finish your breakfast."

Sam turned and walked toward the kitchen, and they were alone.

"I didn't get much sleep last night," she said. "I was thinking about what I said to you, how I've been acting."

"You haven't done anything wrong. I was out of line."

"Wait. Let me finish. After I went to bed, I tried to remember the last time we talked. Really talked. Not about Sam, but about us. What happened to us?"

She studied his face as if she were seeing something different about him. "There was a time we could talk, when there was nothing we couldn't say to each other. Remember?"

He nodded.

"I don't think we can ever get that back, but I know we can do a lot better than we have. And we owe it to each other to try."

"It's been a long time," he said. "A lot has happened." He wanted to tell her he would try. But she'd asked him not to lie. "I'm not that man anymore, Becky. I don't think I'll ever be that man again."

"So talk to me about who you are now."

He shook his head. "Why? We'll be out of here soon. You'll go back to your life, and I'll go back to mine."

"We're stuck here, at least for a little while. Wouldn't it be nice if we could get along? Maybe not like we used to, but we could learn to be friends again, couldn't we?"

"You'll only be disappointed."

"Let me be the judge of that, okay?"

He reached over and brushed her soft cheek with the back of his hand. "Don't say I didn't warn you."

She rewarded him with a smile. "All I'm asking is that we try. Now, go call Cliff. Tonight we'll see if we can remember some of the old words, okay?"

He nodded and let his hand drop. He wanted to say something reassuring. To tell her he still knew how to be her friend. But he wasn't sure it was true. "You keep Witherspoon in the kitchen. I'll call from here."

He watched her walk into the kitchen. She wore beige stretch pants that disappeared inside her ankle boots. Her legs were long and slim, and he liked the way the pants hugged her. The sweater was beige, too, and bulky with knitted flowers. She'd put up her hair—a French braid, he thought. He'd watched her do that one night, fascinated by the dexterity of her fingers, and amazed that she could make something so pretty just by touch.

Mike forced himself to forget about her, for now at least. He turned to the telephone and dialed the Denver office of the FBI. The phone rang four times. It took a few minutes for the switchboard operator to locate Cliff. He listened to an old Beatles' song and then a few more rings.

"Mike." Cliff's voice was tinny. He was on the cellular phone.

"Tell me something good, Cliff."

"You were wrong about him. He never showed up at Becky's."

Mike swore. "That makes no sense."

"Ten to one he's heading for Canada. Damned if I know how, though. We had road blocks up. His picture has been plastered all over the television. Every police agency in three states has been notified. The man has vanished."

Mike walked around the couch and sat down. "Tell me about the nurse."

"His hostage."

"Yeah."

"She was pretty new at the prison. She got hired about five weeks ago, but she'd worked in prison hospitals before. Single, no kids. Good at her job, from what the doctors say. Not too talkative."

"They haven't found her body yet?"

"Nope. He's still got her."

"If Mojo still has her, then she's no hostage. She's an accomplice. She got him out of there."

"We already thought of that. We couldn't..."

The phone line filled with static for a moment, then settled down again.

"...known her."

"I didn't catch that."

"There was no way he could have known her. He'd never been to the infirmary before that night."

"It doesn't matter. She's working with him. It's the only thing that makes sense. Find out what other prisons she's worked for. I'll bet you Mojo's path crossed hers somewhere along the road."

"Nope. We checked that. The only time they've been in the same state was this last year, when he was already in prison. Her record is spotless."

"Still, she's not dead."

"We don't know that."

"If he'd killed her, he would have dumped her by the side of the road. He did it with the banker's family, and he did it in California. Why would he change his MO now?"

"Maybe because the whole world is looking for him."

Mike could tell Cliff was getting impatient with him. Mike could picture him, fidgeting with his necktie, tugging at his collar. Cliff was only comfortable when he was in sweats and a T-shirt, sitting in front of a football game, drinking a diet soda. He got the "itchies" when he was bored, or when, like now, he felt outfoxed.

Dammit, Mike knew he was right about Mojo. "He used the nurse to get him out of prison. He's on his way here. I'm not wrong about this."

"That's what you said about Becky's house."

"So he skipped that step. That doesn't mean he's leaving the country."

"How would he know where you are? No one but me knows about the cabin, and I haven't talked to the man. Besides, even if he did know where you were, he couldn't get to you. Not with that storm. According to the weather service, that's going to get a lot worse before it gets better. The only thing you need to worry about is staying warm."

Mike rubbed his eyes. He suddenly felt bone weary. He wanted to go back to bed and sleep for two or three days. "You're gonna have to believe me on this one, buddy. Forget what you think, what you know. Just trust me. Morris Jones is on his way here. He'll find a way to get through the storm. It's all he cares about. He's a smart son of a bitch and he's made me a promise."

Cliff didn't say anything, and all Mike heard was static. When the line cleared, his partner said, "I believe you, Mike. But I don't know how much good that's gonna do. I don't call the shots around here."

"Do whatever it takes. I mean it. Get up here and bring as many men as you can. You're gonna feel like a jerk if I turn up dead."

Cliff laughed, a short, rueful retort. "You would haunt me, wouldn't you?"

Mike wasn't smiling. "Till the end of time."

Cliff wasn't laughing anymore, either. "Okay. I'll be there."

"Hey, I need you to do something else."

"Yeah?"

"Check on the phone service up here, would you? See if it's possible for Witherspoon's phone lines to be down, when this phone works just fine. I don't like his explanation."

"Witherspoon's all right, Mike. I've known him for years."

"Well, check anyway. For me."

Cliff sighed. "Anything you say."

"Thanks. And listen, pal, Mojo doesn't care if he dies. I think he wants to die. But he won't go before he tries to get me. And my family."

Becky poured Witherspoon a second cup of coffee. She overfilled the cup and a little of the hot liquid spilled on the table. "I'm sorry," she said, as she put down the pot and reached for a sponge.

"No harm done."

She wiped up the spill, still trying to hear what Mike was saying. It was useless. The sounds of the storm were too loud. She hated the storm, the noise, the frantic beating of the branches on the windows. If she had to listen to it all day, she knew she would go mad.

Sam ate his cereal. He used a soup spoon which was too big for him, so he strained to get the flakes in his mouth. He seemed to enjoy the challenge though, so she didn't give him a teaspoon. If only she could concentrate that hard on something other than Mojo. Or Mike.

She poured herself a cup of coffee and sat down next to Mr. Witherspoon. "It must be lonely up here, all by yourself," she said.

The old man shrugged. "I'm used to it. Doesn't bother me much. I've got my ham radio friends. I talk to them from all over the world. Even Russia."

She smiled and tried to work up some enthusiasm, or at least think of some questions for him. She wanted so desperately to go to the living room and find out what Mike had heard that it was hard to keep still. But she didn't want to scare Sam anymore this morning. "That must be fascinating."

Witherspoon nodded. "I came up here nearly twenty-two years ago. With my wife and boys. They used to love it up here. The boys loved to ski in the winter. They loved the boating in the summer. You really should try and come again in season, you know. You can't tell about this place when it snows like this."

"Where are the boys now?" Becky took a sip of coffee and brushed some loose hair behind her ear.

"I'm the only one left," he said, his voice soft with tenderness. "Ted and Roy were killed eighteen years ago. Car accident."

Becky's heart sank. She lowered her cup slowly, then looked at the old man. "I'm so sorry," she said. "I know how hard it is to lose a child."

He didn't say anything for a minute. He just looked at her with his pale blue eyes. Then he reached over and patted her hand. "It's not so bad," he said. "They're still with me. So's my wife. She passed on two years ago. But they're all right here." He tapped his temple. "Every day. I can hear them laughing and arguing, and I can see them sleeping. It gives me comfort." He gave her a gentle smile. "Truth be known, I won't mind at all when it's my time. Nope. I won't mind seeing them again at all."

Becky had to look away. She checked on Sam, worried that he might be upset. However, he was still working on his cereal, and busy reading the back of the box. He didn't look troubled.

"I couldn't leave, you see. I've got too many memories here," Witherspoon said.

Becky tried to smile back at him, but she couldn't. His words had taken her to a place that had no smiles. "I envy you," she said. "My memories aren't so sweet."

"Lost someone close, did you?"

She nodded, and glanced again at Sam. "Maybe we shouldn't talk about that right now."

"I don't mind," Sam said. He put down his spoon and looked at Witherspoon. "My little sister died. She had cancer. She was four."

Witherspoon smiled. "I bet she was pretty."

Sam shrugged. "I guess."

"You miss her?"

"I don't remember her very well. I was only six and a half, you know. When she died."

Becky stood up. She couldn't listen to this. "Sam, are you finished with breakfast? Why don't you scoot upstairs, huh? I think Mr. Witherspoon has some business with Daddy."

Sam looked up at her, puzzled. "Did I say something wrong?"

She shook her head, and tried to calm her rapid pulse. It was hard to speak with the lump in her throat. "No, sweetheart. You didn't say anything wrong. But I still think you'd better go upstairs."

Sam pushed back his chair and stood up. He took his empty cereal bowl in both hands and walked over to the sink.

Becky watched every move, her heart aching and heavy. He didn't remember Amy. He would grow up not knowing how special his little sister had been. He wouldn't teach her to ride a bike, or help her with her homework. He wouldn't fight with her or laugh with her, or tell her all his secrets. It wasn't right, she thought. It wasn't fair. *Dammit, it wasn't fair.*

He turned from the sink and walked to the door. He didn't look her way or say anything more.

"I'm sorry if I stirred up trouble."

She heard Witherspoon, but she didn't answer him. She couldn't. He didn't press it, and for that she was grateful.

"I'll just go downstairs and check the wires," he said.

She heard the scrape of his chair, the shuffle of his booted feet. She even heard the basement door open and close. But all she saw was her daughter's face.

Chapter 6

Mike stopped cold when he saw Becky standing in the middle of the kitchen. "What's wrong?"

She moved her head slowly until she met his gaze. Her eyes were so filled with pain that he stopped breathing. He walked to her, and took her arm. "Becky, what happened?"

"He doesn't remember Amy. He was too little."

"Are you talking about Sam?"

She nodded. Her eyes glistened with unshed tears. "He said so. He talked about her as if she'd been a stranger."

Mike folded Becky in his arms. He felt her sag as her cheek rested on his chest. He held her tight, and rocked her back and forth. Then he lifted his hand and stroked her hair. "It's all right," he whispered. "We'll help him remember. We'll give him our memories."

He felt moisture on his shirt, and he envied her tears. The scent of roses, the silk of her hair beneath his fingers, the ache of her soft sigh against his chest sent Mike back to a time when Becky had been all his. He felt a desperate need to comfort and protect her.

"The day after Amy was born," he whispered as he rocked Becky back and forth, "I brought Sam to see her. He was only two. I lifted him up and held him close to the window. I pointed to the second row, third from the left. She was on her back, all wrapped up in a tight pink bundle. No hair underneath her little knit cap. Her face was all scrunched up. Sam laughed when he saw her. He pointed at Amy, then he looked at me. I knew he was asking if that was her. If that was his new sister. When I said yes, he looked at her again. He smiled. Then he got the hiccups. I'll always remember staring at that brand new baby, with Sam's head bumping my chin with each hiccup. Thinking I was the luckiest man on the face of the earth."

He stroked her hair again, and continued to rock her, as if *she* were a child. The memories of that long-ago day hung over him like a low cloud. How scrawny Amy had been, how tiny. How helpless. He didn't know then, that they would have her for such a short time.

Would he have loved her more, knowing? Could he have loved her more? He'd struggled with that for a long time. What he could have done, how he should have acted. Regrets, like sharp arrows, pierced the soft haze of recollection.

Becky sniffed, then leaned back and met his gaze. Even with red-rimmed eyes and flushed cheeks, she looked extraordinarily beautiful to him.

"Thank you," she said.

While he looked into her eyes, feelings swept through him. A shimmer of joy from the day he'd proposed. A stab of lust from their wedding night. A heartbeat of agony from the moment they'd learned of Amy's illness.

Then sadness.

No flash this time. No glimpse back to feelings he barely remembered. Just the dull, familiar ache of being without Becky and his family.

"What's wrong?" she asked.

He focused again on Becky. Her smile was gone, replaced by a look of concern.

He stepped back so he was no longer touching her. "They don't have Mojo yet," he said. "He didn't go to the house. They think he might be headed toward Canada."

Becky wrapped her arms around her waist and shook her head. "You really have great timing, you know?"

"You asked me to tell you the truth."

"For a minute there, I thought we might be sharing something. I thought I was seeing the old Mike. The man I'd married. I guess I was wrong."

"Look, I have to go get the second snowmobile," he said. "I don't want to talk about this now."

"You have to leave because you started to feel something, and it scared the hell out of you."

It was true. He had to go because if he stayed in the kitchen, looking at Becky and seeing the disappointment in her eyes, he would remember too much. The days of watching Amy die while he stood helplessly by. The agony of seeing his family fall apart in front of him. The memories would grow dark and ugly, and crippling.

Becky needed him strong, now. Not filled with questions that couldn't be answered, pain that would never go away. He shoved the past behind him, out of his mind and his heart, to a place where it couldn't hurt either of them any more.

"Did you hear me?"

He nodded. "I heard you." He reached back and pulled his gun from his holster. "I want you to take this. Mojo isn't up here, I promise you that. I wouldn't leave if I thought there was any immediate danger. But I want you to keep this close by. I think you'll feel more comfortable with it while I'm gone.''

Her mouth opened as her gaze went from his eyes to the gun in his hand. "You know I can't use that."

"You can if you have to."

She looked up at him again, confusion and hurt clouding her expression. "Don't leave," she said.

He straightened his shoulders and clamped down on the words he wanted to say. That he didn't want to leave, now or ever. That it scared him to death that Mojo might find them alone in the cabin while he was away. That he missed her so much it hurt clear through to his bones.

He breathed deeply until he could say what he had to. "You need to be prepared. I may not be able to protect you. Or Sam. What I can do is make sure we have an escape route. What you can do is take this gun, and let me teach you how to use it."

She reached for the gun, then hesitated. "What if I mess up? What if I accidentally shoot Sam?"

He turned the gun butt end toward her. "This is the safety. If it's engaged, you can't shoot. Don't take off the safety unless it's your only choice."

"What if I can't use it when I need to? I honestly don't know if I could shoot a person."

He lifted her hand and placed the gun on her palm. She slowly closed her fingers around the butt. "If Sam's life is in danger, you'll do whatever you have to. Trust me."

"Oh, God," she whispered as she turned her hand so the gun was pointing at the ground. "I hate this."

He walked behind her, and brought his arms around her so that he was holding the gun with her. Again, the soft scent of roses filled him with regret. He refused to let it get to him. Teaching Becky to use the gun was truly a matter of life and death, and he wasn't going to let his weakness interfere.

"It's very simple," he said. "Slip the safety off with your thumb, like this." He demonstrated, then engaged it once again. "You do it."

She followed his example.

"Okay. Hold the gun with both hands. Make sure you're standing with both feet planted firm." He widened his stance a bit, and she did too. "Lift the gun in front of you so you can see where the barrel is pointing. When the target is in your eyesight, squeeze the trigger. Be prepared, because it's going to jerk in your hands after the shot. Grip it tightly."

She grasped the gun and pointed, and he stepped back and eyed her stance. "Don't lock your arms," he said. He noticed that the gun wasn't steady. She was shaking.

"I don't know if I can do this," she said again.

"You'll do fine."

She lowered the weapon. "Go. Get it over with and get back here. Please don't take long."

He nodded. "I'll be as quick as I can. Hold the gun for a while. Get used to the feel."

She looked at the weapon and her lip curled in disgust. "I'll never get used to it. Ever."

Footsteps coming from the basement made them both turn. Witherspoon walked into the kitchen and his eyes went immediately to Becky's hand and the gun.

"Don't shoot me," he said. "I'm innocent."

Becky smiled, although she didn't think anything would be funny ever again. "Don't worry, Mr. Witherspoon. Mike was just showing me how to use it."

The old man grinned. "Good for him." He turned to Mike, who had moved farther away from her, toward the door. "The mice haven't gotten to any of the wires down there. At least the ones I could see. But I left you the cable, so if you have trouble you can fix it yourself."

"Mice?" Becky asked.

Witherspoon nodded. "I told your husband earlier that they come in from the cold from time to time. Don't worry. They won't hurt you."

"You ready?" Mike asked.

The caretaker didn't answer him. Instead, he walked over to Becky. "The way I see it, we'll be gone for a little over an hour. But don't get scared if it's more like two. The storm is getting worse, and the wind might slow us down. I'm taking him to my place to get the second snowmobile, then to the back road. Okay?"

She nodded. "Thank you."

"My pleasure." He turned to Mike as he walked past him toward the living room. "What are you standing around for? Get your coat. We've got places to go."

Becky started to hug her waist, but the gun stopped her. "Here, take this." Mike unsnapped his shoulder holster and took it off. He held it for her as if it were a jacket. She slipped into the leather harness. "Wait," Mike said. He reached over and tightened the straps.

She slid the .45 in its pocket. When she looked up, she could see how concerned he was.

"Lock the door after us," Mike said.

She nodded, but she didn't follow him into the living room. She forced herself to take the gun out again, to stand with her feet apart and her knees bent. To look down the barrel of the weapon, just the way he'd shown her. But her hands were trembling, and she couldn't hold it straight no matter how hard she tried. She brought her arms down, and she heard the front door open, letting in the wind, then close. It took all her self-control not to run and bring Mike back.

She walked into the living room and pulled the drape back. Mike was so bundled up, she couldn't see any part of his skin. But as he struggled against the wind, she recognized the tilt of his head, the long, even stride of his walk. Witherspoon climbed aboard the snowmobile first, then Mike behind him. She prayed their journey would be safe and quick. Then she locked the door.

After she heard the whine of the engine, she left the window to check up on Sam. She debated leaving the gun downstairs, but decided against it. The whole point of having the weapon was to protect her son. She slipped it into the holster and tried to act casual as she went into the bedroom.

Sam was sitting on his bed, his geography book open in front of him. He looked up at her, then his gaze traveled down to the gun. He didn't seem shocked.

She walked over to him. He had a pencil in his hand and a paper on his lap. When she looked at it, she saw he'd been busy. His neat script filled the entire page.

"You don't like guns."

"You're right. But Daddy had to go with Mr. Witherspoon for a little while, and we thought it would be best if I held on to this one till he got back."

Sam nodded. "Can I hold it?"

"No. It's very dangerous. I don't want you touching this, or any gun."

He shrugged. "Okay."

There wasn't much room, but she sat next to him anyway. "It's hard to be scared, I know. But if we stick together, everything will turn out okay." She slipped her arm across his back. "You want to talk about it?"

He shook his head.

"Hey, I think that's enough homework for now. Why don't we pull out your computer and play something?"

Slowly, he obeyed her. He closed his book and put it on the floor along with his schoolwork. He pulled his computer from the bottom of the bed and opened it. His movements were sluggish and clumsy, his features expressionless. It worried the hell out of her.

She climbed on the bed so her back was against the wall. Then she had him move so his back was to her. She wrapped her arms around him and kissed him behind his ear.

He ducked away. "Gross."

She squeezed him tight. "I love you."

"I know," he whispered. Then he turned on the computer.

She laid her cheek on his head and closed her eyes. She breathed deeply, smelling the little-boy scent that was all Sam. She'd fallen in love with that smell the moment he was born. It had changed since then, but not that much. She thought that when she was an old woman and he was a grown man, she'd still find that sweet, clean scent that was so uniquely his.

When she opened her eyes, she saw that Sam hadn't brought up a game to play, but his word processing program.

"What's this? I thought we were going to play a game?"

"We are. But I have to send a letter first. Is that okay?"

"Sure." Becky watched as Sam manipulated the data on the screen with wizardlike speed. A whole slew of files flashed by—all called Daddy, but with a different numeral after each one. "What are those?"

"Dad's e-mail."

"You save them?"

He nodded. "I like to read them sometimes."

She kissed the top of his head. "That's great, kiddo. He must write nice letters."

"Do you want to see?"

"Not if it's private."

"Well, some are." Then he shrugged. "It's okay." He pressed another button and the screen changed again.

I'm sorry I had to cancel our hockey game. I promise I'll reschedule soon. We'll go sledding, too, okay? I'll take you out on dead man's hill—just don't tell your mom!

How is she? Did she like that picture of the boat? I bet she put it up on the refrigerator, huh? She's real proud of you, Sam. And when she tells you to go outside and play, she isn't being mean. She loves you, and she wants you to do all kinds of things. She knows you're crazy about your computer, but there are other things that are important, too. Have you used those ice skates she bought you yet? What about that scout troop I told you about? I'm sure Mom would be glad to take you to the first meeting.

So be nice to her, okay, and don't give her any trouble when she tells you to go outside. She's really smart, and she knows a lot more about us guys than you can imagine. Listen to her, Samson. And give her a kiss for me.

Mike had written that letter only two months ago. That's when he canceled the hockey game, and that's when Sam had given her the picture of the boat. Mike had been right—she had put it on the fridge and kept it there for three weeks.

She'd never read one of his letters before, even when she'd had the opportunity. She'd wondered about them, though. She'd hoped Mike wouldn't say anything negative about her, just like she didn't say anything bad about him. But she'd never expected anything like that.

For the first time since the divorce, she felt better about the computer relationship between her son and Mike. No, it was much more than that, she realized.

There was still a part of the old Mike alive. Hidden behind that wall he'd built. She read the letter again. It was as if he'd written it five years ago, instead of two months ago. It was thoughtful and loving. Most of all, kind. She hadn't seen that kindness for a long, long time.

Thank God he could be that way for Sam. She had no illusions that Mike would ever be that way for her. Too much had been said, and done, in anger. This trip had shown her very clearly that she and Mike could never go back to the way it had been. He'd closed himself off to her, emotionally. He came by the house twice a month to get Sam, and he was always polite. He never failed to ask her if she needed anything. She had to admit that there was still a physical attraction. But the man she could confide in, who could confide in her, was gone.

She was glad she'd seen the letter, though. Glad that Sam could see the good in his father. They both deserved that.

She hugged Sam once more. "I don't blame you for keeping them, Sam. I'd keep them, too."

The ski mask didn't stop the snow from biting at Mike's face. His eyes watered continuously as he followed Witherspoon. Ice burned his mouth and his nostrils. He knew if he hadn't worn the mask, he would have been frostbitten in minutes.

The snowmobile was easy to manage even in the fierce wind. He'd been riding them since he was a child, so he knew how to lean into the turns and when to ease back on the power. Thankfully, with the face mask and the parka, the noise wasn't too bad. If it wasn't for the circumstances, he thought the ride might have been exciting.

It had taken longer than expected to go to Witherspoon's place and get the second snowmobile. To make up for lost time now, the old man had set a brisk pace. Mike stayed close as they sped past the houses by the lake. The farther they went, the thicker the trees became, until finally, there was a road only wide enough to travel single file.

Nothing had been through here in a long time, Mike noted. The snow in front of Witherspoon was pristine, white powder. With this storm, their tracks would disappear as quickly as they made them. But the storm wouldn't last.

If someone was trying to find them, and the wind wasn't blowing, it wouldn't be difficult. He tried to see between the trees on his right and then his left, but there was no room for a snowmobile. This was it, the only way out. He would have to pray for speed, then, in the event of a chase. He wouldn't be able to duck out of sight.

They continued up the trail. It was clear Witherspoon knew the route well. His speed varied, taking curves and bumps more slowly. Mike had to concentrate to follow suit. What would this road be like in the middle of the night? With Sam sitting in back of him, holding on to his waist?

He would have to get a rope and tie his son on. Sam wouldn't be able to hang on without help. That is, assuming he and Becky could navigate the trail in the dark. It was shadowy here already from the large trees. It would be a nightmare run after sundown.

He wasn't sure just how far they'd gone—two miles, three?—when they hit the clearing. He hadn't realized how much the trees had blocked the wind, but when he passed the edge of the forest, he and the snowmobile nearly tipped over. It was louder now, too. Even through the material around his ears, he could hear the fierce, howling wind and the high-pitched roar of the vehicles.

Ahead, he saw the sharp rise that led deeper into the mountains. This place was a meadow, probably filled with wildflowers in the summer. Now it was a shifting desert of white wind and ice.

Witherspoon slowed down, and Mike pulled up next to him. They both stopped. Mike saw that the old man was talking to him, but he couldn't hear. He held up his hand, then pushed his snowmobile right next to Witherspoon's. The old man leaned so close he was nearly touching Mike's ear with his mouth. "Get your bearings," he shouted.

"Once you're in the meadow you have to head straight north. The road goes east for a while, but don't go that way. Go north. You'll pick up another trail after a while."

The old man sat back, holding up his hand. It was a huge effort to talk, to be heard against the wind. Mike thought this whole trip must be hard on him. He thought about telling him to go back, but threw out the idea immediately. He didn't want to hurt the old guy, but Becky and Sam were at stake here.

Witherspoon motioned and leaned forward again. Mike struggled to listen.

"If you're in trouble, there are some caves due west of here." He pointed with his thick fingers. "Don't go there unless you have to. It's dangerous there. Avalanches. Try to head straight north, over the mountain. Once you get to the other side, it's not far to the gate and the road. You go down from there, till you hit the highway."

Mike nodded. "Let's go."

Witherspoon waved, and started up his snowmobile again. He took off, straight ahead. Mike had to remember to bring a compass. Straight north. Caves to the west. He looked at the slate gray sky above him, at the black clouds churning in the far distance. If it came down to it, he could get his family out of here. He prayed he wouldn't have to.

Mike had been gone two hours and ten minutes when Becky heard the sharp whine of the snowmobile.

"Daddy's back. I'm going to go make some hot chocolate. Want to come help?

Sam shook his head. "I'm almost at the pirate ship."

Becky glanced at the computer. A beautifully detailed animated ship was docked at a mythical port. Amazing. "All right." She climbed off the bed, took the gun from the night table then bent low to kiss Sam on the cheek. "Just don't be too long, sweetie."

She hurried downstairs. Mike didn't park in front, so she cut through the hall to the kitchen to meet him at the back door. It was only when she went to turn the dead bolt that she remembered the gun strapped to her side. She unsnapped the holster and put the whole contraption on the kitchen counter, glad to be rid of the horrid thing. Then she went to let Mike in. The wind was so strong it knocked the edge of the door into her forehead, hard. She couldn't even let go to rub where it hurt. Snow flew inside, twirling at her feet like a swarm of white mosquitoes.

If she'd thought the noise from the storm was bad inside, out there it was end-of-the-world loud. Oddly, she felt a sense of relief. No one could get through this, she thought. Mike was even crazy to go on the snowmobile. Mojo might be resourceful, but he couldn't fight something this big.

Mike stomped in, shaking snow off his body in great clumps. She pushed the door closed behind him, and double-checked the lock. When she turned, he'd already started taking off his snow gear. Going to the stove, she turned the burner on under the teakettle. She'd promised Sam chocolate. A hot drink wouldn't do Mike any harm, either. He must be freezing.

"That was unbelievable," Mike said.

"How did you find your way back?"

He'd already taken off his parka, face mask and gloves, and had his holster back in place. His face looked red and chapped. He rubbed his hands together as he sat down at the table.

"There are markers. Witherspoon showed me before he headed home. Everything okay here?"

"Fine. Sam's upstairs on the computer."

"Does he know I'm here?"

She nodded. "He's finishing up a game." She got three mugs and poured the packets of premixed chocolate into the cups. He looked up at her. His skin tone was better, but not normal.

"I need him down here. We have to talk."

Becky stopped what she was doing and turned to face him. "What happened?"

"It's brutal out there. I don't think Mojo could get through to us. Certainly not in a car or even a truck. But I want you both to know what to do if things go wrong."

"I don't want you scaring him. He's already having a tough time."

"Isn't it better that he's scared instead of dead?"

Her heart dropped. "I can't take this. If we're in so much danger here, why don't we leave? We can get on a plane. Go to Europe. To Africa. I don't care where, just someplace he'll never find us."

Mike stood up and came close to her. He put his hands on her shoulders. She screwed up her courage and looked at him, even though she knew he was going to tell her things she didn't want to know.

"And run for the rest of our lives? We have one real chance to get this bastard." His voice shook with emotion. "It will be in the next forty-eight hours. We've got the very best men on the job. The whole bureau is looking for him. We'll never have as narrow a window, do you understand?"

"But what if they don't catch him? What if he finds us first?"

"It's a very remote chance. There are only six people in the world that know we're up here. You, me and Sam. Witherspoon. Cliff and the chief, that's it."

"I don't care. If it was really safe, you wouldn't be handing me your gun, or going out in this blizzard to map out an escape route. You think he's going to find us. I know you do."

"I want to be prepared. That's not the same thing."

"Please, can't we just leave Sam out of it? Why do we have to frighten him?"

"He needs to be prepared, too. Believe me, I don't want to scare him any more than you do. But if there's even one chance in a million, I want him to be ready."

She turned and broke the contact between them. His hands went to his sides.

"I don't have a choice then, do I?"

"No."

"There will be consequences. You know that, don't you?"

"What do you mean?"

"Even if Mojo never shows his face, Sam will be afraid. He'll have nightmares, just like he did after Amy died. He's not strong."

"I'm trying to save his life."

She stared at Mike for a moment, then pushed past him and went to the staircase. "Sam. Come on down, honey."

While she waited, she made an effort to collect herself. She didn't want Sam to sense her fear. He would have enough of his own. She needed to be strong for him. She prayed she could be strong for him.

She watched him walk down the stairs. He looked so sweet in his jeans and his blue flannel shirt. He seemed more lively than he had this morning. The game had helped. She was glad of that. What she was afraid of was how he was going to react to Mike's talk. He retreated inside himself at the drop of a dime. A bad test score would send him to his room for days.

"Is it lunchtime?"

She smiled. "Are you hungry?"

He stepped down from the last stair. "Sort of."

"Daddy wants to talk to us first. Then I'll fix lunch. Soup and sandwich sound good?"

He nodded. "Alphabet soup?"

"Sure. Whatever you want." She walked him to the kitchen. If only she could think of a way to protect him from this. But she knew she would never be able to live with herself if the worst happened and he didn't know how to be safe.

"Hey, Samson." Mike was standing by the sink. He had a glass of water in his hand. Becky noticed his skin color was back to normal. Looking from him, in his red flannel shirt and jeans, to Sam, she saw how alike they were. As far as looks went, that was a good thing. Mike was a handsome man, and Sam would grow into one. What concerned her was that Sam was quiet, like Mike. Mike had shut them out of his life, and Becky was afraid Sam would follow in his footsteps. Hold himself apart from friends and family. Keep himself separate and alone.

"Have a seat, Sam," Mike said. The teakettle whistled, and he turned the burner off.

Becky went to fix hot chocolate, but Mike waved her to a seat. While he poured, she sat down next to Sam, scooting her chair to be close to him. She wanted to be able to touch him. To reassure him.

Mike brought over two mugs. He gave one each to Becky and Sam, then went back for his. He finally sat down across from his son.

"You know that there's a man out there who wants to hurt us, don't you?"

Becky shut her eyes. He didn't waste any time, did he?

"Yeah," Sam said. His voice was so quiet she barely heard him. It seemed to her as if the wind were trying to break in. The trees hitting the side of the house sounded loud and ominous.

"The FBI is looking for this man," Mike continued. "You remember my partner, Cliff?"

Sam nodded. God, he looked so young, she thought. So innocent.

"Well, Cliff and a whole bunch of other agents are looking for him right now. No one knows that we've come up here. I believe we're completely safe."

Sam nodded again. His mouth had opened just a little. Becky could see a hint of his white teeth. His eyes were as round as saucers, staring at his father.

"But just in case, I'm going to tell you what to do if that man should find us."

"He won't though, honey," Becky said. "Do you hear the wind out there? He can't get through that."

Sam turned his head to look at her.

"You know how we told you about talking to strangers?" She leaned forward and took his hand in hers. "It's like that. Just because we're talking about it doesn't mean it's going to happen."

"Do I get to have a gun?"

She smiled at him. "No. No guns."

"This is what I want you to do," Mike said.

Sam turned to face his father. His fingers slipped away, and Becky felt empty and helpless without them.

"I want you to know where your flashlight is all the time." He leaned forward and put his hands around his mug. "If you hear Mommy or me say hide, I want you to run, not walk, but run to the closet in your bedroom. Take the flashlight with you. Get down and climb underneath that big pile of sleeping bags and blankets. You got that?"

Sam nodded. He nibbled on his lower lip, but Becky could swear he hadn't blinked since he sat down.

"You might hear bad sounds. Gunshots. Or yelling. But don't come out. Don't come out until Mommy or I come to get you. Do you understand?"

He nodded again. "What if he kills you?"

Mike looked at Becky. She could see he hadn't anticipated that question. She couldn't help him.

"Cliff will come to get you. Or Mr. Witherspoon. You stay hidden for as long as you can. We're going to put some food in the closet so you won't get hungry."

"What if I have to go to the bathroom?"

"You might have to go in the closet, Samson."

He wrinkled his nose.

"Remember, this is all just in case."

"Okay."

His voice was too calm. Becky reached over and grabbed his hand. "Sam?"

He looked at her, completely composed and serene. It was as if they'd been talking about school or baseball. He registered no fear, no worry. "Did you understand what Daddy said?"

"Yeah. I'm supposed to hide in the closet if the bad guy comes. I have to stay in there no matter what until someone comes to get me. Even if he kills you."

He had her worried now. My God, it was as if she were seeing a miniature version of Mike with his stolid refusal to get emotionally involved in his own life. "It's okay to be frightened, Sam. This is scary stuff."

"I'm not scared."

"But—"

"Can I go back upstairs now? Until lunch is ready?"

She didn't know what to do. Should she make a scene so Sam *would* be scared? Or let it go? She glanced at Mike. He didn't look worried. No surprise there. She turned back to Sam. "Okay, honey. Go on. I'll call you when lunch is ready."

Sam got up quickly and headed for the door. He didn't look back at either of them. She heard him run up the stairs. "They've got to catch him, Mike," she said. "They've got to catch him soon."

Chapter 7

Mike leaned back in his chair, still cold, all the way to his bones. "I think he handled that pretty well."

Becky looked at him quizzically. "You've got to be kidding."

"What do you mean?"

"You didn't recognize his behavior? It didn't seem at all familiar to you?"

"What are you talking about?"

"Your son just gave a brilliant imitation of his father. Down to the last detail. 'I'm not scared. Can I have a gun?' Where do you think he got that?"

Mike waited for the punch line. Becky didn't move. She didn't say anything more. She just looked at him with weary eyes.

"You're saying he was trying to be brave for me? To please me?"

She shook her head. "No. I don't think bravery entered into the picture at all. To be brave, he would have to realize there was a dangerous situation."

"Of course he knows it's dangerous."

"No," she said. She scooted her chair closer to him so her eyes would be level with his. "He didn't. He denied there was any problem at all. Think about what he said. How he acted. It was as if we were telling him about someone else's life, not his own."

If he leaned forward he would be able to take her hand. That's how close she was. "Maybe he just accepted the situation. Maybe he didn't think getting hysterical would accomplish anything."

She moved her hand and put it on his leg. "He's nine years old."

The small imprint of her palm was the only spot of warmth on his body. He knew if she kept her hand there much longer, he wouldn't want to talk anymore. He stood up and took his cup to the sink. "You're reading too much into this."

"I don't think so."

"I'm going to build a fire. It was damn cold out there." He heard the scrape of her chair, then she was next to him.

"Do me a favor?"

He looked into her green eyes. He wanted to erase the worry he saw there. To comfort her and ease her pain. But he didn't have a clue how. "I'll try."

"Think about this. Don't just dismiss it. Something important happened here. How we deal with it is going to matter. This isn't about you and me. This is about Sam."

The tone of her voice, more than the words, made him stop. She was really serious about this. She truly believed that Sam's behavior had something to do with him, and that it was real cause for concern. "I know you mean what you're saying," he said. "I'm trying to understand."

"I asked the wrong question," she said gently. "I don't want you to think. I want you to *feel*. Trust your instincts. I know you can do that. You may be rusty at it, but dammit, I know you can if you try. Don't be logical. Don't make it fit into one of your neat boxes. Sam is in trouble. And we have to help him.''

He lifted his hand and brushed her cheek with his thumb, pleased beyond all measure that she was so near. "You're really something, you know that? I want to do this for you and Sam. I want to make you happy."

She moved her head. Just an inch. Just enough to break contact with his hand. She caught his gaze in a fierce lock with her own. "Don't do it for me. Do it because it can save your life."

She wanted something he couldn't give her. How was it possible that two people could see the exact same thing and come away with two completely different interpretations? But that's what always happened. He'd meant it when he said they were from different worlds.

"What I saw was Sam listen to the facts, understand them, and move on," he said. "He didn't whine about it or complain. If the worst happens, he'll do well. Looking at things logically isn't so terrible. That's just survival."

"Survival, yes. But is that all you want? To go through the motions of your life without feeling anything? Without caring?"

"You think I don't care?"

She shook her head. "I think you've forgotten how. You were hurt, so you turned yourself off. Like a light switch. And now you just wander around in the dark."

"Talking a problem to death isn't going to solve it. Since when did analysis ever fix anything? There's a real live man out there. Not some textbook villain. If he finds us, he's going to do everything he can to kill us. What the hell difference does it make if he hated his father, or if his mother left when he was ten? We'll be just as dead. You think if Sam gets upset and crazy about this he's going to react as quickly? Survival *is* everything. Don't you see that?"

"What good is surviving if you end up dead inside?"

"This isn't getting us anywhere. I didn't mean to upset ou."

She sighed. "Go on upstairs. Make sure Sam is okay. 've got to fix lunch."

Mike hesitated. He didn't want to leave it this way. He lid care. Too much. Every day they'd been married he'd ried to show her that. Even after the divorce, he'd hon-red her wishes. He'd stepped into the background. He adn't caused any trouble. All he'd ever wanted was her appiness.

He left when she went to the sink.

Climbing the stairs was an effort. The trip to the back oads had worn him out, made him feel old and tired. It adn't helped that he'd gotten so little sleep in the last few lays.

Sam wasn't in his bedroom. He must be in the bath-oom, Mike thought as he walked over to the window on he far side of the room. Pelting snow swirled in a dizzy-ng pattern. The pine trees swayed and trembled in the vind. Mike felt as though he were in one of those glass globes that he used to shake when he was a kid. His favor-te had been one of a little village. There had been a cabin ike this one inside the glass.

He turned away from the window and saw Sam's open omputer on the bed. It was on, but he saw only a screen aver—revolving triangles of color on black. He'd felt sure hat Sam would be knee-deep in a game by now. Well, naybe he was between battles.

As he headed toward the door, he heard a sound com-ng from the closet.

He whirled around and checked the floor beneath the vindow. It was completely dry. There were no signs the vindow had been opened. He turned back to the closet and eached for his gun. He eased the safety off with his humb, then slowly pushed the sliding door to the side.

At first all he saw were sleeping bags and blankets. The he saw Sam's running shoe. "Sam? You okay?"

"Yeah," Sam said, his voice muffled.

A large pink blanket moved and when Mike bent over he saw the side of Sam's face. Mike felt relieved and a little foolish. Better to be a jerk than to be caught unaware He engaged the safety and slipped the gun back into hi holster.

"Scoot over." Mike lifted a handful of bedding and shoved it aside. There wasn't much room, and he had to get down on hands and knees to make it, but finally he sa right next to Sam. The blankets settled back down, cut ting off his view of the room. "It's a little warm, but no half bad," he said.

"It doesn't smell too good."

"Maybe Mom can think of a way to fix that."

"Probably."

As they settled into silence, Becky's words swirled i Mike's head. The last thing he wanted was for Sam to grow up to be like him. To go to work every day and not give damn. To eat alone every night. To fall asleep in front o the TV set. The only bright spot in his life was this little guy.

"You want to talk?" Mike looked to his side. Sam sa cross-legged, with his hands folded in his lap. His hair wa all messy from crawling around, but he seemed to be do ing fine. He didn't look up at Mike, but straight ahead through a small gap between a Mickey Mouse sleeping ba and an afghan.

"About what?"

"About what we discussed downstairs."

"No, that's okay."

"You scared?"

Sam shook his head. "Nope."

"I am."

That got Sam's attention. He turned to look at Mike. He seemed surprised. "You are?"

Mike nodded. "Sure. It's a scary thing to have someone want to hurt you."

"But you're in the FBI."

Mike smiled. "You think FBI men don't get scared?"

"Uh-uh."

"We do." He reached over and took Sam's hand in his. The small palm and fingers were soft and delicate, and reminded him again of just how fragile his little boy was. "Being brave doesn't mean you can't be scared. Being brave is doing what you can even when you're scared. Facing trouble, even though all you want to do is run for the hills."

"But you don't act scared."

"Maybe I don't talk about it. But I feel it sometimes. Just like you."

Sam's squeezed his hand tighter. "Where will I live if that guy kills you?"

He wanted to tell Sam that it would never happen. That there was no chance that Mojo would get to them. But he couldn't lie. Sam already knew too much about death. He'd seen it firsthand. He may be only nine, but he still deserved the truth.

"*If* that happens, you'll live with Grandpa."

"Will I still go to the same school?"

"I think so. But you know, we probably aren't going to get killed. What's likely is that my partner Cliff is going to catch Mr. Jones and put him in jail for a long, long time."

"But if he does, I'll be an orphan then."

"Do you know what a long shot is?"

Sam shook his head.

"It's when there's a chance something will happen, but only a tiny one. Like the Cubs winning the series. It could happen, but it's really, really unlikely."

"But you said . . ."

"The reason I said those things downstairs was to prepare you for the very worst. But the very worst is a long way from what's probably going to happen. So you don't have to spend a lot of time worrying about it. As a matter of fact, now that you know what to do, you don't have to think about it at all."

"I'll try."

He leaned over and kissed the top of Sam's head. "Listen, kiddo. If you remember the safety rules, you'll be just fine. You got that?"

Sam leaned a little bit to the right, just enough so that his shoulder and arm made contact with Mike. "I like it when you live with us."

"I know, Sam. I know." He sat in the quiet of the closet. He couldn't hear the wind outside, or the trees banging on the roof. All he heard was the soft, sweet breathing of his son.

Becky had been right. Sam hadn't been stoic, just scared. Why had he resisted her words so fiercely? What was he trying to prove?

All he knew for sure was that he would do anything to keep his son safe and happy. The safe part was simple. Find Mojo and make sure he would never have a chance to hurt his family again. He still believed the letters in his duffel bag held the clues to Mojo's plans. When Sam went to sleep, he would go look at them again.

As for keeping Sam happy, well that would be a little trickier. Becky would know how. He would ask her. And this time, he wouldn't argue. He would just listen.

He closed his eyes.

The sound of a footstep woke him. Mike felt disoriented for a moment, until he realized he was still in the closet. He felt the weight of Sam's body leaning against his left side. When he turned to look, he saw that his son was out. His eyes were closed, but his mouth wasn't. He was as limp as a dishrag. If Mike had been in that position, he would have been in traction for a week. Sam wouldn't feel a thing.

"Mike?"

"Yeah." The sleeping bag in front of him moved, and then Becky was staring at him.

"It's time to get up. You guys have been asleep for a long time."

"I'm not sleeping." Sam yawned as he sat up. "I was just resting."

"I see. Well, it's too late for lunch. So how about coming down for dinner? While you two were wasting the whole afternoon, I baked cookies for dessert."

It took Sam a lot less time than Mike to crawl out. He managed, but a lot of bed rolls came out with him.

"What kind of cookies?" Sam asked.

Becky smiled. "What kind do you think?"

"Chocolate chip?"

She nodded, and Sam raced out of the room.

"Not till after dinner," she called after him. Then she turned back to Mike.

He was busy rubbing a kink out of the small of his back.

"Whatever you did, it worked."

"Huh?"

"Sam. He's acting like his old self again."

"How can you tell? You saw him for two seconds."

"I'm his mother. I can see when he's upset and when he's not. Now, come on. What happened?"

"We just talked a bit."

She narrowed her eyes. "This couldn't have anything to do with our earlier conversation, could it?"

He shrugged his shoulders. "Seems you were right."

She studied him some more. Her gaze traveled over his face, searching for clues. "I was, huh?"

He nodded. "He was scared. He didn't want to admit it."

"What did you say?"

"I told him I was scared, too."

She smiled. It changed her whole face. She looked soft and beautiful, and he was glad to have those eyes looking at him. "You confuse the hell out of me, you know that?"

He smiled back at her. "It's my job."

"Come on down. Chocolate chip is your favorite, too."

She turned and he watched her walk out of the bedroom. His gaze traveled down the length of her, admiring her sleek body and the way she moved. All that and brains, too, he thought. He had a good feeling about the night to come.

He didn't go right to the kitchen. First, he went to his bedroom and washed his face. The nap had done some good, but he still felt achy and stiff. He needed a solid night's sleep. If Cliff didn't call with good news soon, he doubted he would get one.

Mojo could be out there, on the mountain. It would be hard to travel in this blizzard, but it could be done. He would need a snowmobile. A map and a compass. Some luck. On the other hand, even if he knew they were staying at the lodge, he would have to know which cabin they were in. Mike thought about the smoke from the fireplace. He would wait until it was fully dark before he lit the next fire.

He sat on the edge of his bed and opened his duffel bag. The letters were on top, and he pulled out the stack. He heard Sam's laugh coming from the kitchen. Then he read.

Dear Mike,
You never write, you never call. It's starting to hurt my feelings. We have so much in common, you and I. We really should be closer, don't you think? It's not as if you didn't have the time. That restaurant you frequent, George's Café? You could bring a pad and pen in there. No one would bother you. Just like al-

ways, you could sit for hours in the back booth, nursing your coffee, eating your tasteless meals. I think it would look less pathetic if you busied yourself with correspondence, don't you?

There was more, but Mike didn't have the stomach to read it now. Every time that lunatic mentioned something personal he wanted to tear his throat out. Where the hell had he gotten his information? How had he known about George's Café?

He folded the letter and put it back with the others in his duffel bag. He would work on this some more tonight. The letters held the key. He knew it.

Becky and Sam had already started eating by the time he got to the kitchen. An empty bowl and a thick sandwich waited for him. "Smells good in here."

Becky got up and took his bowl to the stove. She ladled some of Sam's favorite alphabet soup, then brought it back to him. The steam filled his nostrils, and he realized just how hungry he was.

"Did you see?" Sam asked through a mouthful of tuna sandwich. "Mom baked a cake, too."

"Swallow first," Mike said. She'd been busy. A golden cake sat cooling on the counter. Next to that were the cookies, big ones, lots of them. On the stove, next to the soup, a larger pot boiled loudly. He turned to Becky. "Bored, were we?"

She gave him a Mona Lisa smile. Something had shifted. The atmosphere had changed. The tension from this morning had disappeared. Sam, for the first time since they'd been here, acted like Sam. He ate his soup with a vengeance and swung his legs beneath the table. Becky was different, too. It was nuts, but the way she was looking at him—she was being coy. Flirting.

Had all this come about because he'd told Sam it was okay to be scared? That didn't make sense.

But what else could explain it? They were still stuck in this little cabin. The blizzard still howled. Mojo was still out there.

"None of us will be bored tonight," Becky said. "I've made plans."

Mike looked at Sam and raised his eyebrows. "Uh-oh."

Sam giggled.

"Let's play checkers, then we'll work some more on that puzzle. After that, I thought we would play these word games." She got up from the table and went to the counter by the phone. There was a brown bag there, and she brought it with her back to the table. "Look," she said. She pulled out a thick tablet. "It's a game. Full of stories that have a bunch of words left out. We make up words to fill in the blanks. Then we read them out loud. Sounds great, huh?"

Mike nodded. All he'd wanted was to sit by the fire and turn in early. But he didn't want to spoil the mood. "Can't wait."

He ate his sandwich and watched his family. *What used to be his family.* Sam hummed the theme from *Star Wars* as he chewed. Becky looked relaxed and comfortable. Even though he knew it was an illusion, he didn't care. He wanted to have this moment.

He wandered back in time, shaking out old memories. Nothing had given him more pleasure than quiet times with his family. Not his job, not vacations. Nothing. He would sit in the living room, pretending to read the newspaper, while Becky and the kids puttered around the house. He'd felt like king of the world, with a sense of satisfaction that he'd never found again. He never suspected that it all would be taken from him in the blink of an eye.

Now, the only real pleasure he had was to remember what was. Except for Sam. He watched his boy take another letter from his soup and put it on his plate. He'd collected quite a few. Mike saw he had spelled the name

Darrelyn with the pasta. Wasn't nine too young to be interested in girls? In his time, maybe, but it was a new world.

He took another bite of his sandwich. It was the best meal he'd had in ages.

Becky took her empty dishes to the sink. She felt hopeful for the first time since this nightmare had begun. Mike had really made an effort with Sam. When it came to his son, Mike was capable of going the distance. She believed that with all her heart. He'd proved it again today, when he'd talked to Sam about being scared. What a difference he'd made.

She turned at the sink and leaned back, just watching her little boy. He was playing with the letters from the soup. His hands were gooey, but she didn't care. He wasn't that sullen, withdrawn kid anymore. At least for now. She would do anything she could to keep it that way.

She thought about the letter she'd read on Sam's computer. Maybe, just maybe, if Mike could be that way with Sam, he could be that way with her. Had Sam shown her that letter in an attempt to bring them back together? Was he really clever enough, old enough, to plot something that subtle?

Her gaze moved to her husband. Her ex-husband. He'd really listened to her concerns this afternoon. She knew he was frightened to let down his guard. It didn't take a genius to figure that out. What puzzled her was what he thought he was going to lose. Did he believe the Tin Man act would save him from being hurt again? Maybe. Tonight, she would bring it up. After today's success with Sam, he might even be willing to listen.

But what if he did listen? What if he said he wanted to change? Did she really want to get involved with him again? Her life worked now. She was busy and productive, and her days—and nights—weren't filled with dread about Mike getting hurt. Maybe she should just leave well enough alone. "You guys ready for dessert?"

Sam nodded. "I want five."

"Five? These are big, Sam." She lifted the plate and brought it over to the table. Each cookie was the size of a saucer. "Are you sure you can eat that many?"

"I'll bet you I can."

"What kind of a bet?" She sat down and looked from Sam's smiling face to Mike. He grinned, too. He seemed younger. More handsome. The humor in his eyes captivated her, and she remembered, a little too clearly, how she had always been a sucker for that look.

"If I can eat five cookies right now, we don't have to work on that stupid puzzle tonight."

She laughed. "Stupid puzzle, eh? And what happens if you can't eat all five?" She knew he could, of course. He would be sick afterward, but he could do it.

"Then we put the puzzle together."

She shook her head. "Oh, no. That's not nearly enough. If you can't eat all five cookies, then you have to—"

"Clean the kitchen for a week," Mike said.

Becky grinned. "And help with the laundry."

"What?" Sam screeched. "That's not fair."

"You called the puzzle stupid, Samson," Mike said, suddenly serious. "You know perfectly well how your mother feels about puzzles. Now you have to pay."

Sam grabbed a cookie. "I'll eat six!" He took a huge bite.

Mike got up. He moved slowly behind Sam's chair. Sam swiveled around to look at him. "What are you doing?"

"Don't talk with your mouth full," Mike said.

Becky didn't know what he was doing, either. Then Mike motioned for her to join him. She did.

Sam, still chewing, tried to scoot his chair back so he could get up.

"Nope. You have to sit right there."

"That wasn't in the rules."

"Sure it was." Mike wiggled his fingers so that Becky could see he wanted to tickle Sam.

She shook her head, and leaned very close to him. "He'll choke," she whispered.

Mike stopped. Clearly, she'd foiled his plan. He looked at her with raised eyebrows.

Then she knew just what to do. She smiled. Only one thing bothered Sam more than being tickled. Big sloppy kisses. She winked at Mike, then went down on her knees so her face was level with Sam's.

Mike followed quickly.

Sam looked at her, then spun to look at Mike. He was trapped and he knew it. "No fair!"

"That's only one cookie," Mike said. "Five to go."

"Get away!"

"Nope," Becky said. She nodded at Mike. As a unit, they leaned forward and smooched Sam's cheeks.

He screeched.

Becky had to stop. She was laughing too hard to keep going. Mike was still at it, making unbelievable sounds as he kissed Sam, who flailed around in a desperate attempt to escape. "Five more to go," she said and moved in for another round.

Just before she made contact with his cheek, Sam disappeared. He slid from his chair, under the table in one smooth move. Suddenly, she was staring at Mike, her face and his only inches apart.

She froze. Mike did too. They stared at each other for a long minute. Then Mike leaned forward.

Chapter 8

Becky watched his face come nearer. She held her breath as his lips brushed against hers, softly, like a whisper. She closed her eyes, and he kissed her again, harder this time, but not by much. Just enough to send a little shock wave through her system.

"I've finished. All six!"

Becky's eyes snapped open and she pulled back. Mike gave her a wistful smile, and she felt her cheeks fill with heat. She turned quickly away, afraid that he would see her reaction to his kiss.

He'd barely touched her. His lips had been warm but closed. And he'd made her tremble.

She sat back and watched as Sam held up both hands to show he'd eaten all the cookies. The smile on his face was worth a million dollars. His eyes looked alive and spirited and his giggles were filled with delight. Then she saw the cookie-shaped lump in his pocket, and she grinned. She wouldn't say a word.

Mike reached forward and grabbed Sam by the waist. He pulled him into his arms and gave him a bear hug that Becky almost felt. She pictured herself in Mike's arms, then shook away the image as quickly as she could. What was she thinking? Mike toppled to his side and brought Sam with him. Their laughter filled the room as Mike got down to some serious tickling. Sam wiggled like a fish under his teasing hands.

She started to move toward them, to join in the fray, but stopped short. It was wonderful to see Sam and Mike so free and easy, but she was a fool if she thought it was for keeps. They'd all been so tense for so long, it was only natural that they would seek relief. That had been her original intent, hadn't it?

She'd planned the games and baked the goodies with one thing in mind. To release the stranglehold of fear that had encircled them all. She couldn't do anything about Mojo from here. Just wait and be careful. But she would be damned if she was going to let him squeeze the life out of her boy. Not without a fight. A fight she was winning, for now.

That didn't mean that Mike was his old self, and would never again retreat behind his icy facade. Any minute, he could turn on her, shut her out. But seeing him like this was like seeing an old friend. He even looked like the man she'd married. The laughter took years from his face and, more importantly, swept away the haunted expression that had plagued him for so long.

It wasn't hard to understand why this man made her think of being in his arms.

She got up, and went over to the guys. In those short seconds, the tables had turned. Sam sat on Mike's stomach. He was trying hard to tickle his dad, but he couldn't keep Mike's hands out of the way. She sat down again, facing Sam and above Mike. She grinned and grabbed Mike's wrists, pulling them to the floor.

"Hey, no fair." Mike struggled, but not very hard.

Sam attacked with all ten fingers, and she laughed until she cried.

The sound of the phone stopped them all. She froze, with Mike's wrists still captive in her hands. Sam sat up with wide eyes. The ring came again, high-pitched and urgent.

Mike broke out of her grasp instantly. He lifted Sam and sat him down by his side, then he was on his feet. He turned to her. "Stay here." He ran into the living room, out of her sight.

The next ring stopped abruptly, and she began to pray.

"Who is it?" Sam asked.

She turned to him. He was still sitting where Mike had put him. His smile had disappeared, and in its place was a worried frown.

"I don't know," she said, trying to keep the fear from her voice. "Probably Daddy's office."

"What if it's him?"

She knew who he meant. "Daddy will take care of it, honey."

He didn't ask her any more questions. He just stared at the kitchen doorway with unblinking eyes. She couldn't do much more herself. She was so afraid to hope.

Time seemed to come to a crawl. She didn't move, didn't dare breathe. Then she heard his footsteps.

He was smiling.

She let her head drop into her hands as the relief washed over her.

"Hey, sport," Mike said. "Why don't you go set up the checkerboard while Mom and I clear the table?"

Becky looked up again. Sam was on his feet, worry still evident on his beautiful face. Mike put his arm around his shoulders. "It's okay, kiddo. Don't worry. We're gonna be fine."

Sam's smile came slowly. "Did they catch him?"

Becky heard Mike take a slow breath. "No," he said. "They haven't caught him. But they do know he's headed north. He's not coming this way tonight."

"Are we going home?"

"Not yet."

Sam sighed. What a sound coming from such a little guy, she thought.

Becky got to her feet, and walked over to her son. "It won't take us long in here, Sam. You go set up the checkerboard, like Daddy said. We'll be there in a minute."

He nodded, and walked out of the kitchen. As soon as he was gone, Becky turned to Mike. "Tell me."

"It's good news. They've picked up his trail. He's in, or he was in, Laramie. Heading north. That was as of this morning. He's probably in Casper by now."

It was hard to believe it was over. That they were safe. "When can we go home?"

"There's no guarantee that he's not going to double back. We're not leaving till he's caught."

"That could take days or weeks. What if they don't ever catch him?"

"They will. At the very least, they'll be able to verify he's in Canada. But you'd better pray they catch him. The last thing we want is for him to get away. We would never know another minute's peace."

"But tonight?"

"We can breathe a little easier. Just don't let down your guard. He could be here tomorrow or the next day. Until we know, we keep to our game plan.

"All right." He stood by the fridge and she walked over to him. "But we do have this night. Let's relax and have fun. Sam needs it. I need it."

His dark brown eyes softened. "Yes, ma'am."

She reached over and took two of his fingers in her hand, but she didn't let go of his gaze. "It's nice to be friends again. I've missed that."

He nodded. "I've missed you."

She didn't move, and except for the light pressure of his fingers, he didn't either. She swallowed and found her throat felt thick and her mouth dry. She captured her bottom lip with her teeth, and his eyes followed the movement as if spellbound. She knew what he was feeling. A pull as strong as the tide had her in its grip, too. What he couldn't see under her thick sweater was that her breasts felt heavy and her nipples hard. Warmth spread inside her and her pulse quickened.

She stepped back, dropping his hand and breaking the spell.

"I've got to clean up," she said, afraid to look him in the eye.

"Becky..."

"Don't, Mike." She looked up at him again. He did want her, there was no mistaking that. She knew this man better than she knew herself. "We can't do this. You know that. Now go on out there and be with Sam. I need to do the dishes."

She could see the strong muscle of his jaw tense and relax. "No, no. I'll clean up in here."

"Thank you," she said, wondering if he understood that she meant far more than the dishes.

"Go on, get out there," he said. "I can only be noble for so long."

She caught his gaze. The haze of desire still lingered in his brown eyes. The temptation to go to him surprised her with its strength. It was the situation, she thought. The news that Mojo was far away, and that they could all relax. She turned and took three deep breaths to clear any foolish notions from her head. Sam needed her.

He sat on the floor by the fireplace, with the checkerboard in front of him. He flipped the box top over and caught it with one flat hand, then flipped it again. When he looked up at her, it fell to the floor.

"Sorry I was so long."

He shrugged. "I want to be red. Can I?"

She nodded as she sat across from him, the checkerboard between them. "Sure can. That means you go first."

He studied the board, while she studied him. His dark hair was getting too long. It came down below his collar and half covered his ears. She would take him for a trim when they got home. For the first time in a long while, she felt as though they would be going home. That life would be getting back to normal.

He would go to school, and she would finish the decorating job at the hotel. He would go back to his computer generated world, and she would get busy with the PTA, or volunteering at the museum, or a hundred other little pieces of business that would help keep her mind off the lonely nights.

How long would it take her to get over Mike this time? Another year? If they made love, would she ever get over him? God, why was she even thinking that? She wouldn't make love to him. Not tonight or ever.

"It's your move."

Sam's voice startled her and she looked down at the board. It took a minute to remember what she was supposed to do. "I haven't played checkers in a hundred years," she said.

"A hundred?"

She smiled at him. "Maybe a thousand."

"Maybe you played it with dinosaurs," he said, giggling.

"That's it. Me and Tyrannosaurus rex. I kept winning because his arms were too short to reach the board." She put her hands close to her sides and wiggled her fingers.

Sam mimicked her and roared like a dinosaur with all his might.

Mike walked quietly into the living room and stood by the couch. Watching Becky and Sam goof around was the best thing that had happened to him in a long time. He'd better enjoy it. After all, the chance would probably never come again.

The world they were in wasn't real, and he knew it. The fear, the close quarters, the intensity were all extraordinary. They'd been granted a temporary stay, and emotions were bound to go overboard. But he'd seen the look in her eyes. In the old days, all she'd had to do was give him that glance, and they would have headed for the bedroom.

Christ, he wanted her. He wanted to take off that damn sweater of hers and feel her beneath his tongue. He wanted to know her body again, to explore all the hidden curves he'd once worshipped.

Making love with her once would never be enough.

Many things had changed in the last few years, but her effect on him wasn't one of them. Just looking at her now, sitting on the floor, was enough to send his pulse into overdrive. It was more than her beauty. It was the way she looked at him, the way she smiled. The way she tucked her hair behind her ear. Hell, every move she made was enough to make him crazy.

"He's killing me, Mike," Becky said. "He's crowned me, and he doesn't even care that I'm his mother. You would think he would show a little mercy."

Mike fought down the urge to pull her to him right then and there. He struggled to smile casually as he walked over to the fireplace. It was dark out, although he wasn't sure if that was nightfall, or just the black thunderclouds carpeting the sky. It didn't matter. Mojo was in Wyoming. And while he was there, he couldn't see the smoke from the chimney.

He crouched and grabbed some tinder. "Sam, don't let her trick you. She's ruthless when it comes to checkers."

He heard them both laugh. The sound filled him with something he'd nearly forgotten existed. Peace. He crumpled some newspaper and stuck it under the grate. "There's not enough wood here for the night. I've got to get some more."

"Outside?" Becky asked.

"Unless you want me to chop up the dining room table."

That set Sam off again. When was the last time his boy had had the giggles? Years, he thought. Before Amy had gotten sick.

The thought of his little girl was a sharp jolt, bringing him back down to earth. He was a fool to think things had really changed. One night of laughter didn't go very far to erase years of pain.

He stood up. "Is the game over?"

Becky nodded. "He won. You're next. We'll see if you have better luck." She lifted her hand to him, and he took it, pulling her to her feet.

She stood very close to him, close enough for him to smell the soft scent of roses. Before he could back away, she touched his arm lightly with her hand. His mind went right back to where he started. Wanting her. Needing her.

He had to go outside. Now. It was as if he was back in high school, when he'd had to carry his books in front of his crotch to hide his overactive hormones. "What are you waiting for, Samson? Set up the game. I'll get the firewood, and then I'll whip your butt."

"Not a chance," Sam said. "Not in a billion years."

Becky went back into the kitchen while Mike donned his parka and gloves then turned to look at Sam, leaning over the checkerboard, setting up the pieces. Mike hadn't realized how much he missed the little things about living with his family. The quiet times, and the silly games. Watching Sam grow from day to day. How could a week in the mountains make up for years of being a part-time father? The thought of going back to the way it was hurt like hell. Maybe Sam didn't need him, but Lord, he needed his son.

He headed for the kitchen. Becky stood by the stove, her back to him. He didn't move for a minute, just let his gaze wander over her, feeling his heart thud as he looked at the soft curve of her bottom.

What was the matter with him? It had been a long time since he'd made love, but this was out of hand. He rushed past her to the back door. When he opened it, snow and ice hit him with a blast. It was almost enough to douse the flames.

"Damn fool," he muttered, as he lifted the logs. "She's off-limits. She doesn't want you. Get over it." He balanced the last piece he could manage, then pushed the door open with his foot. Before he went inside, he turned and looked around.

The snow was falling at a sharp angle from the wind. The trees that had been so laden were now bare, as the fierce storm kept any snow from sticking. Huge drifts had come up above the deck and against the side of the house. The windows would be buried soon. The sound of the gale was thunderous as it whipped the trees into a frenzy.

The sky itself was black and turbulent. He couldn't make out individual clouds, just a churning mass of darkness. He pitied anyone who didn't have a warm home tonight. Except one man. He hoped the storm went all the way to Wyoming, and that it kept Mojo far away from here.

Mike didn't believe Mojo was heading to Canada. He didn't care that he'd been spotted in Laramie. The man had made a promise. One thing Mike had learned—Mojo didn't give up. He might not come after them tonight, but he would come. Mike would stake his life on that.

He went inside and kicked the door closed behind him. He couldn't manage the lock, not with his arms so full. Hurrying to the living room, he stopped in front of the fireplace.

Becky and Sam were there to help. They each lifted split logs from the pile and placed them next to the grate. As soon as they were done, he went back to the kitchen and locked the door. Only when he heard the click of the dead bolt did he feel comfortable enough to slip off his gloves and his jacket.

"Come on, Dad. Mom's talking about doing the puzzle again."

Mike didn't go yet. He grew still, and let his feverish mind calm down. Nothing was going to happen, except a nice, quiet evening. He would play checkers. That's all. No use thinking about anything else. He breathed slowly and deeply, letting the air out in a long sigh. Then he went back into the living room.

Becky sat on the couch, with Sam bent over the armrest, his butt high in the air. Mike remembered how he'd called him Monkey Man, after Sam had just learned to walk. Sam had loved to climb. Over chairs, people, toys, it didn't seem to matter. He fell as often as not, and Mike remembered coming to the rescue. Picking him up and holding him tight until the wailing came to a halting finish.

A lump came to his throat and he felt foolish and sentimental. What the hell was happening to him? "Hey, come help me with this fire."

Sam was up in a blink, and by his side. Together, they fashioned a decent pile of paper, kindling and logs. Mike lit it in several places, then sat back on his haunches to watch it come to life.

"Pretty good job, Dad."

When he looked over at Sam, he saw the boy mimic his stance exactly. His hands were on his thighs, his bottom resting on the backs of his legs. Even the smile on his face copied his own expression. "Thank you, son," he said. He had to swallow pretty hard before he could talk again. "So, what's up next? Checkers?"

"Yeah. I'm red."

Mike positioned himself comfortably across from Sam. When he turned to look at Becky, he saw she'd risen from the couch. She came over to join them, and sat down, facing the fire.

"Come to watch my inglorious defeat, eh?" he asked.

She nodded, and gave him a crooked grin. The light from the fire made her look soft and lovely. "You bet. I don't want to be the only one to go down in flames tonight. I warn you, he's tricky."

With some effort, he turned his attention to the game. It moved along quickly, as Sam was pretty ruthless. The fire was the perfect accompaniment to the evening, crackling away and turning the room into a warm cocoon.

He would remember every detail, he thought. Every move, every sound. He would memorize the way Sam bit on his lower lip while he concentrated. The way Becky hugged her knees up to her chest while she watched them. The warmth that came more from contentment than the fire.

In the nights to come, after they'd all gone back to the real world, he would travel back here, to this night, and replay the scene in his mind. It would be enough. It had to be.

After the second game, which Sam won, of course, Becky made hot chocolate. When she came back, she sat closer to Mike. Close enough to touch.

He was incredibly aware of how near she was. If she leaned just a little to her left, their legs would brush. He sipped his hot chocolate and burned his tongue. That seemed to amuse his son.

"You have a mean streak," he said, turning his gaze to Becky.

"I know," Sam said.

Becky only smiled, and let her hand drop to his knee. The contact was hotter than the burning liquid. The electric sensation traveled straight through to his groin. He moved just enough to dislodge her hand. Then he forced himself to concentrate on the game.

A log shifted and he jumped.

She touched his arm.

He almost groaned out loud.

Sam saved him this time. He kicked the checkerboard and scattered the pieces. Mike moved quickly to retrieve them, making sure he was just out of Becky's reach.

Was she doing this intentionally? Did she have any idea what her casual moves were doing to him? If she did, she was crueler than he'd ever imagined.

He set up the game again. He focused on the board, on his cocoa, on the fire, but he didn't look at her. What if he saw that her touches had been a signal? That she, too, was thinking about making love? Worse, what if they weren't?

Sam crowned his man, and Mike cursed. When Sam's mouth dropped open, he realized he'd said the word out loud. "Sorry," he said, risking one glance at Becky.

It was one glance too many.

She smiled at him mischievously, shaking her head at his faux pas. When she moved, the soft tendrils of hair that had escaped from her braid shimmered in the firelight. Her lips seemed moist and inviting, and her skin looked softer and sweeter than anything mortal man would ever touch.

"Don't you mean fudge?" she said.

He nodded.

She turned to face Sam, and he let out his breath. He hadn't realized he'd stopped breathing. He had to get the hell out of here, that's all.

"Well, I'm gonna turn in now," he said, stretching his arms way out to the side. "Too much excitement for me."

"Good idea," Becky said. "We'll play that word game tomorrow. It's time for you to go to bed, too, Sam."

Sam got to his feet. "Can't we play one more game? I know, let's work on the puzzle."

Becky laughed. "Not on a bet. Upstairs, kiddo."

"Do I have to?"

"Yes," Mike said, a little more forcefully than he'd intended.

"You go on and get in pj's while I help Daddy straighten up down here. Then I'll be up to say good-night."

Sam looked at Becky, ready to start pleading his case. Mike stood up, and spun Sam around so he faced the stairs. "Bed," he said. "Now."

Sam gave one pitiful glance back and headed for his room.

"And no computer tonight, either," Becky said. "You can read for a while if you want, but that's all."

The exaggerated sigh matched his slow, dragging steps up the stairs.

Becky watched him until he was out of sight, then she turned to Mike. "So, are you really sleepy, or did you just want to stop playing checkers?"

"How did you guess?"

She laughed as she stood up. "I could see your eyes start to glaze over."

"Four games is about my limit."

"Don't run off," she said. "I'll be back down in a minute. I'm just going to make sure he gets to bed."

Becky didn't look back at him as she headed up the stairs. She wondered, not for the first time that evening, just what had gotten into her. She felt as if she were infused with electricity, that if she touched anything she would see a spark. The night had been the best she'd had in a long, long time. Seeing Sam so relaxed was a tonic. And Mike. My God, it felt as if he'd come back from the dead.

Had he noticed that she had trouble keeping her distance? That she'd found herself touching him, just to reassure herself that he was really there, and that they were really having such a wonderful time?

She didn't want it to end. She wanted to go back downstairs and talk to him, like they used to. She felt as though he'd let down his guard, and she wanted to take full advantage of it. How she'd missed him.

More than ever before, she realized all she'd lost. Mike had been her best friend. She'd been able to say anything to him, and he'd understood. He'd confided in her, too. They'd shared so much. His love had been the very center of her life, and losing him had cost her dearly.

Seeing Sam in his pajamas, sitting up in bed with the covers pulled over his lap, filled her with a completely different kind of satisfaction. Tonight had been so good for him. He missed Mike, too. She went over to the bed and kissed Sam on the cheek. "'Night, sweetie."

He gave her a reluctant grin.

She walked to the door. "You want to read? I'll leave the light on."

"No, that's okay."

She smiled and blew him a kiss before she turned off the light and pulled the door closed. She rested her head against the hard wood, and said a silent "thank you."

She got halfway down the stairs before she saw Mike. He stood by the fire, watching her. He caught her gaze, and held it steady.

Somehow, the heat from the flames had invaded his body, and his eyes were ablaze.

She stopped still, feeling her own temperature rise.

He'd unbuttoned his shirt, and it hung open and loose. Dark, curly hair in an inverted V played over the muscles. She felt her mouth go dry as she scanned his washboard stomach. His jeans rode low on tight, slim hips, and his hands were tightly fisted by his side.

Her pulse accelerated, and she stopped thinking about anything at all. Without her willing it, her hands moved to her head and she began to loosen her prim braid.

His gaze zeroed in on her hands, and she moved slowly and deliberately. She shook her head and felt the soft curls touch her cheeks.

She wondered if he could hear her heart beat.

He moved to the staircase, his gaze never leaving her face.

She walked down, drawn to him as if by a magnet. My God, she'd missed this, too. So much it frightened her. She took another step, and then he was in front of her. They were eye-level, with him on the step below. He reached out and touched her hair. Then his palm moved to her cheek and his rough hand caressed her with infinite tenderness.

He pulled her toward him, and she fell into his kiss.

Chapter 9

She closed her eyes as he closed the distance between them. His lips touched hers softly. She trembled as he deepened the pressure. Her arms wrapped around his neck, while his hands moved up and down her back in slow circles. He brought her closer, pressing his stomach against hers, and she felt the hard evidence of his desire.

She opened her mouth to him, and he moved his head so he could join her more intimately. She tasted him, hot and sweet and familiar. She breathed his clean, sharp scent and that only made her want more. She ran her hand down his chest, letting her fingers tease the soft hair, feeling the tense muscles underneath. She kept on moving, past his waist and over the bumps of his pockets. Then her hand slipped over the thick curve of his erection and she felt, more than heard, his low moan.

His flesh pulsed beneath her hand. Even through the layer of denim, she felt his heat. His hands cupped her buttocks and drew her closer still.

She wanted him inside her. She wanted to be swept away on a wave of sensation to a world where there was nothing but pleasure and release.

His hand moved down her legs, and he lifted her into his arms. She wrapped her hands around his neck and buried her head in the crook. He smelled wonderful, clean and masculine.

Often, in the last years, she'd come across something he'd left behind, a shirt or a sweater, and she'd caught that scent. Each time, it had made something deep inside her ache. But now the ache had a name, and he was carrying her away.

He moved down the rest of the staircase. His labored breathing was more from want than anything else. He was remarkably strong. She'd seen what his body had become. Muscled, taut, fierce. She wanted to explore him again, to feel the differences.

They passed the kitchen, and he kicked open his bedroom door and flipped on the light with his elbow. She closed her eyes as he shut the door behind them and carried her to his bed. He laid her down gently, and she felt the mattress dip as he sat next to her. When she opened her eyes, he was looking at her, very close. He was braced by one arm, a breath away.

Her heart pounded and a deep throb of anticipation swelled in the pit of her stomach. A faint stir of alarm played at the back of her mind. This was foolish, dangerous. How would she ever get over him now?

"Becky," he said, his voice a bare whisper, raw with emotion.

She lifted her hands to his chest, and she heard his sharp intake of breath as her fingers made contact. She had always loved the feel of him, the texture of his smooth skin. Now, with his well-defined muscles, there was even more pleasure in tracing his flesh. She let herself linger near his nipples, teasing herself as well as him, before she continued her journey. She moved up to his shoulders and she pushed back his shirt.

"I want to see you," she said. "You've changed so much."

He shifted his position, putting his legs beneath him and stretching up above her. He pulled his shirt off the rest of the way.

He was magnificent. His shoulders were broad and heavily muscled. His chest expanded with each breath, and the sight of him was overwhelming. She moved her gaze down, searching until she found an old scar on his rib cage. It was small, barely discernable, and wonderfully familiar. He'd gotten it the year after they were married, while training at the obstacle course at Quantico. She touched the smooth skin there, and heard him gasp.

He lowered himself until he was sitting. He still towered over her. Reaching slowly, he took hold of the bottom edge of her sweater and lifted. His hands brushed her skin lightly as he bared her chest, and she shivered. He sighed once before he brought the sweater over her head and past her arms.

He looked at her with dark flashing eyes, his desire for her thick and vibrant. He leaned forward and down, bringing his lips to the hot flesh beneath her breasts. She moaned as he kissed her, writhed as he tasted her. Moving slowly, kissing her tenderly inch by inch, he moved up her body. When he reached the cleft between her breasts, he paused, but only long enough to undo the clasp of her bra.

He lingered there for a moment, his hot breath sending shivers of desire to her very center. Then he eased his fingers under the silk and pushed the material aside.

He moved back so he could look at her. His eyes told her he was pleased. His smile told her he was just beginning.

She held her breath as he leaned forward. He kissed the rounded flesh of her right breast, while he caressed her left with his hand. It was impossible to be still. Something quivered and pulled tight low in her stomach. The touch of his hand sent shocks of pleasure coursing through her. His tongue on her rigid nipple, swirling and teasing, made her grab the cover beneath her and squeeze until she shook with the effort.

He let her catch her breath while his hands found the waistband of her pants. She struggled to push off her boots and in another minute he slipped the pants down her legs, onto the floor. The cool air hit her wet flesh, and made her already taut nipples even harder.

Mike slid down off the bed, and stood looking at her naked body. While he undid the buttons of his jeans, he drank her in, drowning in the silk of her thighs, the swell of her breasts, the triangle of soft hair between her legs. His Becky. His woman. He never thought he would see her like this again.

He'd been starving for too long. His hands shook as he reached the last button. He was harder than he'd ever been, swollen beyond his endurance. He let his pants drop, and the cool air on his skin was almost painful.

She was looking at him now, seeing how much he wanted her, what she could do to him. He ran his hand down his length as he gloried in the hunger in her eyes.

He couldn't stand it any longer. He climbed on the bed again.

She opened herself to him, spreading her legs to welcome him home. He sank down, not yet letting himself touch her there. He caught her gaze and held it with his own. "Do you know what you've done to me?"

She nodded.

Still he held himself away. Reaching with one hand, he touched the soft mound at the juncture of her thighs. He knew this, the feel of her, the way her body curved. He'd dreamed of this night after night, the reality of her now so much more than he'd remembered. He moved his hand down, teasing her lightly, then slipping his fingers inside the moist warmth.

She moaned and lifted her hips.

Liquid velvet. He wanted to take it slow and easy, to learn her body all over again. Then she touched him.

He bit back a groan as she urged him to replace his fingers with his swollen manhood. He sank inside her, penetrating slowly. She grew still, somehow knowing if she moved, he may not be able to control himself.

He went deeper, until he was completely inside her, and they were no longer separate people but joined as one. He felt complete for the first time in years. The ache that had haunted him every night and every day was finally, mercifully, assuaged. All he could do was whisper, "Becky."

She held her breath as he moved inside her. She felt as though he belonged there, as though her body had been designed with him in mind. The sensations were familiar and new, all at the same time. His eyes, his lips had been a part of her forever, but running her hands down his back offered tantalizing surprises. His body was streamlined and powerful, and as he moved into her, she felt his muscles contract and release.

He pulled back until he was just barely inside her. She lifted her hips, not willing to let him go. She opened her eyes and found him staring at her. While he thrust in and out with agonizing slowness, he entered into her very soul.

He was a dangerous man, but she'd been a fool to think she would ever escape from him. He had infiltrated her mind and her heart years ago. The tragedy of their lives had not succeeded in tearing the connection, only stretching the thin line that held them together to the limits. She would always be a part of him, and he a part of her.

He quickened his pace, and she started the long, slow, spiral that would take her to release. She wrapped her legs around his hips and kneaded his back with her hands, wanting every part of her body to touch his, to feel the powerful strokes and his thudding heartbeat.

He kept her gaze captive with his own. As she stared into the dark brown eyes, she felt the tremors begin low in her stomach. She could feel the blood pulse through her veins as she rose higher and higher until she was on the very edge of a cliff.

She fell, and he was there to catch her.

She cried out, and he held her tighter, still thrusting, still coming deeper and deeper inside her. Then she felt him tremble and heard his primal cry as he let go. He thrust again, and she contracted around him, and then there was no more movement, only the shaking, quivering release and the slow journey back to breathing and seeing and hearing.

Finally, he sank down, resting his whole body on hers. She brought her hand up and stroked his hair, and whispered his name softly in his ear. It took a long time for them to stop trembling and lay quietly entwined.

She listened to him breathe, felt his chest expand and contract. She didn't want to think yet. Only to feel. She closed her eyes and let her senses take over.

She was glad they'd made love. She felt as though a healing had begun. When he'd been inside her, she'd remembered so much of what their love had been. Close, sweet, secret. Nothing had been taboo between them, nothing too scary to talk about. Even in the very beginning—when they'd both been inexperienced and shy, they'd been able to love each other. They'd learned about sex together, and about intimacy. He'd asked her once if she ever regretted not having more partners, and she'd told him no. He was everything she had ever wanted, and more.

It was still true. She didn't want another man. In the year they'd been divorced, she'd gone out only a few times, but she'd never made love. She had convinced herself that it wasn't important. That making love wasn't necessary. But she'd been wrong.

Tonight, her soul had needed touching. His touch.

Her breath caught in her throat as the realization hit her. It wasn't that she just needed his touch. She still loved him. She had never stopped loving him. The breakup, the bitter words, even the fear that Mike would end up getting killed hadn't been enough to change that one basic fact.

She ran her hand down the length of his back. His skin was smooth and cool and more familiar to her fingers than her own flesh. His scent was imprinted in the deepest part of her, sultry and sharp like no other on earth. The way he moved, the sounds he made, the look in his eyes. She would never be able to forget them. She didn't want to. No matter what the future held, he was the man she loved. He had captured her heart and made it his own.

It was no use thinking she would get over him when she went back to the real world. The sting of their separation would lessen, the yearning would mellow in time, but she would always want him. The nights would be long and empty, and sleep would be hard to find, but she would survive. She would take this night, the memories of the way he held her, and relive it in her dreams. She lifted her head and kissed the soft crook of his neck, then she closed her eyes.

Mike lay in her arms as he tried to recover. Making love with her had been better than he'd dared hope, and for that he was sorry. Not for the experience, but for the memories he would take with him. If only he could stop the world now. His world at least.

How was he supposed to go on, knowing that in her arms he was whole again? How could he survive going back to his empty apartment, his empty life?

He lifted himself off her, and rolled onto his back. He felt cold without her, hollow. What had he been thinking? Why the hell hadn't he just left her alone?

"Mike?"

He turned his head and looked at her. Her hair was wild on the pillow, her skin luminous and soft. Her eyes were filled with dreams and promises, and he wanted to turn away.

"Do you remember the first time we made love?"

"What do you think?"

She smiled. "It was pretty awful."

He thought back to that night, so many years ago. The dingy motel room that had seemed so exotic, the scratchy blanket on the lumpy bed. His fumbling attempts that had ended embarrassingly quickly. "We were just kids."

"I knew that night that you were the one I wanted to spend the rest of my life with."

The ache in his chest grew. They had been so young. So naive. He'd wanted to give her everything. A big house and nice cars. More than that. He'd wanted to give her children. Lots of them. But that was long ago, when he'd believed in happy endings. He knew better now.

"What's wrong?" she asked.

"Nothing."

The softness left her eyes. "Nothing? Come on. Don't hide. Talk to me."

"Maybe this was a mistake."

She rolled over on her side, facing away from him.

For a long time she didn't speak. When she did, her voice was bitter. "Couldn't you even wait five minutes before you spoiled it all?"

"I didn't mean to spoil it. It's just—"

She turned to face him, her gaze filled with fury. "It's just what? I'm such a jerk. I keep pretending that you'll come back. That you'll snap out of it and be Mike again. But it's been two years. You're not going to change. Ever. Why can't I get that through my thick head?"

"I tried to tell you—"

She grabbed her sweater and pulled it on. "What gets me is that you don't see what a waste it all is. That you don't care that you've thrown away your family. I can understand that you don't love me anymore, but what about Sam? How can you let your self-pity keep you from that little boy?"

"Self-pity? You think that's what it is?"

She held her pants in her hand, but didn't move to put them on yet. "Yes, I do."

He grabbed his jeans, pulling them on quickly. He walked over to her side of the bed and made sure she was paying attention. "You don't get it, do you? I screwed up, big time, or don't you remember? I let you down, I let Amy down. You didn't hesitate to remind me of that every single day. Is it coming back now? Is it clearer? I was never there, you said. But even when I was there, I wasn't enough. I did everything wrong, and you let me know it."

He tried hard not to remember the heated words and accusations from that horrible time, but they were permanently etched in his memory. "I had to work, Becky. I had to keep on going or I would have gone insane. Gordon tried to get me to take a leave of absence, you begged me to stay home, but I wouldn't. I insisted on working, insisted that we check out that warehouse. Gordon died because of me. I killed him, not Mojo. I am responsible for his death, just like I'm responsible for the death of our family. So don't tell me it's self-pity. I'm just aware of the facts. And when you're thinking a little more clearly, you'll remember them, too."

She almost turned away, but he captured her chin in his hand. "The only thing I did right was to let you go."

She jerked out of his grasp, and rubbed her chin where he'd touched her. "What arrogance," she said, as she stood up to face him. "Did you think you could heal Amy with your touch? She had cancer. You didn't do that to her. You didn't kill Gordon, either. You did your job. He knew the risks going in."

"So nothing's my fault, right?"

She shook her head. "Leaving was your fault."

"You were the one who left. I just didn't stop you."

"Why not? Weren't we worth it? Didn't the fact that I loved you matter? I left because you stopped being my husband. You lived with me and shared my bed, but you had gone. Somewhere I couldn't find you."

"I had no right to keep you there."

She pushed her shoulders back and stood very straight. "I want you to understand this. I didn't leave you because Amy died, or because Gordon died. I left because it hurt too much to see what you'd done to yourself. You could have had me and your son. We could have been a family. But you gave us up without a fight. I hope you're happy with your guilt. That's all you'll ever have. I won't make this mistake again."

The ache started in his gut, and went straight through his heart. He couldn't seem to move, or form words. He just watched as Becky finished dressing. What had he done? What the hell had he done?

"You know," he said quietly. "Amy died on me, too. Not just you."

"I know that."

"I did what I thought was right. It wasn't. So you took Sam and you left."

She ran her fingers through her hair, trying to tame it into submission. Then she dropped her hands and wrapped her arms around her waist. "All I ever wanted was for us to hold on to each other. Was that too much to ask?"

He took a step back from her, trying hard not to let the pain bring him to his knees. "That's not true. You wanted me to save you. To save Amy."

"I never said that."

"You said it with every look, with every touch, with every tear. You hated me for letting Amy die, and don't try to tell me you didn't." He turned his back on her. "I'm going to take a shower."

"Wait," she said.

"Why? What's left to say? I don't want to rehash the past. I don't need any more of your guilt. I've got enough of my own."

Becky took a long, slow breath, then let it out in a sigh. She hurt inside. So much sadness, so much grief. They'd been through hell, and had never managed to find their way back. "Come and sit down. Please. Let's talk about this. I don't want any more bitterness between us."

He hesitated, looking at her as if she were setting some kind of a trap. Finally, he sat at the bottom of the bed.

She sat down, too, but not so close that they could touch. She hadn't grown used to his chest, the broadness of his muscles. He was a new man in many ways. But not altogether. "I know how much you loved Amy," she said. "And how much she loved you. I don't know what you remember, but I never doubted that. Not for an instant. You gave her everything you could. I probably did ask too much of you. I was crazy back then, I know that. But what I can't figure out is what happened to us? You were the one person who knew what I was going through. You knew how it felt to watch her slip away and be powerless to do anything. So why didn't we help each other, Mike? Why did we turn against each other?"

He looked like she felt. Wounded, battered. "I don't know what you want me to say."

"I'm trying to understand," she said. "Doesn't our past mean anything to you? You're the only man I've ever loved. That has to count for something."

He sat straighter and she could see his muscles tense all through his body. She wanted to comfort him, to hold him in her arms until he was peaceful again, even while she was angry and hurt by his actions and words.

"You loved someone else," he said, his voice cold and low. "You loved the man you thought I was. You were mistaken."

Her heart sank. Maybe it had gone too far. Too much had gone wrong. The pieces were shattered and couldn't be put back together again. "Did I?" she asked. She stared at her hands, afraid that if she looked up she would start to cry. "That makes me pretty foolish, huh? Wasting all those years?"

"We both made mistakes." He stood up and started toward the bathroom. Her hand caught his and held on until he turned to face her.

"I don't want to think loving you was a mistake. Sam showed me something while you were gone," she said. "A letter you wrote him."

"Which one?"

"The one about the boat picture."

He still looked at her suspiciously. "I don't remember."

She sat further back on the bed, tugging lightly on his hand, hoping he would sit back down. "When you had to cancel the hockey game. You told him to listen to me, that when I asked him to play outside it was because I loved him."

He nodded, but he didn't join her. "Yeah, okay. What did I do wrong?"

She dropped her hold on him. "Nothing. The letter was wonderful."

"So what's the problem?"

"I'm trying to say something nice here."

He still looked fierce and mistrustful. Had it really been so bad between them? Had they lost all connection?

"That letter *was* wonderful," she said. "It was sweet and thoughtful. You handled Sam like I wish I could. You know what I thought when I read it? I thought, that's Mike. That's how he is. Funny and kind, always ready to listen. Not afraid to get mushy. That's the man I lost. He left me over two years ago, and I didn't see him again until tonight. How come, Mike? Why did that man leave me?''

"I wasn't the one who left."

She sighed, and bowed her head. "Oh, God. It is too late, isn't it?"

He left the room.

Chapter 10

Becky gathered the rest of her clothes and left Mike's room. The house was dark and quiet, all of the warmth from the early evening had gone. The warmth had gone out of her, too.

How could it hurt so much to see the truth? Hadn't she learned yet that Mike was never going to change? That he would never again be the man she'd married?

When would she wise up and listen to her head instead of her heart? She should never have let him touch her. Or kiss her. Letting him make love to her had been the ultimate mistake.

She moved toward the stairs, but stopped after taking the first step. Had she just *let* him make love to her? Wasn't that her way of denying her own responsibility? She hadn't *let* him love her. She'd gone willingly. More than willingly. She'd wanted him desperately.

Mike had changed, but so had she. She'd learned to be independent, to stand up for herself and her son. She'd struggled hard to build herself a life. But in the two years since she and Mike had been apart, she'd never really accepted the fact that she still loved him. Instead, she'd chosen to ignore her emotions, to concentrate on everything else, to keep herself so busy that she didn't have time to feel the emptiness inside her. Tonight, she'd had to face the truth. She still loved Mike. She still ached for his touch, for the comfort of his arms. She needed him to be there for her, to talk to and to listen to her.

She couldn't go upstairs. Not yet. Sam might wake up, and she couldn't deal with any questions right now. Instead, she turned around and went into the living room. She could hear the water going through the pipes as Mike took his shower. That was the only sound in the house. Moving over to the front window, she pushed the curtains aside and saw that the blizzard had ended. Snow was falling quietly, gently. She let go of the drape, and walked over to the couch. She sat down, pulling her legs up and into her arms.

How had things gone so wrong? It wasn't so long ago that she'd had a perfect life. A wonderful husband, two beautiful children, a future as bright as the sun. Slowly, painfully, each part of her world had been torn apart.

Making love had been a terrible error. Having Mike inside her again had awakened a sleeping giant. She'd never stopped loving him. Damn him. Damn her own weak heart.

She leaned to her side, resting her head on the thick cushion. She really needed to go upstairs and put herself to bed. She would just close her eyes for a minute. Then she would get up.

At eight-thirty, Mike went to fix the coffee. He'd slept, which surprised him. He figured his talk with Becky would have gnawed at him, but he'd been out the minute his head hit the pillow.

As he walked toward the kitchen, he saw her. She was sound asleep on the couch, no blanket over her, just a back cushion covering her bare feet. He walked over to where she lay. Her hands were curled up tight against her chest. Her hair was loose around her face. She looked sweet and beautiful, and a deep regret filled him until he could barely breathe.

"Why couldn't things have been different for us?" he whispered. "All we needed were a few breaks, that's all. Just some luck."

Becky stirred, but didn't awaken. He reached down and touched her shoulder gently. Her eyes slowly opened.

"Morning," he said.

"It's cold."

"You don't have a blanket."

She pushed herself up with one hand, while she rubbed her eyes with the back of the other. "Where's Sam?"

"Upstairs. Sleeping."

"What time is it?"

"Close to nine. Why don't you go take a hot shower while I fix breakfast?"

She nodded. As she got to her feet, she bumped her arm against his chest. She stepped back so quickly she nearly fell.

He reached to steady her, but when he saw the look on her face, he dropped his hand. He'd really done it this time, he thought. Last night was the clincher. She didn't want to have anything to do with him.

That's what he'd wanted, wasn't it? He'd finally told her the truth—almost—and it had ended any pretense there might have been. He hadn't been able to save her, or Amy, or their family, or even Gordon. He was supposed to feel better now that it was out in the open, that the words had been spoken. But he didn't. He felt like hell.

She gathered her underclothes and her shoes, and walked around him. She hurried to the staircase and nearly ran upstairs.

He'd shown her, all right. He'd hammered his point home, so she would never forget it. She'd asked him to be her hero, and he'd failed her. Last night he made sure she would never think of him as her hero again. The last piece of his heart, of his hope, died without a whimper while he stood alone in the empty room.

He went into the kitchen and filled the coffeepot with water. He lost count as he spooned the dark granules, and had to start again. He heard the pipes complain as Becky started her shower. Then he got the milk from the fridge and the hot-cereal box from the cupboard. It was important to keep focusing on the food, on the preparation. To measure everything carefully, and to stir the cereal constantly. When the coffee was ready, he poured himself a cup, then set the table for three. He heard her footsteps approach, and he had to struggle harder to still his thoughts, to keep moving as if he were a real person, instead of an empty shell. The one hope he had was that Mojo would be caught today, so they could leave this prison and go on with their lives.

At home, this wouldn't be so difficult. If she wasn't in front of him, close to him, he would be okay. The real problem was being near her.

She came into the kitchen. Her hair was still wet. She'd put on jeans and a white sweatshirt. She was fresh and pretty, and he couldn't bear to look at her. He turned his back and forced himself to feel nothing.

"There's something we have to talk about," she said.

He heard her pull out her chair while he poured her a cup of coffee. It wasn't as hard as he'd imagined, walking over to her. He gave her the mug and sat across from her. "What?"

"Sam," she said.

He watched her take a sip. Nothing. No reaction.

"After last night, I'm real clear on where we stand with each other. That's fine. But Sam shouldn't have to pay. You're not spending enough time with him. He needs you."

"We write just about every day."

"Writing isn't enough. He needs to be with you. He needs a father."

"He has one."

She shook her head, and he found that if he didn't look at her, if he concentrated on his hands, and on his coffee, it was easier to speak in a normal tone.

"You weren't there when he had the chicken pox. Or when he broke his little toe. You haven't been there for a long time, Mike."

"I knew about all that," he said. "Just because I wasn't there in person, doesn't mean I didn't know what's going on."

"Really? Did you know that after he signed up for little league, he used to ditch practice and go to the library? That he lied about playing baseball? I didn't find out for over a month that he'd quit the team. Even then, I found out by accident. I wanted to surprise him at a game, and when he wasn't there, I talked to the coach. He told me Sam had never played. Not even once."

"Why didn't you tell me?"

"He made me swear that I wouldn't. He was so ashamed, Mike. He thought you would be ashamed of him, too."

"Dammit, you should have said something."

"I don't take promises lightly. You know that. I wouldn't even mention it now, if I didn't think it was so important." She reached across the table and touched his hand.

He moved away quickly. He couldn't deal with her touch right now.

"I don't like the way he thinks of you. It's not good for him."

"And just how is that?"

"He worships you. You keep him at arm's-length, so he doesn't see. You don't tell him that he has to go to bed early on school nights. Or make him clean his room. You've let me be the bad guy for too long."

Mike got up from the table and went to the stove. While he spooned cereal into two bowls, he thought about the last couple of years. He had kept himself away from Sam—no, that wasn't accurate. He'd kept his distance from Becky. He'd thought the letters were enough, but even he could see she was right. The last thing in the world he wanted was for his son to worship him. It would kill him to see that look of disappointment on Sam's face when he realized what his father was. It was all he could stand to see Becky look at him that way.

"I'll do whatever you say," he said, his voice as flat and emotionless as the deadness inside him. "Whatever you want."

He brought the food to the table, and handed Becky her bowl. He wasn't hungry any more.

"I think you should keep up the e-mail. It would hurt him if you stopped. But you need to see him a lot more. You need to take him to ball games and to the park. He loves to go sledding."

"I know that," he said, "Despite what you think, I do know him."

She nodded. She wasn't looking at him with angry eyes, or blaming him with her tone.

He wanted to ask her if she felt anything, or if she, too, had decided that feeling had too high a price?

"What about on the weekends?" she asked.

"It doesn't work like that. You know I can't be sure I'll have the time off."

"Can't you explain to them that you have a little boy who needs you? That he has to be able to count on you? Or don't they believe in families?"

He started to say something angry, but stopped. After a deep breath, he said, "I'll talk to them. Maybe we can work something out. I don't know for sure, but I'll try."

Why was she looking at him like that? What would make her get weepy now? Her green eyes glistened with unshed tears, and her lips curved up in a slight smile.

"That would be wonderful," she said. After a long minute, she looked away, and picked up her spoon. "Where is he, anyway? I told him to come down. His breakfast will be cold soon."

Mike was still confused. Was she that pleased that he had agreed to talk to his superiors about taking time off? Was it so unexpected that he would want to be there for his son? He pushed his chair back and stood. "I'll go get him."

He walked upstairs quickly, thinking about that look she'd given him. What kind of an ogre was he supposed to be? It's not as if he never saw Sam. At least once a month, he'd taken the boy for a few days. It wasn't enough, he would give her that. Especially after this extended 'vacation,' he'd seen how much he missed Sam. He needed the boy as much—no, more than Sam needed him.

He opened the door to the bedroom. Sam's bed was empty. Mike went over to the closet and pushed the sliding door to the right. But Sam wasn't in there, either. He hadn't heard him come downstairs. Maybe he'd wanted a shower. "Sam?"

The hairs on the back of his neck stood up. Something was wrong. He felt it. Sam would never voluntarily take a shower. Not in this lifetime. He took one last look at the room. It was messy, with some clothes and shoes on the floor. He didn't see the computer anywhere. The window was still locked, and he could see it hadn't been disturbed by the way the snow clung to the pane.

He reached for his gun. He didn't like this. Not one bit.

Becky finished her coffee while she waited for Mike to bring Sam down.

Mike had surprised her. He truly had. She'd expected him to stand tough. To fight for his position and deny there was any problem with Sam. It probably wasn't fair of her. Even though he didn't want her, he still loved Sam. She'd always known that. It made her feel a little guilty for not talking to him about this before. She'd had plenty of opportunities to bring up the subject. Actually, she had, but never straightforward like this morning. She'd hinted, made vague references, then she'd gotten angry when he didn't take any action.

All she'd had to do was ask.

"Becky?"

She dropped her spoon. The tone of his voice had her out of her chair in a second, out of the room in two. "What's wrong?"

"Sam's not upstairs."

There was an urgency in his tone that made her blood go cold. "Sam!" She called his name, trying hard not to panic.

Mike moved past her and went into his room. She ran after him, the adrenaline shooting through her veins.

"Sam." Mike's voice was angry. Scared. He ducked into the bathroom, and she went into the closet, but all she found were clothes and shoes.

Mike came out of the bathroom. The look of worry on his face cranked up her fear a couple of notches. But it was the gun in his hand that started her panic.

"He's got him. He's got my baby."

"Don't lose it now," he said. "I need you." Mike ran from the room, and she forced her legs to move, to follow him.

He headed for the front door. "It's unlocked. From the inside." He flung open the door. There was no wind this morning. Only gray skies and snow.

She got to Mike's side. Starting at the front door, she saw one set of footprints. Small footprints. Sam's.

"Where did he go?"

"Get your coat," Mike said, as he ran to the closet beneath the stairs "He can't have gone far."

She was shaking so hard it was difficult to put on her gear. Especially her gloves. Sam was out there. Why? she thought. Why did he leave?

Mike came back with his rifle. In a second he had his parka on, then he handed her the .45. "Take this."

There was no hesitation this time. The gun felt solid in her hand. If Mojo had touched Sam, she would kill him without blinking.

The air was frigid and still outside. Everything was blanketed in a thick pile of snow. Sam's trail went to the right, up the hill. She looked for signs of another pair of boots, but to her eye it seemed as though Sam was alone. "Is he really by himself? Does Mojo have him?"

Mike shook his head. "I don't think so. Come on, he's headed toward the woods."

Mike took the lead. Getting through the snow was slow work for them, it must have been terrible for Sam. Some of the drifts came up past Becky's knees; they would have come up past Sam's waist. She tried to figure out why he would have done this. Boredom? Mischief? It didn't make sense. They hadn't been cooped up that long. Maybe he just wanted to go sledding? No, he would have headed in the other direction, toward the hills past their cabin.

Mike had moved a lot faster than her, and he was nearing the third cabin—the last cabin before the woods. She pushed herself to catch up to him. He stopped. She thought he was waiting for her, but when she reached his side, she saw he was looking at the deck of the cabin.

Sam was standing there, toward the back of the deck, looking at them. The sound that came out of her was a strangled cry of relief. She tried to run to him, but the damn snow held on to her boots and her legs. Mike moved ahead of her, and just as she reached the steps, he grabbed Sam and hugged him to his chest.

She had a moment to register that Sam had his backpack on.

"Where were you going?" Mike asked. "You scared the hell out of us."

She reached Mike's side. She wanted to hold Sam herself, but she saw that he had a death grip on his dad, and she contented herself with touching him to make sure he was really there.

A muffled sob told her that Sam wasn't in great shape. She pulled back his hood, and saw his face was tear-streaked and pink. His eyes were swollen, and he looked absolutely miserable. Her heart lurched in her chest. She wanted to hold him. He needed her comfort.

It was a tremendous effort to let Mike console the boy. She'd grown so used to being the only one there for him. His father was here, now, and she couldn't bring herself to interrupt this moment. They both deserved it.

"What happened, Samson?" Mike asked.

Sam couldn't talk yet. He was still crying too hard.

Mike looked at Becky. "Let's take him home."

She nodded. She knew he meant the cabin, but she wanted to take him to their real home. Back to their real lives. Mojo was gone. He was in Canada by now. She wasn't going to wait any longer. They would go home today.

She followed Mike down the steps, back into the heavy snow. It was easier going back, using their old path as a road. Halfway there, she finally felt the cold. Her nose burned with it, and her hands ached. The worst of it was her head. Her hair had been damp, and now it felt as if it were turning to ice.

She moved ahead of Mike when they reached their cabin. She opened the door, and stood back to let them in. When she closed the door behind her, she bolted it, then rested her head against the cold, hard wood. She didn't know whether to curse or cry. He was safe, and that's all that mattered to her. There was no way she would have survived if something had happened to him. Her heart wasn't strong enough.

"I'm taking him upstairs."

Mike's voice made her turn around. He was already at the staircase.

"Put him in his pajamas. With socks. And give him some more blankets. I'm going to put on some water to boil, then I'll be up." She didn't want to go to the kitchen. She wanted to be with Sam every second. But he needed warmth from the inside, too.

She watched Mike climb the stairs, Sam still clinging to him for all he was worth. What had made him leave? It was so unlike him.

As they turned to go into the bedroom, she put the gun on the coffee table and hurried to the kitchen. It took only a minute to fill the teakettle and light the burner, but it felt too long. She needed to see that Sam was all right.

On her way to the stairs, she unzipped her parka and shrugged it off, leaving it right where she dropped it. She ran up the stairs and into Sam's room.

Mike had him on the bed. His backpack was on the floor, and his down parka was halfway off. She hurried over to him, and tugged the other arm free.

Sam's face was still pink, but the tears seemed to have stopped. He sniffed, and she touched his chin so he would look up at her. His eyes broke her heart. So big and round and filled with sadness. "What is it, honey? What happened?"

Sam just stared at her, blinked his eyes, and sniffed again.

"It's all right. We'll talk later. You just get into your pajamas, okay? Let Daddy take off your boots."

Mike worked quickly and efficiently. He had Sam's boots and socks off, and before he put the new socks on he took Sam's feet in his hands and rubbed them briskly. Becky helped Sam put on his pajama tops, but her gaze was on Mike.

The way he was touching Sam was as tender as anything she'd ever seen. He rubbed those little feet with infinite care. His eyes were filled with concern and with so much love it was palpable. She hadn't been wrong to ask Mike to be with Sam more often. They needed each other so much.

It didn't take long to finish dressing Sam. She pulled back his blanket and he crawled in.

"Why don't you get in there with him?" Mike said. "Maybe that will stop your shivers."

Shivers? She looked at her hands. She was shaking. A quick tremor raced up her spine, and she realized her teeth were chattering. "Move over, kid," she said. Sam made room for her, and she slipped off her boots, then crawled in beside him. It was a bit cramped in the twin bed, but she didn't mind at all. Having Sam tight against her, safe in her arms, was the best possible medicine.

"The water is probably boiling," she said. "Mike, would you mind fixing some hot chocolate for the Popsicle next to me?" She looked down to see if Sam was smiling, but her tiny joke didn't even elicit a grin. He still looked sad and weepy.

Mike stood over the bed near Sam. "You want to tell us what you were doing out there?"

Sam turned to his side and curled up next to Becky.

"I think we should wait to talk about this. He needs some rest now."

"Did you talk to anyone? See anyone out there at all?"

"Not now Mike." She glared up at him. Was he trying to make things worse?

"I'm sorry. I have to know." He bent over and touched Sam's shoulder. "You need to tell me if there was someone out there, son."

Sam shook his head, but didn't say anything. Becky could tell Mike wanted to press the issue, but she held up her hand to stop him.

He didn't go on. He turned and walked out of the room, and she heard his heavy footsteps on the stairs. She closed her eyes, and snuggled closer to Sam. She wanted him warm and safe. Her shakes had not all been caused by cold. The adrenaline from her terrible fear was still coursing through her.

She vowed again that she would take Sam home today. Without a doubt, Mike would argue, but she wasn't going to acquiesce on this one. It wasn't clear to her why Sam had left the cabin. But with all the talk of killers and hiding, she had a pretty good guess. If they stayed here any longer, she didn't know what would happen to him. She wouldn't take the chance.

When she looked down at him again, she saw his eyes were closed. His even breathing told her he'd fallen asleep. She closed her own eyes, but not to sleep. To say a silent thank you to the Fates for keeping her boy safe.

"Is he sleeping?"

Becky opened her eyes and looked up to see Mike standing by the bed. He had two mugs in his hands. She must have dozed off herself; she hadn't heard him come in. She nodded.

"You want some hot chocolate?"

"I don't want to move," she whispered. "I don't want to disturb him."

Mike put the mugs on the dresser, then came back to the bed. "I'll let you two get some rest. I'm going out to check the snowmobiles and the truck. I want to make sure no one's touched anything.'' He turned to leave.

''Wait,'' she said.

He stopped and came back to the bed.

''I want to go home,'' she said, careful to keep her voice low.

''So do I. But until I hear from Cliff—''

''No,'' she interrupted. ''I don't care. I want to go home today.''

Mike's lips pressed together and his eyes narrowed. ''I told you before. It's too dangerous.''

''And this isn't? Don't be ridiculous. Being up here is scaring him to death. I won't have it anymore.''

''I don't think we should talk about this now. He might wake up.''

''You're right. We won't discuss it. We'll just leave. I want to be out of here by sundown. I won't back down on this. If you don't take us, we'll go by ourselves.'' She saw his jaw muscle tense, a sure sign he was furious, but she didn't care. Not anymore. She couldn't hide here any longer. Not just because of Mojo. But because it was too hard to be here with Mike. She needed to be home, where she could think. Away from his anger and his tenderness and his voice. All she felt now was confusion, and a weariness that went all the way down to her toes.

She closed her eyes again. As soon as she woke up, she would pack. For now, though, she would sleep.

Mike stared at Becky and Sam for a long time. All he wanted was to keep them safe. That's it. He had no other purpose in life. Just to keep them away from harm.

He'd almost lost it earlier. When he'd realized Sam was gone, the terror had been overwhelming, blinding. He'd only known that kind of fear once before. When Amy had died.

Nothing would happen to Sam. He swore it as an oath, and he hoped that God was listening, because there would be no bargaining this time. He didn't give a damn what he had to do—take them to another country, change their names, kill Mojo with his bare hands. Whatever it took, no one was going to harm his son. Or his wife.

No, she wasn't his wife. He'd given her up, just like he'd given up being a real father to Sam. He couldn't turn back the clock or make up for his mistakes, but he could keep them safe. And when Mojo was dead or locked away for good, he would try again with Sam. He would change his schedule, and he would be there in person when Sam wanted to talk. He would take him sledding or to the ball game or anywhere he wanted to go. He would learn to be a father, instead of words on a computer screen. All he needed was the chance.

He reached out very carefully and touched Sam's cheek. He had to swallow hard a couple of times. "I promise, Samson," he whispered. "I won't let you down again."

He turned quickly, and headed to the staircase. When he reached the living room, he pulled his gloves from his pocket. He still had to check the vehicles. As he zipped up his parka, Becky's words came back to him. More than her words, her determination to leave this place.

Maybe they should go home today. Maybe Mojo was in Canada, and they had nothing to worry about. He wanted to believe that, but he didn't. His gut told him it wasn't over yet. Even if Cliff could prove that Mojo was out of the country, it wouldn't make a difference. For all he knew, Mojo hadn't been able to trace them to this cabin, and he was waiting for them to go back home so he could strike.

That's the scenario that was most logical, but it also made the future difficult to plan. He couldn't keep Becky and Sam here forever. But how long should he wait? A day, a week, a year? If Mojo was waiting until they got home to make his move, maybe the best course of action was to accommodate him. Set a trap for him in Boulder.

If only he knew how Mojo had gotten his information. If there was someone in the bureau who was feeding him, it would be incredibly dangerous to take them back home.

He slipped off his right glove, then went to the phone and dialed the office. Cliff wasn't there, so the operator put him through to the cellular. His partner answered on the second ring.

"Good news, amigo," Cliff said, after Mike's brief hello. "We found the son of a bitch."

"Where?"

"Jackson Hole."

"And?"

"He's got hostages."

"The nurse?"

"Yes, and a kid, a teenager who'd been working at a convenience store. I've got backup coming, and I've called in the sharpshooters. I would say your man will be dispatched in a few hours."

"We had him trapped once before, remember? And all we ended up with was a dead family."

"Mike, we've got him. He can't get out. I'll call you the minute it's over."

"Hey, what did you find out about the phones up here?"

"Oh, yeah. Witherspoon was right. There are four different lines going up to the mountain. If one goes down, it only affects a quarter of the service. So don't sweat it."

"Right."

"I'll see you soon."

The line disconnected, but Mike didn't put the phone down right away. He was thinking about the banker's family, and how Mojo had dumped them so unceremoniously on the highway. They'd had the bastard cornered that day, and he'd gotten clean away. Would this time be different?

He put the phone on its cradle and pulled his glove on once again. Mojo was in Wyoming. He couldn't possibly have touched the truck or the snowmobiles. But Mike was going to check them out just the same. The one thing he knew was that until Mojo was certified dead, until his heart stopped beating, he couldn't let down his guard. He would keep Becky and Sam here until he was absolutely certain they were safe. With Mojo, there was no risk worth taking. None at all.

Chapter 11

The wind howled again. Becky opened her eyes and listened to the trees scratch against the window. She had no idea how long she'd slept. It was dark, but she didn't think it was night. She couldn't have slept the whole day away.

Sam was still next to her. She looked at him now, and was surprised to see that he was awake, too. "Hi," she said.

"Hi."

"How you feeling?"

"Okay," he said listlessly.

She didn't buy it. Tossing back the covers, she scooted up the bed until she was sitting up. Sam didn't seem inclined to move, so she grabbed him under his arms and pulled. Once he realized she wasn't going to let him be, he cooperated. They sat shoulder to shoulder.

"You want to tell me what that was all about?" she asked.

He shook his head while he stared at his hands in his lap.

"I think you'd better, honey."

"I was going to see a friend."

"Oh?" She tread very carefully, wanting to make him feel safe enough to tell her the truth.

"She lives in Denver."

"Were you going to walk?"

He shook his head slowly. "Only to the highway. I thought I would get a ride from there."

"The snow was a little scary, huh?"

"Yeah."

She let the silence come again. She wanted to know why he'd done such a foolish thing, but she held back. He would tell her. But she couldn't help remembering that fit of panic when she thought Mojo had kidnapped him. She never wanted to be that scared again. Ever.

"I'm sorry I quit baseball." His voice was so low, she barely heard him.

"Baseball?"

He still wouldn't look at her. He was toying with a small rip in the blanket, working his little finger through the material.

"What do you mean, honey?"

"I know you wanted me to play baseball. I wasn't any good. They laughed at me. That's why I quit. I didn't mean to make you mad."

"I wasn't mad."

He looked up at her then, turning his head so she could see his annoyance. "You were so."

"I wasn't mad because you didn't want to play baseball. I was upset because you didn't tell me. What if something had happened to you when you were at the library? I wouldn't have known where to find you."

He didn't say anything. He just kept looking at her with accusing eyes. His lower lip quivered just a bit, but he didn't cry. He turned suddenly, so she couldn't see his face. "You promised you wouldn't tell."

He'd heard her talking to Mike. So that's what this was about. She tried to remember what she'd said this morning, but the conversation was a blur. She touched Sam's hand, but he pulled away from her.

"Daddy isn't mad at you."

"Yes, he is."

"No, sweetheart. He cares about you. He worries sometimes, but all parents do that."

"Why doesn't he want to live with us anymore?"

She hadn't expected that question, although she should have. Sam had never really talked to her about the divorce. She'd tried to explain many times, but he'd only listened in silence. She'd accepted that as understanding. "Do you think Daddy doesn't live with us because of something you did?"

He nodded as he brought his knees up to his chest and hugged them close to his body.

"Sam, look at me," she said. "Come on. Turn around."

He moved slowly. She could tell he didn't want to look at her, that he didn't want to hear the answer to his question. The wrong answer, at least. Finally, he let go of his grip on his knees, and he turned enough so that she could see him. But he didn't look at her.

"Daddy and I got divorced because we couldn't live together anymore. It had nothing to do with you. We both love you very much. You didn't do anything wrong."

"If I had died instead of Amy, he wouldn't have left."

Becky's heart skipped a beat. Had he been living with that idea for two years? My God, how could she have missed it? She looked at him again, but it wasn't enough. She got to her knees and grabbed him, pulling him tight against her in a fierce hug. "Oh, Sam. No. That's not true at all. We didn't want to lose Amy, but we never stopped loving you. Not even for a minute."

She laid her cheek against his soft hair, and closed her eyes as she tried to transmit her love to him through her fingers and her hug, and to stop the guilt that had her stomach in knots. When she opened her eyes again, she saw Mike standing in the doorway. She hadn't heard him come up the stairs, had no idea how long he'd been there. Had he heard Sam's confession? She met his gaze.

He had. Her own anguish was mirrored in his face.

Sam held her tightly, and she felt his little body shake with his tears. She rocked him gently back and forth.

"You're so wonderful," she said. "I wouldn't trade you for anyone in the whole world. Not anyone. You hear me?"

Mike came into the room hesitantly. She watched him, still holding on to Sam for all she was worth. He needed to be here, too. Sam needed them both so much.

"Hey, kid."

Sam grew still. Becky loosened her grip on him, and he turned to look at his dad.

"It was never your fault," Mike said. "Mommy left because I couldn't be the kind of husband she needed. It had nothing to do with you. I was always sorry I couldn't be with you more. But that's going to change. I promise. You wait and see—" His voice broke and he looked away quickly.

Sam scrambled out of the bed and ran to his father, who bent low and scooped him into his arms.

Becky watched the two of them and wished with all her heart that things could be different. That they could go back to the way they were before Amy had gotten sick. It was a foolish wish, she knew that, but she couldn't help it. Life had been so very sweet then.

At least Mike was trying. She truly believed that he would be there for Sam. He'd changed in the last few days. This experience had been a nightmare, but at least Mike had had the chance to spend time with his son, to see how important it was for him to be a real father.

She should be happy. Her son was the most important thing in her life, wasn't he? Seeing him connect with Mike should be enough. But it wasn't. She wanted it all. She wanted Mike to love her again, too.

Mike eased his bear hug and leaned back. He looked into his son's brown eyes and saw all the innocence in the world. Sam needed him to be strong, to be wise, to keep him safe. He wanted to be all those things, but wanting wasn't enough.

He would disappoint his son. Maybe not today, but he would. Sam would look at him the way Becky had in those last months. The way Amy had.

The image of his daughter's face came to him clearly. She was in the hospital. It was her last day. Her last moment. And she'd looked at him with such anger, such distrust in her eyes that he could barely stand from the weight of it. She hadn't let him touch her. She'd died not wanting him near.

He put Sam down on the floor. "Go on," he said. "Go to your mom." He physically turned Sam around so he was facing Becky. It took no more prodding than that. Sam went back to the bed and climbed up. Becky's arms went around him as he fell into her lap.

Mike couldn't look any more. "I'll be downstairs," he said.

"Wait," Becky said. "Don't you want to—"

He didn't stick around to hear the rest. He needed to think. To sort out some things by himself.

The cabin felt cold and strange. He hated this place, the damn flowers on the couch and the ugly curtains. He couldn't even bring himself to look at the kitchen. When he got to his room, he kicked the door open. It sounded as if he'd broken the lock. Good.

Too much was happening here. Memories he'd managed to bury for two years were surfacing with alarming frequency. Amy, the funeral, the look on Becky's face when they'd lowered their baby into the ground. It was more than he could take. He wanted to go back to that place he'd found where he didn't think and didn't feel. He'd mastered his emotions once, he could do it again.

The closet door was already open. He gripped the chinning bar with both hands and stiffened his body. He lifted himself slowly, feeling each muscle in his arms and shoulders pull and strain.

He wanted it to hurt. He wanted to be swallowed up in physical pain, to blot out everything but the muscles and the sweat and the effort. Again and again he pulled up and down, forcing his breath to be even and rhythmic, his mind to go numb.

But this time, Amy wouldn't go away. Becky was still there, too. Both of them accusing him with their eyes, with their thoughts, with their tears. His mind filled with ghosts of the past, and worse, the present.

"Is there something else you want to tell me?" Becky stood by Sam's bed. He was sitting up with his computer on his lap. She was reasonably sure their reassurances had calmed him, but something was still bothering him. She could tell by the way his dark eyes seemed shadowed, and the tentative smile he couldn't manage to keep steady. There was more to his story, she was certain.

"No. I'm okay," he said, concentrating on his video game.

"Will you do me a favor?"

He nodded.

"Don't scare me like that again. If something bothers you, you come and talk to me about it. Or you can talk to Daddy. Running away doesn't solve anything."

He nodded again, unconvincingly.

She turned to look outside. The winds had picked up sharply, and the snow was coming down hard and fast. If he went out in this weather, he would never make it to the first cabin. "Promise?"

"I promise," he said.

She wasn't going to get any more out of him now. Maybe tonight, when he was sleepy. He told her things in the dark that he didn't have the courage to say in daylight. "All right. I'm going downstairs. If you need me, you holler."

His thumb moved furiously on the joystick and his gaze darted across the monitor. At least he was safe while his nose was buried in the computer.

She left him, and didn't shut the door on her way downstairs. The events of the day had worn her out and even though she'd just gotten up, she longed to go right back to sleep. She couldn't stop thinking about what Sam had said. He really believed that if he had died instead of Amy, Mike and she wouldn't have split up. It was completely untrue, but he hadn't known that until today.

How had she missed it? Where had she been?

She didn't see Mike in the living room, and was a little surprised to find herself in the kitchen alone. She put up some water in the kettle, then went to the window above the sink and pushed the curtain aside. The storm had come back, and it seemed angrier this time, as if the lull had stoked its fire. So much for going home. They would never be able to drive in this, and she wasn't about to put Sam on a snowmobile unless she absolutely had to. But, God, she wanted out of here. She needed time to herself, time to think about what she was feeling.

Sam wasn't the only one bothering her. Mike confused the hell out of her, too. She didn't understand him at all. Every time she thought she'd figured him out, he did something totally unexpected.

Why had he left so abruptly? He was this close to making a real connection with Sam and then, boom, he shut down completely. The only thing she knew for sure was that she didn't dare keep her hope alive. It didn't matter that she still cared about him; he was as deadly as the storm, as tricky as the wind. She needed a constancy and commitment that he could never give her, and wishing it could be different had accomplished nothing.

He would come through for Sam. That would be enough.

The kettle whistled, and she went to make herself some tea. As she poured the boiling water into the cup, she thought about her life back in Boulder. She'd been so busy filling up her days with work and school and meetings that she hadn't even noticed that her son was crying for help.

The hot water spilled over the rim of the cup. After putting the kettle down on the stove, she poured a little of the water into the sink, then went to the table and sat down.

She stared at the darkening liquid, too tired to stir in a packet of sugar. She couldn't remember ever feeling this weary. She didn't want to think any more, or worry, or care. She wanted someone else to be the grown-up.

"Is he okay?"

She looked up. Mike stood in the doorway. His hair was damp and she could see that he'd been sweating. "You've been on the chinning bar I see."

He nodded. "I was going to take a shower, but I wanted to make sure Sam was okay first."

"He's upstairs. Go see for yourself."

Mike didn't turn around. Instead, he came to the table and pulled out the chair facing her. He sat, ran his sleeve across his forehead, and sighed. "Poor kid. I had no idea he blamed himself for the divorce."

"Takes after his father that way."

His brows went down. "What do you mean?"

"Blaming himself then running away. It's something of a pattern with you two."

Mike stood up so quickly, his chair nearly toppled backwards. "Forget it."

"No," she held out her hand. "Wait. I'm sorry. I shouldn't have said that."

"Why not? It's what you believe. It's always been easy for you to point the finger, hasn't it?"

"I don't want to fight with you."

"Why the hell not? Because we're focusing on you for a change?"

She looked up at him, really confused at his anger. "No, that has nothing to do with it."

"Of course it does. You're damn good at holding the mirror up to everyone else, but you run whenever it turns to you."

"Mike, it's been a really bad day. Can we have this fight another time?"

"I'm not fighting. I'm just telling you the truth. You're always accusing me of hiding behind some mask. Well, I've got news for you. The only difference between you and me is the packaging."

She stood up, too. "Don't put your demons on me," she said. "I'm not the one who runs off at the first sign of an emotion."

"No?" He walked toward her. One of the dining room chairs was in his path, and he tossed it aside so roughly it clattered to the floor. He didn't stop until he was right in her face. "Let's look at some hard facts, shall we? When Amy was diagnosed, and I wanted to talk about it, what did you do? You joined three different cancer support groups. Three. When I didn't want to go to a damn meeting every night of the week, you told me I didn't love her enough. Or did you forget that?"

She backed up, trying to get away from his eyes and his accusations. The stove stopped her, and she tried to dart to her right, but his hand caught her and held her steady.

"Let me go."

"No. You're going to listen."

She closed her eyes, but she couldn't shut out his words.

"Every time I tried to help with Amy, you told me I was doing it wrong. I didn't know how to bathe her properly, I wasn't gentle enough to sit with her during chemo. My stories scared her, my beard hurt her skin. And when I wanted to make love, when I needed you in my bed, you turned your back on me. It wasn't because you were too tired. It was because you were afraid I would give you another damaged child."

"No." She dared another look at him.

His lip curled in a mocking smile. "She was a smart little girl, our Amy. She learned her lessons well. In the end, she only wanted you. Remember? You taught her that. You stole her from me."

She slapped him. The sound was sharp, like a rifle shot. She could see the imprint of her fingers on his cheek.

He let her go.

She ran then, to the only place she could think to get away. She threw the basement door open and nearly fell as she went down the steps, blinded by her tears, shaking with horror at what he'd said.

The dark room swallowed her up, but she didn't stop moving until she hit the big dryer. She put her hands down on the cold surface, afraid that if she didn't, she would fall where she stood. Then she wept.

Mike stood at the door to the basement. He couldn't see into the darkness, and he thought about turning on the light for her. He heard her cry, a deep wellspring of sadness, of anger. He touched the side of his face, where she'd slapped him. She'd surprised him with that, all right. But she'd also knocked the fight out of him. There was no satisfaction in this. He'd had no intention of saying those things, even though they were true.

There had been too much pain. Enough. The word reverberated in his head. *Enough.*

He flipped on the light, and headed down the stairs.

She was leaning on the dryer, bent almost double. Her sobs ripped a hole in him, and he felt awash in shame. What could he say now? Sorry didn't come close.

Chapter 12

He stood for a moment, in the cold sterile room, listening to her weep as the wind wailed in accompaniment. Then he moved slowly forward, until she was very close. Finally, he reached for her arm and turned her around. The tragedy, their tragedy, was etched on her face, seared in her eyes. He pulled her close and wrapped his arms around her. She fell against him, her cheek next to his. He wasn't sure whose tears fell to his shoulder.

Becky hung on to him as wave after wave of pain and guilt swept through her. All she had left inside her were tears and memories. She didn't want to believe the horrible things Mike had said, she would give anything for him to take them back, but it was no use.

She remembered watching Mike hold Amy, and how she would try to be patient and calm, but then she couldn't stand it another minute and she would take her from him. Those nights when she'd found Mike singing softly to his little girl, and instead of being comforted by his gentle love, she'd been filled with an inexplicable rage.

She shut her eyes more tightly, as if she could somehow hide from the pictures in her mind. But they came, tumbling one on top of another, terrible in their intensity. Amy's shrieks of pain, the bars on the side of her hospital bed. The smell of medicines and sickness, the sound of rubber soles on linoleum. Over it all, the fear that had turned her inside out, that made her want to scream until she had no voice, to cry until she had no tears. The anger at a heartless God who could hurt an innocent child.

From somewhere far away she heard a voice.

"Shh," he said. "It's all right."

Closer still was a tender hand on her hair, petting her slowly. It was hard to breathe, but the hand and the voice made it easier. She seemed to fall from a great height, and when she opened her eyes, Mike was there, holding her up.

She let go of him long enough to wipe her face with her sleeve, then she grabbed on to him again. She looked up into his face, expecting to see his rage, but it was gone. Somehow that was worse. She broke free and leaned once again on the dryer.

"I want to say it's all lies," she said. "I want it to be lies, but it isn't."

He moved closer to her, but she stepped away. She didn't deserve his touch.

"I shouldn't have said anything."

She heard her own bitter laugh. "That's my job, right? To tell you what you've done wrong?" She had to swallow hard and hold back another wave of tears. When she could talk again, she said, "How hard it must have been for you. To keep quiet all this time. Why? Why didn't you say something before?"

His gaze shifted to something in the dark part of the basement. "Because I believed you."

She stared at the man she'd loved with every ounce of her being and knew she'd hurt him beyond repair. Funny thing is, she'd never pictured herself as the villain. It was always the cancer or God or Mike. She winced. That was the truth, wasn't it? She'd painted him the monster, turned him into the object of her hate. All this time, she'd blamed him for the breakup of their marriage, when she was the one at fault.

It was too much. She felt as though she'd fallen through the looking glass into an upside-down world. Black was suddenly white, light was dark, and she was spinning out of control.

"I never once thought of asking myself what part I played in our little drama," she said. "It was easy to blame you. It couldn't be random, not that kind of pain. How could it be? It had to be someone's fault. Your fault." She closed her eyes. "How insufferable I've been. How self-righteous. No wonder you stayed away."

"I stayed away for my own reasons."

She looked up again, surprised at his calm tone. "Did you? I don't know anymore. I can't see straight."

Suddenly, her legs weren't strong enough to hold her. She sagged, grabbing on to the side of the dryer. Then she felt him next to her, holding her so she wouldn't fall.

She let her head rest on his chest. She didn't want to think anymore.

"You okay?"

She looked up at him. "I don't think I'll ever be okay again."

"I'm sorry," he said. "I didn't mean to—"

She placed her fingers on his lips to stop him. "Don't. You don't have to. I was the one who hurt you." Fresh tears came, and she fought them back.

"We hurt each other."

She shook her head. "I blamed you. I did. It wasn't fair. It *wasn't* your fault. I was so scared. I know that's no excuse."

"I should have understood."

She studied his face, the strong jaw, the high cheek-bones. The deep chocolate eyes that showed her nothing but compassion. "I don't know how you can even look at me. Not after…after everything I've done. You have every right to hate me."

"I'm too tired to hate you. I just want, I don't know, to move on. To put all this behind us. I've had enough."

"I feel like I've been living someone else's life. My God, no wonder I didn't see that Sam was feeling so bad. I didn't see much of anything." She let go of him and stepped back. "It was all my fault."

He laughed. "Sorry, that position has been taken."

She couldn't smile because she knew he really meant that. It was no joke to him. She'd done one hell of a job convincing him that he was to blame for all the pain they'd gone through. Could she ever make up for that? Were there enough words to make him believe that he'd done nothing wrong?

A chill ran through her, and she realized where she was. She had no recollection of coming down the stairs. She didn't like it down here. It was too cold and creepy. Looking up to the small window, she saw that it had been completely covered in snow. For some reason that made it even worse down here.

"Let's go upstairs," he said. He was leaning against the clothes dryer. His shirt was damp from her tears. He looked big and reassuring, with his broad chest and muscled arms. She could lean on that man, and he wouldn't fall. But who could he turn to?

For three years, all she'd done was point her finger at him, diagnose his problems, analyze his behavior. All because she hadn't been able to look at herself.

She felt her cheeks flush with heat. So much hurt. Too much, for such flesh and blood creatures.

"I could use a cup of coffee," he said.

Even his voice was forgiving. She didn't deserve it, but she was grateful all the same.

She led him up the stairs and into the kitchen. It had grown very dark outside. The storm had turned into a blizzard, whipping the snow into a frenzy. She shivered again, wrapping her arms around her waist. "Why don't you light a fire," she said, "while I fix the coffee."

He nodded. "You gonna be okay?"

She managed a smile. "I think so."

As he passed her, he touched her arm, squeezing it gently. She watched him walk away. A new sadness settled on her like dust; the realization of how much time they'd wasted wounding each other, when they should have been helping each other to heal.

She moved slowly, each step an effort, and filled the kettle with water. Her teacup, from a thousand years ago, was still on the table. Her whole universe had changed in an instant. Nothing was the same. All she knew for certain was that she had to fix the coffee. He liked his with sugar and milk.

It was good to concentrate on the simple task. To focus on something outside herself. Of course, she was only putting off the inevitable. She had to look, and look hard, at who she was and what she'd done. He'd jolted her with the truth, and she couldn't turn back.

The whistle of the kettle startled her, and she got busy again. A few minutes later, she took the two mugs into the living room.

The fire was blazing and Mike was sitting on the couch with his legs stretched out in front of him. He looked tired. There were dark circles under his eyes, and the lines that bracketed his mouth were deep. Even so, he was incredibly handsome. She'd always thought so, but right now, he was more than just good-looking. His eyes made the difference. The shutters that had kept them hidden and suspicious for so long were gone. With a start, she realized she was really seeing him for the first time in years. She'd fallen in love with those eyes, once upon a time.

She handed him his mug, then curled up on the opposite end of the couch. She didn't want to be too close to him, not yet. There were some hard things to say coming up, and she needed room to say them.

The fire crackled and she spent a moment staring at the dancing flames. Where to begin? So much had happened, it was impossible to know what to say.

"Remember when we went to California?"

She hadn't expected Mike to speak. Putting her mug on the table, she turned more toward him. He wasn't looking at her though. His eyes were focused on the past.

"When we took the kids to Sea World? That was a good time," he said. "It was all perfect, remember? The kids, us. Everything was funny. God, how we laughed. I think that's the last time we all laughed like that." He turned to her. "Until last night. It felt like the old days for a minute there."

"For me, too."

Again, they fell into silence. She found herself thinking of that magical vacation. A smile crept up on her as she pictured Sam and Amy and Mike in that big king-size bed at the hotel. Mike had them all singing a horrible song about eating worms that the kids thought was the funniest thing in the whole world. "I think Amy would feel awful if she knew what had become of us. I think it would hurt her feelings."

Before he had a chance to respond, she reached over and touched his hand. "Why did you stick around so long?"

He met her gaze. "I'm not sure. I guess I got used to it."

"Being mad at me?"

"Yeah."

"I thought I knew you," she said. "I thought I understood everything about you. But I don't. We're strangers, aren't we? We've been strangers for a long time."

He shook his head. "It's this place. Being trapped up here. It makes everything feel different."

"No. If anything, this place has given us a chance. In a way, I'm glad. Not that Mojo is out there, but that we were forced together. I doubt this would have ever happened back in the real world."

"Probably not."

"We would have gone on, chipping away at each other for years and years."

He ran a hand through his thick hair. "I feel like we've been up here half our lives."

"I haven't changed my mind about going home, you know. I realize we can't leave in this storm, but as soon as it's over I want to leave."

"We'll see," he said.

She took a sip of coffee, then got her nerve up. "Are you sorry?"

"For what?"

"That we made love?"

Now she dared a glance. The look on his face was more important than his answer. She could see he didn't regret it.

"I'm sorry we only did it once."

She laughed, more with relief than anything.

"Are you sorry?"

She shook her head. "No. But I've learned something. We've both changed. A lot. I made love with the memory of who you were, who we were. I can't do that again."

He sighed. "I suppose so. But damn. It was a good memory."

She uncurled her legs and moved over on the couch until she was sitting next to him. His arm went around her shoulder, and she rested her head against his chest.

There was a long road in front of them. Today had only been the first step. She didn't know if they would be together when they reached the end. But she hoped so.

* * *

Mike grabbed for the phone by his bed, anxious not to wake Becky. "Yeah."

"Mike?"

It was Sully, the bureau chief. Something was wrong. "Where's Cliff?"

The silence that followed clinched it. Mojo wasn't in custody and he wasn't dead. He had escaped.

"Cliff is dead." Sully's voice seemed to come from far away.

The floor dropped out from under Mike. "No," he said. It wasn't possible. It was some kind of sick joke. Cliff would be on the line in a second, and he would laugh. "That isn't funny."

"I'm sorry, Mike."

He swore only once. What he wanted to do was bash something, tear the room apart. "How?"

"Mojo."

"Tell me he was killed in the crossfire, Sully."

"He escaped. He's still got the woman. The kid is dead. We believe Mojo is headed back into Colorado."

"I know exactly where he's headed. Get us out of here, Sully. Now."

"I'm trying."

"Don't tell me you're trying. Do it."

"Have you looked outside? It's the worst storm in Colorado in fifty years. Air transportation is grounded. Cars aren't moving anywhere. Half the state is immobilized."

"You think the storm will stop him? You're out of your mind."

"Look, if it's this tough for us to get to you, Mojo is on the same boat. He can't drive on these roads, either."

"He'll get here. He'll figure out a way. Dammit, don't you see? You can't stop him. Nothing can stop him."

"Calm down. The safest place you could be is right where you are."

"Wrong. There is no safe place where that bastard i concerned."

"You have ammunition? Weapons?"

"Yeah. Not that they'll be enough."

"I'm doing everything humanly possible to send help. won't let him get to you."

Mike stared out the bedroom window at the furiou wind. This was not where he intended to die. He though about Cliff. And his wife. Mike cursed again. "Have yo told Ellie?"

"Yeah."

"God."

"Hold tight, Mike. I'm sending the cavalry."

"Just get them up here. I don't care how."

Sully hung up, and Mike lowered his phone to the cra dle. Cliff was dead. It was an unbelievable notion, lik thinking the ocean was pink. He couldn't be dead. He ha a family. His wife was a year younger than Becky. His kid were all in grade school, and Terry, his oldest, was Sam' age.

Another partner had died trying to protect him. I wasn't right. Why should he still be alive, and those tw men dead? He went over to the closet door and laid hi forehead against the cold wood. Nothing made sense any more. He'd thought, for one minute there, that things wer going to get better. That he and Becky had a shot at start ing over. That there was a future.

He curled his hand into a fist and slammed it into th door. Pain radiated up his arm, but it wasn't enough. H wanted to smash through the wood, to tear the cabin dow around him. He wanted out.

Becky fought to stay asleep. She didn't want to b awake, to remember. She shivered and opened her eyes The fire was still burning, so why was she so cold? She fe as though she would never be warm again. She woul never be in her own home. That she would never see another spring. Everything would happen for the rest of her days in snow and ice.

She wrapped her arms around her knees, hugging her legs to her chest. Where was Mike? He'd been here, comforting her. His kindness bewildered her. How could he be so nice, after what she'd done to him?

But that was Mike, wasn't it? The man she had married. He'd been a sweetheart back then, a gentle and considerate lover. Before she'd turned against him. Now there was something to be proud of.

No, she wouldn't go down that path. All it would lead to was more hurt, and like Mike had said, they'd all had enough of that. What was important now was to start over. To learn to be kind again, to Mike, to Sam, to herself.

Someday, she might understand why she'd done those terrible things. Why she'd found it necessary to hurt him so deeply. But for now, she would just stop. Stop pointing fingers and stop the blame.

It was nearly five o'clock. She'd slept for a long time. How could so much have happened in one day? She'd had a year's worth of revelations, a lifetime's worth of sorrow. Enough. That's what Mike had said. Yes. Quite enough.

She got up and stretched. Her muscles ached and her neck was sore. There was a bathtub in Mike's room. Maybe later she would soak for a while and try to get out the kinks. In the meantime, Sam had been upstairs alone all afternoon.

She took the stairs slowly. Her legs felt heavy and sluggish. His door was open, and when she walked in, she saw he was on the bed playing on his computer. Didn't he ever get tired of that thing?

She shouldn't complain. It was probably good for him to have someplace to go. So what if it wasn't the real world? The real world wasn't all that hot sometimes.

"Hey, kiddo. How you doing?"

He looked up at her, a little startled by her voice. "Hi. I'm on the fifth level. Only one more to go." Then his gaze went back to the screen.

"The fifth level? Wow." She hadn't a clue what he was talking about, but if he was impressed, she would be, too. She walked over to the bed and looked at the screen. It was a jumble of lights and figures, streaming beams and flashing icons. She couldn't make heads or tails of it.

Then she turned her attention to Sam. His fingers were moving with unbelievable swiftness, his eyes darting back and forth as he followed the game. She loved him so much it was hard to breathe.

Had he known? Had he watched her turn against his father? Had he seen the accusing stares, heard the bitter words? Is that why he took refuge in a machine?

She reached a tentative hand out and touched his hair. What she wanted to do was take him in her arms and hold him, but she simply ran her hand down the curve of his head, and then let go. He didn't acknowledge her in any way. Not a smile or a frown. It was the game that had him transfixed, she knew that, but it didn't make her feel any less alone.

She turned and went to the window. A maelstrom of wind and snow and tree branches smashed against the glass. What was that poem, about the world ending in ice? She could believe it. Her world had ended. Her belief in herself, the very foundation of her existence had been swept away in a gale of cold words and colder truths. She had thought of herself as a decent person most of her life. Now, all she believed was that she was afraid.

"Dammit!"

Becky turned quickly, startled at Sam's outburst. "What?"

"I got killed. Two more men, that's all I needed. I was so close."

She tried to get her pulse to slow. "I'm sorry you didn't win. Next time, win or lose, you need to find another word to express yourself."

He looked at her, puzzled. "What did I say?"

She laughed. "Never mind. Anyway, you've been playing that thing too much. Put it away and come downstairs. I need some help with dinner."

"I'm starving."

"No wonder. You haven't eaten all day."

"Yes I did. I fixed myself a peanut-butter-and-jelly sandwich."

"When?"

"I don't know. Earlier. You and dad were downstairs."

Had he heard them? She dearly hoped he hadn't. He didn't need one more thing to worry about.

He started typing again. She guessed he was saving the game for another time.

"Mom?"

"Hmm?"

"I'm really sorry about this morning."

"Don't sweat it, kiddo. Just don't do it again."

His fingers stilled. "I didn't mean to make you cry."

She rushed over to the bed and sat down next to him. "Did you hear me crying in the basement?"

He nodded, making sure he didn't look anywhere but straight in front of him.

She put her arm around his shoulder and hugged him. "That wasn't about you. I promise. I was crying about a lot of things, honey, but not you."

"You sounded...bad."

"I'm sure I did. But it wasn't bad. Sometimes crying can be a good thing. It can help you express feelings that are deep inside. I was very sad for a long time, but today was the first time I could cry about it. So it seemed worse than it was."

"Okay."

She touched his chin with her finger and turned him so she could see his eyes. "You mean it?"

He nodded.

She kissed him on the nose. "Thanks for caring, sweetie."

His cheeks got a little pink, and he turned back to his computer. She watched him hit a number of keys, then the screen went black. He shut the cover. "Mom, what's for dinner?"

"How about spaghetti?"

"Yeah."

She stood up, and Sam scrambled off the bed. He was out of there and clomping down the stairs before she reached the door. She was pretty sure he believed her, but tonight, before bed, she would check in with him again. Reiterate that he hadn't done anything to upset her. She would have Mike say something to him, too.

Speaking of Mike, she thought, where had he gone? He wasn't in the living room or the kitchen. Maybe he was napping.

Sam had already started setting the table. He seemed okay to her. But then, she'd thought he was fine last night, and all the nights before. How was she ever going to trust her judgment again?

She got out the big pot and filled it with water. After she put it on the stove and started the fire beneath it, she turned to Sam. "Can you finish setting the table by yourself?"

"I'm almost done."

"Don't forget glasses. Use the chair to reach them. I'm going to go talk to Daddy for a minute."

He nodded, and she hurried out of the kitchen. She'd managed to give herself one heck of a headache. After she talked to Mike she would go upstairs and take some aspirin.

His door was shut. She almost turned around, but she needed to talk to him. Wasn't it ironic that she was turning to him for comfort? She knocked softly.

"Just a second."

He'd answered so quickly that she didn't think he'd been asleep. But it took him a while to come to the door. When he opened it, she saw he hadn't changed from the flannel shirt and jeans he'd been wearing all day. "I thought you were going to shower."

"I was." He stepped aside and let her in. "The day got away from me."

She nodded. "I think it got away from all of us." His room was messy. The bed was unmade, a towel was on the floor. His duffel bag was sitting open on his pillow, next to yesterday's dirty clothes. She didn't care. Moving a pair of jeans, she sat down on the edge of the bed and turned to him. "Sam heard me crying."

She didn't think he heard her. He was staring at the bed, his eyes fixed and his brow furrowed.

"Mike?"

He turned his gaze slowly toward her. "Yeah?"

"Where are you?"

He blinked and seemed to come back to earth. "Sorry, I was thinking about something else. What did you say?"

"Sam heard me. When I was crying in the basement."

"What did he say?"

"He thought I was upset because he tried to run away."

"I'll talk to him."

"I told him that I wasn't, of course, but I think you should. I—" She rubbed her eyes, and told herself she was *not* going to cry again. "I don't trust my judgment. He may still be very upset."

Mike came over to the bed and sat down next to her. "You want to explain that?"

She picked a piece of lint off her sweater. "How am I supposed to make up for everything? I let him down. I let you down. I just don't know what to do to make it right."

"It's over. Forget it."

She looked straight at him. "How am I supposed to forget it? Sam tried to run away today because he thought we didn't love him. I chased you away because I couldn't deal with my own craziness. How do you expect me to forget that?"

He reached over and took her hand in his. "The worst thing that can ever happen to a woman happened to you. You did what you needed to, to survive. We both did."

"Throwing away your love was how I needed to survive? No. Leaving you nearly killed me."

His eyes closed and she heard his sharp intake of breath. When he looked at her again, he seemed in pain. "Leaving me was the smartest thing you've ever done."

"What? How can you say that?"

"Because it's the truth. This thing about blame, it doesn't cut it. It wasn't my fault or your fault. Or maybe we were both to blame, but it doesn't matter now. It's over. We had something once, a long time ago. We can't ever get it back again." He got up off the bed and walked to the bathroom door. Instead of looking at her, he stared at this shoes.

A great hand came around her heart and squeezed. But what had she expected? That he could forget what she'd done? That he could ever forgive her for the way she'd come between him and Amy? "Of course," she said. "You're right." She tried to smile, but it was a dismal failure. "Go on and shower. I've put dinner up. By the time you get out, we'll be ready to eat."

He hesitated. She thought he might say something, but after a while, he just opened the bathroom door and went inside.

One good thing had come of this. She didn't hurt anymore. She just felt numb. What could she have been thinking? He didn't love her. She'd taught him not to.

Mike let the hot water pound on his back. He wanted to stay in here forever.

He had to tell her. Even if he didn't, she would soon guess that something was wrong. She knew him too well. But damn, he didn't want to.

Why now? Why not wait until tomorrow? Let them get a good night's sleep. That would be the kind thing to do. What was the use of terrifying her tonight? Even Mojo couldn't get up here that fast.

Could he pretend for the whole night? Could he look at her without betraying this awful fear? He was no actor, but for them, he might be able to pull it off.

Then he thought about that last letter. The one he'd gotten the day Mojo escaped from prison. Mojo had known about Becky's job at the hotel. He'd known her hours, her habits, including the fact that she worked out to exercise tapes every day at four. He'd known about Sam, too. Where he went to school, how old he was, even his favorite food.

How? Who had told him?

Maybe the storm would ease up by morning, Mike thought. Enough at least for them to take off on the snowmobiles. He knew the route. They would take backpacks of food and water, sleeping bags and a tent. If the winds weren't too bad, they would be on the road for four or five hours, he guessed, until they could find shelter. If everything went right.

But things never did. Something always went wrong. With his family at stake was he willing to risk it?

At least here, they could fortify themselves. They had food, water, shelter. It would be Mojo who had to fight the elements.

He turned and grabbed the shampoo. Maybe he was worrying for nothing. There was no evidence that Mojo knew where they were. Even if he did, how was he going to get up here?

No. He couldn't afford to believe that. Mojo had managed to do the impossible time after time. Only a fool would believe he couldn't do it again.

However, Mike was beginning to think that running was the last thing they should do. Literally. They should stay in the house, make it as impenetrable as possible. Becky could handle his gun if she needed to, and he had his rifle. Sam already knew about the closet.

The decision was made. Now all he had to do was act as if nothing was wrong.

It was going to be a long night.

Chapter 13

Becky stirred the spaghetti, then went back to making the salad. She sliced the last tomato and tossed it in the bowl.

Sam had finished setting the table and had taken his seat. He had the salt and pepper shakers in his hand, and it looked to her as if he were pitting them against each other in battle. She hoped the salt won.

She shook her head at her own foolishness, but a small part of her was relieved she could still smile.

"What are we going to do tonight?"

"I don't know," she said. "Any preferences?"

"Yeah. I want to watch TV."

"Other than that."

He guided the pepper shaker around the fork and the spoon, straight into the salt. It tipped over, and Sam gurgled and grabbed his throat to expire right along with it. He slumped in his chair, eyes closed, mouth wide open, then one second later, he sat up again. "I *don't* want to work on the puzzle."

"No, really?"

"Let's tell ghost stories. I know a really gross one."

"Good. The grosser the better."

Becky turned at the sound of Mike's voice. He was standing just inside the kitchen, smiling at Sam. His hair was still wet, combed straight back, and he had swapped his trademark flannel for a University of Colorado sweatshirt. Tonight's jeans fit him better. They were snug against his slim hips and long legs.

He walked to the table and pulled out his chair. "Anything I can do?"

She shook her head. "It's almost ready. Sit."

He did. Becky watched him talk with Sam. The words weren't important, the way he said them was. He was listening to Sam raptly, interested in everything he had to say. Sam responded in kind, laughing and talking a mile a minute.

Her gaze moved from her son to his father, and she realized with a start that she wasn't the only one who'd been out of touch with reality. Only Mike's was a reality far better than hers. He was a good, decent man, with a great deal of love in his heart. The problem was, he didn't know it.

Of all her crimes, that was the biggest. She'd convinced him that he was cold and unloving. He'd spent the last two years keeping himself at arm's-length from his son, all because of her. They'd both lost in this terrible battle, but no more.

She would prove to him that he still had a heart. Just like the Wizard of Oz, she would show her Tin Man that he was whole and complete. That he didn't need to hide anymore behind that steely facade. She owed him that—more than that.

"What's wrong? You've been staring at me for five minutes."

Becky shook herself free from her thoughts and smiled at Mike. "Nothing. Everything's fine."

The pasta was done, and in a few minutes she had the whole meal on the table and had taken her seat. Strangely enough, she felt kind of good. Clean. It was as if she'd gone to confession. Of course no one had given her absolution, but maybe helping Mike see the truth about himself would be a start.

"Eww, look at the worms," Sam said. "Blood-covered worms all writhing on your plate, and you're going to chew them up so their guts—"

"Hey!" she said, sharply. "Knock it off. That's disgusting."

Sam hung his head, but she caught him sneaking a peek at Mike and then the two of them laughed.

"Do you think we could hold off on the gross stories until after dinner? Please?"

Mike looked stonily at Sam. "Your mother's right. We won't say another word about slimy, crawling worms that slither down your throat—"

Becky gasped loudly and threw her napkin at Mike's head. "You're horrible. Both of you. Yech."

Sam was laughing so hard she was afraid he was going to fall off his chair. Mike watched him with a large grin on his face. When her gaze went to his eyes, she lost her own smile.

Mike was staring at Sam as if he would never see him again. There was no mistaking that look, she'd seen it before. What had happened? Was it their talk this afternoon? Had he made some kind of crazy decision to leave Sam for good?

She thought about what he'd said in the bedroom. That running from him had been the best thing she'd ever done. No. It wasn't. It was a horrible mistake, one she would never forgive herself for. She'd nearly destroyed three lives, and she had a lot of mending to do. She had to make him see that he belonged with Sam.

"Come on you two," she said. "Eat your dinner before it gets cold."

Mike nodded his agreement. "Okay. Nothing but serious talk now." He took a big bite of spaghetti, then made a show of chewing. As soon as he swallowed, he turned to Sam. With an exaggerated frown he said, "So, Sam, what do you think about the trade embargo with Cuba?"

That set Sam off again. He giggled and fidgeted in his chair, loving the attention more than the jokes.

But her gaze stayed on Mike. He might be able to fool Sam, but not her. She knew him too well. She didn't know exactly what he was thinking, but she knew it was painful. As soon as dinner was over, she would talk to him. She only hoped he would tell her the truth.

Mike listened to Sam's laughter and tried to memorize the sound. He saw how his eyes crinkled up so he could barely see, and his cheeks turned pink. Nothing was more important than remembering this. It could all be gone in an instant. Just like Cliff's life. Or Gordon's.

There was a time, long, long ago, when he'd believed that good would triumph over evil. That the guys in the white hats would always come out on top. But it wasn't true. Life was a crapshoot, and so was death. Of course, being his friend, or his child, knocked the hell out of the odds.

Amy had loved him, had counted on him, and he'd let her down. Gordon and Cliff had counted on him, too. It was a dangerous thing, believing in Mike McCullough. Downright deadly.

His record was about to get even better. Mojo was out there somewhere, determined to keep his promise. For the first time since this whole nightmare had begun, Mike had no faith that he would be able to stop him.

So he would watch his son tonight, and memorize his every move. He would make him laugh. Give him what little happiness he could.

He tore his gaze away from Sam before he lost it. That wouldn't do him any good. The facade was too critical. Sam and Becky had to believe this was just an ordinary night, not their last. He went on eating, not tasting the food. It didn't matter. Nothing mattered, except tonight. Now.

Becky was staring at him. For how long? he wondered. Had she guessed his secret? No, she would have been scared to death, not just curious. She knew something was wrong, that was clear. She always had been able to read him like a book. He would have to do better, if he was going to pull this off.

He smiled at her, willing his whole body to move into the smile with him. He needed to remember something good. That part turned out to be easy. Becky, in his bed. Loving him. Taking him inside her, crying out his name.

The look of concern on her face melted away. He'd succeeded, for the moment at least, in putting her at ease. He turned his attention back to his dinner, and to listening to Sam. He was talking about the game he'd almost won. How he'd gotten to the fifth level, which was almost impossible—he only knew two people who'd gotten to level five and they were both big kids, in junior high.

Mike had no trouble telling Sam he was proud. Of course Sam had no way of knowing that Mike's pride came from far more than a computer victory. Everything his son did made him proud. He was a good kid, one of the best. He had a generous heart and was quick to laugh. He deserved a rich, full life.

"Who wants dessert?"

Mike was grateful Becky had interrupted his thoughts. "I do," he said quickly, even though it was a lie. He needed more to do, and eating was as good a chore as any.

"Me, too," Sam said.

She got up and took the dirty plates to the sink, then came back with the cake she'd baked yesterday. She'd covered it with chocolate frosting, Sam's favorite.

Becky watched her men eat. Sam was in heaven, having both of them near, without all the tension that normally marred their times together. She glanced at Mike again, but the haunted look in his eyes had faded. Maybe it had never been there at all.

The time sort of slipped through her fingers as she sat back and listened to Sam's chatter and Mike's questions. A peace came over her, one she hadn't known for many years. She felt complete. That was it.

Right now, in this strange cabin, with the blizzard outside and danger just around the corner, she felt as though all was right in the world. She wished Amy could be here, too, but it wasn't melancholy at all. Amy *was* here. In her heart.

"Why don't you and I clean up and let Mom take it easy," Mike said. "What do you say, Samson?"

He didn't look thrilled about it, but he said, "Okay."

"You," Mike said, staring at her. "Get out. We don't want your kind in here."

"My kind?"

"Females. There's man's work to be done. It won't be pretty."

She had to laugh. God, how long had it been since she'd seen this side of Mike? He'd been so funny all those years ago. Then the laughter had stopped. It was a joy to see it come alive again. "Yes sir, captain sir. I'll be in the other room. No fair sneaking more cake."

The way Sam smiled let her know she'd nipped that crime in the bud. She went into the living room, and before she sat down she put another log on the fire. The couch beckoned then, and she stretched out, grateful to have a moment to herself.

She heard laughter from the kitchen, and she closed her eyes. Never before had she been on such a roller coaster of feelings. At least not all in one day. Sleep would come easily tonight. And tomorrow? She hadn't a clue. It would just have to take care of itself.

"How should we wake her?"

Sam was staring at his mom, shaking his head slowly, deep in thought. "I don't know," he whispered back. "But it needs to be good."

Mike put his hand on Sam's shoulder. "We shouldn't do anything that will scare her *too* much."

Sam looked up. "Don't chicken out on me now."

Mike nodded gravely. "It's your call."

Sam brought one hand up to his face, one finger tapping his lips. He studied his mother with extraordinary thoughtfulness and it was all Mike could do not to laugh.

"I think I've got it."

"Hmm?"

"Warm water plus her fingers in a bowl."

Mike burst out laughing. He remembered that trick from years ago, when he'd gone to all-night parties. They would wait until the first person went to sleep then dip his hands in warm water. Inevitably, the poor victim would wet the bed, or the sleeping bag.

"Shh," Sam hissed furiously, waving at Mike to pipe down. But it was too late.

Becky blinked and opened her eyes. "What's going on?"

"Dad just spoiled our surprise."

She pulled herself up to a sitting position. "What? Tell me anyway."

Sam gave Mike a disgusted glare. "Forget it. It wouldn't be any good now."

Mike was still laughing. "Sorry, kiddo. Maybe next time."

"Sure." He hunched his shoulders forward and shuffled past Becky. He plopped himself down in front of the fireplace. "You guys never let me have any fun."

Becky looked questioningly at Mike. All he could do was shake his head. He would tell her later. Maybe.

The wing chair had his name on it. He sat down facing both Sam and Becky. He didn't want to miss a thing tonight. Not one word or gesture. He felt as though he were standing outside of himself, observing more than participating. There—Becky pushed some loose hairs behind her ear. The move was fluid and unconscious and burned forever in his memory. Now Sam toyed with the Velcro on his sneaker, ripping it open, then shutting it again. Mike wanted to stop the world. Right now. Freeze-frame this night, this room, this family. But he couldn't.

Mojo was still out there.

"You said you were going to tell ghost stories," Sam said, looking over at Mike.

"Right. Let's see. You know the one about the hook?"

Sam rolled his eyes. "Duh. That's so old it has mold."

Mike grinned. "How about the one with the beating heart?"

Sam nodded. "Cool. Was it ripped out from someone's chest?"

Mike leaned forward. "You'll have to wait and see."

Becky curled her legs up in front of her and listened as Mike told Sam *The Tell-tale Heart*. He did it well, with sound effects and a spooky voice. Sam was caught in his spell, listening wide-eyed and motionless.

She was caught up, too, but not in the old Poe story. Mike captured her attention. She felt sure, now, that she hadn't been mistaken. Even though he was more like the old Mike than ever before, there was definitely something wrong. If she'd had to, she doubted she could say just what. It was something in his eyes. In the way he looked at Sam. There was an indefinable sadness about him. As if this would be the last story he ever told.

He held a secret, she was sure. But secrets had become her enemy. Nothing good had ever come of them. Only hurt. She could be patient, though. Soon, Sam would be off to bed and she could talk to Mike alone.

When he finished his tale, Sam was delighted. He begged for more, and Mike obliged. She didn't recognize this one. It didn't matter. He could have been reading the phone book aloud. Sam was his. Enraptured, captivated. Nothing had ever held his attention like this. Not even his computer.

By the time the second story was finished, it was nearly ten-thirty. She was still exhausted; her brief naps hadn't been of much help. "It's that time," she said.

Sam groaned. "No. Another half hour. Please."

She shook her head. "Nope. Upstairs. I want you in pj's in five minutes. I'll be up to check."

"Do I have to go right to sleep?" He was on his knees, crawling over to the couch. His hands were pressed together under his chin as he pleaded his case.

She looked into those dark eyes. They seemed to shine, but not from the firelight. It was much deeper than that. He'd been touched by his father tonight. She leaned forward and kissed the top of his head. "You can read. Half an hour. Then it's lights out."

"Thank you, thank you, thank you," he said, then he shot to his feet and raced to the stairs. He came to a screeching halt, turned around and ran back to Mike. "Great stories, Dad," he said, then he was off again, and this time he made it all the way up to his room.

"I think he feels better," Mike said.

She laughed. "I think you're right. How about you?"

He seemed surprised by her question. "Me? I'm okay."

"Really?"

The slight hesitation gave him away. He nodded, and said, "Sure."

She got up, and went over to where he sat. "Stay right there. I'm going to check on the pajama situation, but I want to talk to you. So you sit still."

He nodded without looking her straight in the eye. That convinced her further.

She hurried upstairs. Sam had managed to get his pajama top on before the lure of his book waylaid him. He only groaned at her twice while he changed the rest of the way. Finally, he was in bed, tucked under the covers. She sat down next to him. "It was fun tonight, huh?"

He nodded. "I wish it could always be like this."

She reached over and ruffled his hair. "It can't *always* be like any one thing. But we can sure try to have fun more often."

"What about Dad?"

"He can try, too."

"No," he said, switching his gaze from her face to his hands. "I mean, can't he come home again?"

She took a deep breath. No more secrets, she reminded herself. No more lies. "I don't know honey. I'm not sure he wants to come home. Or even if that would be the best thing. We still have some things to work out."

"But after you work them out?"

"It doesn't happen that way. All I can promise is that everything will turn out for the best."

"What does that mean?"

"That sometimes things happen, and we don't understand the reason right away. But we have to have faith that whatever comes our way, we'll grow and learn, and be happy."

His eyebrows came down and so did the corners of his mouth. "I still want him to come live with us. Why can't that be the way it turns out?"

"We'll see." She leaned forward and kissed his soft cheek. "Half an hour, then lights out."

He nodded and grabbed his book.

Becky got up, reluctant to leave him, but knowing Mike was waiting downstairs. When she got to the door, he stopped her.

"Mom?"

"Yes?" she said, turning to face him once again.

"I love you."

Warmth, like sunshine on a cold day, filled her all the way to the core. "I love you, too."

She left him then, closing the door behind her. She doubted he would last ten minutes, after the day he'd had. In a little while, she would come back up and shut the light.

She took the stairs slowly. She wanted the glow from his words to last, and something told her that her talk with Mike would be anything but warm.

He had done as she asked. He was sitting in the chair staring at the fire. It was hard to believe just a few moments ago he'd been animated and dramatic, when he sat so still now. He didn't even look at her as she reached the floor and walked back to the couch.

"Mike?"

He turned to her very slowly. "Yes," he said.

The tone of his voice scared her. This was the real ghost story, she thought. That word was spoken by a dead man.

"I want you to tell me what's wrong."

He shook his head. "No, you don't."

The couch was too far away. She got up, and knelt by his chair. When she touched his thigh, she felt him flinch. "Haven't we done enough harm? You said so yourself. We've kept too many secrets. It's time to tell the truth."

He looked at her then. The light from the fire reflected in his eyes, giving them life. But behind that, nothing. He had gone to that island, that fortress.

"Don't throw this away," she said, grabbing on to his hand. "Don't you see we've been given a gift. We've got a second chance. If we blow this, if we don't just plow ahead and face everything, then what was it all for?"

She wasn't getting through to him, she could see that. "Please," she said. "Don't shut me out. Talk to me, Mike. If I ever meant anything to you, talk to me."

"Second chance," he said, as if the words hurt his mouth. "That's funny."

"Why?" Her heart was beating faster, and she had to fight the urge to get up and run away.

He closed his eyes briefly, and when he opened them again she could see that something had shifted. It had gone from bad to worse.

"Mojo has escaped."

The breath was knocked out of her. She sat down, hard, on the floor. The thought had crossed her mind earlier, but she'd pushed it away, refusing to think about the real reason they were up here. Now there was no choice. "But I thought he was surrounded. That they had him."

"He killed Cliff. And the kid he kidnapped. I don't know, maybe more."

"Cliff?" She couldn't believe what she was hearing.

"That's right. And it's not over. It's just beginning for us. He's coming. He'll be here. Tomorrow or maybe the day after. It's just a matter of time."

"Then we have to leave."

"How? On the snowmobiles? In this?" He nodded toward the door, toward the howling wind.

"That's right," she said. "He can't get to us. No one could travel in this weather."

"No one sane."

Still stunned, she got to her feet. Her heart was beating like a jackhammer and it was hard to think straight. She walked over to the curtains. She was afraid to touch them, as if they would burn her fingers, but she did. The night was as black as her fear, a swirling, screaming universe of cold and death. Sam would never make it out there. She let the curtain go, and wrapped her arms around her waist. "Are they sending help?"

"They're going to try."

She heard the resignation in his voice. He didn't believe help would come. He didn't believe they would make it.

"Dammit, there has to be something we can do."

"Like what?"

"Set a trap, barricade the house. I don't know. Something."

He laughed, but it was like no sound she'd heard before. Dark, hopeless, unspeakably weary. Not like Mike at all.

She went over to the wing chair, and stood in front of him. "I will not let you give up," she said. "We can beat him. I know we can."

"How can you even say that? Haven't you learned yet that the good guys don't finish first? That there's no logic or reason to any of this?" He pushed himself out of his chair to face her. "Terrible things happen to innocent people. Or don't you remember?"

He was so close, she felt his breath on her face. But she didn't flinch or turn away. She made room, somewhere, somehow, for his anger.

When his breathing slowed and his face softened enough for him to listen, she said, "I know all that's true. But I don't care. I know with all my heart and soul that he can't win. Not against us. We wouldn't have gone through what we have in the last few days just to die. It doesn't work that way."

"Didn't you hear anything I said?"

She nodded. "Every word. It doesn't change a thing. I believe in you. I always will."

"Don't," he said, his voice barely above a whisper. "Everyone who's believed in me has ended up dead."

"Not me." She grabbed his arms and forced him to look her in the eyes. "Not me and not Sam. We're going to get through this. Together. We have too much at stake to lose now."

He opened his mouth to say something, but stopped, and closed it again. He shook his head.

"I've done some thinking about what you said this afternoon."

He looked up to the ceiling. "I should have kept my damn mouth shut. What good did it do except hurt you?"

"No," she said, praying she could get the words right. "The truth may hurt but it's not useless. The truth is, I did hate you. I hated the whole world because Amy had to die and I couldn't stop it. I was so busy hating and being angry that I didn't take the time to be grateful. That's what I regret. We had four years with Amy. Four wonderful years. We got to know her laughter and her tears. Her sweet smell and the way she felt in our arms. We got to see her being born, and we got to be there when she left us. Every moment was precious. It still is precious. I have no idea how much time any of us have, but I'll be damned if I'm going to waste one moment of it."

Underneath her fingers, she'd felt his muscles grow rigid. He was standing so stiffly that one strong wind would snap him in two.

She watched him, silently urging him to feel. To care. To fight. Slowly, like ice melting, the muscles of his face softened. "But Cliff," he whispered. "Gordon."

"It's horrible and sad that they had to die. But it's not your fault. You dishonor them by taking the blame. They were both good agents doing their job. They laid their lives down for something they believed in. Don't take that away from them."

He tried to hold it together. She watched him struggle to keep still, to not give in.

Then one tear broke free and fell on his cheek.

Chapter 14

Becky wrapped her arms around his neck, gently guiding his head to her shoulder. She held him firmly, rocking him like a child as he wept. She felt his body tremble beneath her hands as he let go of months and years of sorrow. Whispering sounds more than words, she ran her hand down the back of his head. She didn't know if he heard her voice or felt her touch.

All that mattered was that he was finally free, that his prison doors had opened. So much pain. Where was the justice, that this good man had to live with such a heavy burden?

Slowly, slowly, the trembling stopped. She heard him take deep breaths, felt his hands on her back, pressing her closer to him.

Then he straightened up and she was able to look at him. Grief still streaked his face, but inside his dark eyes she saw a glimmer of hope, of peace.

She stood on her toes and kissed his cheek, the taste of his tears moistening her lips. Then she touched his mouth with her fingers, learning again his soft contours. It wasn't enough. She kissed him there, gently, like a whisper.

Taking his hand in hers, she led him away from the fire and all the way to his room. Still she said nothing as she closed the door behind them.

He didn't move. He stood by the side of the bed, watching her, his chest expanding slowly with each deliberate breath. The light was too bright overhead, so she turned it off, leaving the small bedside lamp as the only illumination. It was enough, though, to see him clearly.

She grabbed the bottom of her sweater and pulled it over her head. Her bra was next, then her pants. Finally, she stood before him naked.

"Becky—"

She shook her head and moved toward him. "Shh, no more talk."

He let her undress him. The sweatshirt first, then his jeans. As she moved down his fly to the lower buttons, she felt him swell beneath her fingers. She would attend to that in a minute.

Now, she sank to her knees, and untied his heavy boots, slipping them off, followed by his socks and jeans. When she stood, she did it slowly, rubbing her body against his, pressing her breasts to his legs, his thighs, all the way up to his chest.

There was no mistaking his desire. Her own tightened nipples and the heat between her legs made her want to rush, but she held back. This was a gift, and not to be hurried.

She touched his chest, tracing the hills and valleys of muscled flesh, the soft hair teasing her fingers. Leaning forward, she kissed his neck, tasting his sweet, faintly salty skin. She ran her tongue down, circling the hard nub of his nipple. He groaned but made no move to touch her.

She took his arms and moved him backward until the back of his legs hit the bed. He sat. Giving him one brief kiss on the lips, she pressed his shoulders down. When he was laying flat, she climbed up onto the bed, straddling his legs.

She leaned forward to continue her journey. She felt him, thick and hard, pressing against her stomach. She brought her lips once again to his heated flesh, moving slowly down to his firm stomach. Her kisses followed the arrow of thick hair as it tapered off, and was replaced by thicker, denser hair near the junction of his thighs.

She closed her eyes, listening to his uneven breathing, smelling his masculine scent, tasting the light sheen of sweat as she went lower still. She touched him first, circling his heat with her palm. He was ready for her now, straining to be inside her, but first, she kissed him.

His deep moan told her of his pleasure. His hips lifted as she remembered this secret delight, but soon, it wasn't enough. For either of them.

Mike reached down and grasped her arms, pulling her up in one smooth motion. He left her on her back, while he turned to his side. Resting on one arm, he looked down at her. "Thank you," he whispered. "Thank you for my life." Then his mouth was on hers.

It was his turn to taste, to explore. His hands on her skin were reverent, his sigh was grateful and urgent. He nestled his thighs between hers, and then he sank inside her, filling her in the most intimate of embraces.

His head went back as he groaned his pleasure.

She reached around his neck and pulled him closer, only satisfied when she found his lips.

It was sweet and slow. She'd never made love like this before. Every part of her body was electric, every movement brought a new sensation, each one more intense than the last.

She gave herself with her whole heart, holding nothing back. No matter what happened, she would be safe in his embrace. Just as Amy lived on, so would their love. The world couldn't touch this sacred space. When she looked into his eyes, she knew he was there with her, feeling the same connection.

She felt her pulse quicken as he thrust into her more deeply. She wrapped her legs around him and he kissed her over and over as he neared his climax. When the moment came, and he couldn't hold back another second, she held on to him with all her might, straining right on the edge. His cry sent her over, and in that second they were one heart, one breath.

Mike felt her tremble from her core to her fingertips. He buried himself in her a little deeper, not willing to let go. He looked at her beneath him, sloe-eyed and shining. Her mouth opened slightly and her soft lips curved in a hint of a smile. Powerless to resist, he kissed her again. Her hands moved over his back in slow circles. He was where he belonged.

Not willing to break the contact between them, he rolled to his side, carrying her with him. He bent his leg and she curled hers around him, so they were still locked in their embrace.

This is how it felt to be reborn, he thought. He closed his eyes, and for the first time in over three years, he thanked God.

Becky moved her head, nestling against him with a sigh. He didn't move for a long time. He tried like hell not to think, either. Just to feel her next to him was enough. When he finally did look down, he saw her eyelids flutter as she gave in to sleep.

"I love you," he whispered. "Forever."

He was sorely tempted to fall asleep beside her, but he couldn't. There were things to be done, now, tonight, while he still could move in safety. He would wait, though, until she was sleeping soundly.

The wind howled outside as the minutes ticked by, and he struggled to keep his mind on Becky. But Mojo crept in between them, slithered into his brain. He was coming. Mike could feel it in his bones. It didn't matter how bad the weather was, nothing as small as nature could stop him.

Then he felt Becky's warm breath on his chest, and he let go. He didn't want to think anymore. Not about that. He didn't resist this time, when his eyes shut.

Mike awoke in Becky's arms. A rush of memories, of countless days when waking up had been a pleasure because *she* was there, instead of the tortured mornings when the end of sleep meant just another day to get through. Her hair had come out of the tight braid and was wild on the pillow. He'd never seen anything more beautiful.

The room was lighter, but he knew it was barely daylight. Time for him to get up. To prepare.

When Becky shifted, Mike slipped out of her arms. Being alone had never felt colder. He looked at her for another minute, so lovely it hurt. She was his life.

He got up, careful not to rouse her, and put on his jeans. It was chilly, but the sweatshirt helped. He turned off the bedside lamp after donning his shoes and socks. He hoped Becky would sleep for a long time. He had the awful feeling she would need it.

He meant to leave then, but instead, he bent and kissed her cheek once more. "I love you," he said, even though he knew she couldn't hear him. He stole out of the room, shutting the door behind him.

It was cold in the hallway. They'd left the light on in the living room. The fire was dead, of course. He went to the front door and checked the lock. The dead bolt was engaged, just as he'd left it last night. He pushed the curtain aside and peered through the window. The snow was coming down at a sharp angle. It was up past the porch now; maybe three feet had fallen in the last twenty-four hours.

The truck would be useless, but the snowmobiles could travel. He wondered about the back route. Would he still be able to find his way? The thought of taking Becky and Sam out into that freezing hell made him grimace. He would do that only as a last resort.

He let the curtain fall back in place, then went to the closet beneath the staircase. His rifle was just where he'd left it, the boxes of ammo stacked neatly on the shelf.

The sweatshirt was a mistake. No pockets. The jeans, too, were no good. They were too tight. He needed to keep himself loaded for bear, and he didn't want to put on a jacket.

The rifle felt good in his hands. Heavy, formidable. He would give Becky the .45, and he would stick to this baby. All he needed was to get Mojo in his sights. Just once.

He grabbed three boxes of ammo and put them on the table next to the couch. He started for the stairs, but then thought better of going into Sam's room with the rifle. He didn't want to wake him that way. When he was alert, the weapon wouldn't be quite so scary. He put it on the couch, then took the stairs two at a time.

Sam's door was closed. He opened it quietly, not wanting to wake the boy. The light was still on, and above the lump under the covers was an open book. He remembered Becky saying she meant to go back upstairs last night. He was glad she hadn't. Stepping over some of Sam's clothes on the floor, Mike went to the window first, and checked the lock. Nothing looked out of place. When he went to the bed, the lump moved a little. He smiled, and lifted the quilt.

His son was curled up in a tight little ball, sound asleep. An overwhelming rush of love washed over him. No one was going to touch a hair on that boy's head. Not while he still had a breath in his body.

Anger swelled. Fury at the madman who dared threaten his family. He didn't want Mojo back in jail. He wanted him dead.

He covered Sam again. No need to wake him. After he got up, Mike would put the food and water in the closet just in case.

The clock on the nightstand said 6:20. Mike went to the door and turned out the light before he left.

The first thing he needed to do was get an update from Cliff. His throat constricted as he remembered he would never speak to Cliff again. He needed to call Sully. Irrationally, he hoped his boss was sleeping so he would have the pleasure of hauling him out of bed. He hurried down stairs and picked up the phone.

Nothing. No dial tone.

Mike's muscles tightened. *Mojo.* He was here already Maybe just outside that window. Behind that door.

But wait, the storm was a bad one. Witherspoon had said the lines went down a lot during the winter. Before he got all bent out of shape, he'd better check the wires.

He grabbed the rifle and opened up one box of shells. He stuffed a few thick cartridges into each of his pockets. Then he ran to the kitchen. His heart was beating fast, and he tried to consciously slow it down. He needed his wits about him now. No use getting excited until he had to.

The basement was much colder than the upstairs. He flipped on the light and scanned every corner and shadow as he descended. Everything looked still, just as it had the last time he was down here. But he couldn't shake the feeling that it was Mojo, not the storm, who had knocked the phones out.

The coiled wire the caretaker had left was by the far wall. Why hadn't he come down with the old man? Would he even be able to tell if the phone line had been cut?

He crossed the small room and moved aside some storage boxes until he had a clear view of the wall. There were wires there, all right. They all looked fine to his untrained eye. No missing pieces, nothing at all to make him think they'd been tampered with. Besides, if Mojo had gotten inside, they would all be dead by now.

He turned to look out the small window. It was totally blocked by snow so he couldn't see a damn thing. Could he risk going out there? Mojo might be waiting just out of sight, hoping Mike would leave the safety of the house. No. He couldn't take that chance.

He had to assume Mojo *was* out there, and prepare for the worst.

Just as he reached the staircase, a rumble stopped him cold. He froze, adrenaline shooting through his veins. The pipes. The noise was coming from the pipes.

He breathed again. Becky was up, that's all. No danger. Yet.

He went upstairs quickly. She wasn't in the kitchen. That meant she must be in the shower. God, he didn't want to tell her about the phone. How would he be able to stand the look of fear on her face? He'd already done so much to hurt her.

He remembered the sweet ending to last night. How she'd made love to him, with him. They'd been given a chance for a new beginning by the same man who wanted to take it all away again.

The pipes quieted. She was getting out of the shower. A picture of her naked body, glistening with water, came to him like a snapshot. He wanted to make love with her again. Not just tonight, but a hundred nights—all the nights of his life.

It wasn't wise to think about that now. His head needed to be clear, his senses on full alert. He went to the stove and got the kettle. While he filled it with water, he moved aside the curtain to look out back.

The whole world was snow. There was no horizon, only the furiously swirling white. Mojo could be ten feet in front of him, and he would never know.

He put the kettle on the burner. They would need coffee this morning. Lots of it. He intended to take every opportunity to fortify the house, and the three of them, before the confrontation. There was no doubt in his mind that there would be one—the only question was when.

After wrapping the towel snugly around her chest, Becky went to the sink. She used her hand to wipe the fog from the mirror. She didn't look different. It was just her, just Sam's mom. A little older, perhaps, and a lot wiser. She felt as though she'd aged a lifetime in just a few days.

She pulled the towel from her head, and combed her hair. All she wanted was a peaceful, quiet day. Was that so much to ask for? Lord, she needed a breather, some time to get her bearings.

She didn't even know if she and Mike had made up. They were still divorced of course, but were they back together? Did she want to be?

Loving him was a given. It was no use even pretending that she didn't care about him. But that didn't necessarily mean he was right for her.

It was this place. This crazy snowed-in isolation made it all so hard. Would things make sense back at the house? How would it feel when Mike went to work, and there was a damn good chance he wouldn't come home? It had taken her so long to stop worrying about him. Did she honestly want to go through that again?

She put down the comb and focused again on her image. Would being without him be worse than her fear? Could she give him up, after all they'd been through? The woman in the mirror had no answers.

She got busy braiding her hair, forcing the troubling thoughts from her mind. There was no way she could make that kind of a decision right now. So she might as well stop trying.

When she opened the door, the first thing she saw was the rifle.

Everything stopped but the furious beating of her heart. "What's wrong?"

Mike looked at her with pain-filled eyes. "The phone is dead. I think he's here."

She felt dizzy, and grabbed on to the door for support. Mike was at her side instantly. He moved to hold her, but she waved him away. "I'm okay. Where's Sam?"

"Upstairs, asleep. I checked on him already."

"We've got to get him out of here."

Mike shook his head. "The storm is worse. A lot worse. We're safer inside."

She looked at him as she sat down on the bed. "Are you sure about this? That he's here, I mean?"

"No. The weather could have knocked out the phone."

"But the weather...how could he—"

"I don't know. But my gut tells me we'd better be prepared for anything."

She was trembling. It hadn't been real before. Not like this. It had been words and phone calls, and now it was life and death. She'd told him just last night that she believed in him. That she knew beyond reason that they would be all right. Dammit, she still did. "What do you want me to do?"

"Get dressed." He walked to the other side of the bed and got his pistol from the night stand. He checked the clip and the safety and put it back in the holster. "Wear something with pockets. If you don't have anything, take one of my shirts. You'll need room for the ammunition."

Becky stared at the gun, wondering if this time she would be forced to use it. "I'll need a shirt."

While she picked up her clothes from last night, she heard him unzip his duffel bag. When she turned to him, he was holding one of his favorite red flannel shirts. He handed it to her.

She brought it to her face and sniffed. His scent was in the material, just like with his clothes at home. It would make her feel safer, like being wrapped in his arms.

"It's clean," he said.

She smiled. "I know." Then she raised herself up on her toes and kissed his lips.

His arm went around her waist, and the kiss deepened. She tasted his desire as well as his fear. But when he pulled away, all she saw was his love.

"Go on, get dressed. Wake Sam up, and get him dressed, too. I've put up coffee, and we all need to eat."

She touched his cheek, and he closed his eyes and rested upon her hand. Only for a moment, though.

Turning away, she sent up a silent prayer. *Keep him safe, Lord. Please.* She picked up the holster and gun.

"After breakfast, I want you to get the closet ready for Sam."

Her stomach jumped at that. Sam. Oh, God. "I want to stay with him, Mike. As much as I possibly can."

After he pulled his sweatshirt off, he nodded.

"Why are you undressing?"

"I need pockets, too. Now, go on. Hurry."

She looked at him for one last moment. At the stream-lined body that she had just begun to know. At the man she'd never stopped loving. Later, she would tell him. When this was over, she would confess that through it all, even the worst of times, he'd had her heart. Now though, she had a job to do.

"Wake up, honey." Becky touched Sam's shoulder.

He jerked a little, then his eyes opened. "Okay," he said. Then he turned to his side, and went right back to sleep.

"Sam. You need to get up now. Come on."

He groaned, then threw his arms out in an enormous stretch. "Is breakfast ready?"

"Soon," she said.

He was so beautiful. So young and innocent. She would give anything to keep him safe, promise anything to shield him from the fear. "You go wash up, okay?"

He didn't even look at her. It wasn't a slight. He just took her for granted, which was as it should be. She should be here for him, always. Ready to guide him where she could, help him prepare for the rest of his life. Nowhere in her plans was saving him from a lunatic.

When he went off to the bathroom, she hurriedly dressed. She chose her jeans, remembering what Mike had said about pockets. His shirt was way too big, but when she rolled up the sleeves, she found it very comfortable. Instead of her heavy boots, she put on her running shoes. As long as they were going to stay in the house, she wanted to be able to move fast. Then she put on the shoulder holster and made the adjustments so it would fit properly.

Sam's clothes were just as simple to pick out. Heavy jeans, a T-shirt, covered by another flannel shirt. The three of them were going to look like the lumberjack triplets.

"How come you have the gun?"

She hadn't heard Sam come back into the room. She turned to find him at the door, staring at the holster strapped to her chest. The pistol seemed out of place on the pale yellow quilt.

"We have to be really careful today, Sam." She walked over to him and wrapped her arms around his slight shoulders.

His response was quick and urgent. He grabbed her around the waist as tightly as he could.

"If Daddy or I tell you to hide, you know what to do, right?"

She felt his nod on her stomach.

"After breakfast, we're going set up your closet. We'll make it a fort. We'll put in some sandwiches and fruit." She bent so she could see his face. "And all the rest of the cookies."

He smiled for her, a pathetic, scared little grin just for her benefit.

She could be brave for him, too. "So what you do want for breakfast? Pancakes? Eggs? Pot roast?"

"Pot roast?"

She smiled wide as he stepped out of her arms. "Turtle soup?"

He made a face. "Ugh. I want pancakes."

"Chicken."

"No, *pancakes.*"

She laughed and tousled his hair. "I love you, kiddo."

He reached over and took her hand in his. They looked at each other for a long moment, and she was incredibly aware of the bond between them. Nothing could destroy that; it was bigger than life itself.

"Get dressed now. Don't dawdle."

He nodded and let her go and she sat on her bed. When she looked up again she saw that Sam was staring at her. He'd probably guessed that she had slept downstairs. But she didn't want to explain about that now. What would she say, anyway? "You're not dressing."

While he pulled his pajama top over his head, she headed downstairs.

Mike's rifle was on the kitchen counter, in front of the toaster. He was pouring milk into his coffee. He'd changed into a looser pair of jeans and a blue checked flannel shirt. Even from the door, she could see the bulges in his pockets from the heavy cartridges.

He looked up as she walked toward him. "Did you tell him?"

She nodded. "He's trying to be so brave. Mike, are you sure Mojo is out there? I mean, shouldn't we be positive before we put Sam through all this?"

"If we wait, it'll be too late."

She'd known his answer even before she asked the question. Of course they couldn't risk it. "I'm going to fix him pancakes," she said. "Would you get the food ready for the closet, please?"

Mike hesitated as if he wanted to reassure her in some way. He didn't, though. He just nodded, and went to the refrigerator.

She found a big bowl and the prepackaged mix. All she had to do was add water. Her hands shook as she turned on the tap. She dropped the measuring cup in the sink. It didn't break.

She was about to, though.

She bent her head, and put her hands over her face. It wasn't that she wanted to cry—she just wanted to wake up. She wanted to be standing in her own kitchen. She wanted to tell Sam not to run down the stairs, and ask him if he had his homework ready for school. She wanted to see Mike sitting at the table, reading the morning paper.

As if her thoughts had called him, he put his hand on her shoulder. She looked up, knowing none of her wishes could come true.

"Don't fall apart on me now," he said. "You're the strongest woman I've ever known. You've faced the hardest things in the world. You can do this."

She touched his hand with hers, and nodded, not trusting herself to speak. Then she looked into his eyes.

His fear was as real as her own. That should have made things worse, but instead it made her feel better. Whatever else happened, Mike was human again. He could feel, he could hurt. He could love.

He let her go, and went back to fixing the food for Sam's closet.

She poured the water on top of the dry mix, and started stirring. Had last night really changed everything? If they got out of this—no, *when* they got out of this, would Mike just come home? Is that what she wanted?

Not if it meant living with this fear day after day.

Now she knew what it was like to be in the line of fire. There was no way she could watch him walk out her door, and know he was going to face this kind of danger. It would kill her. As much as she loved him, and she had no doubts any more that she did, she couldn't go back to the way things were.

"Should I give him the grape juice or the apple?"

She turned.

Mike was holding up juice boxes, waiting for her decision. As he looked at her, his brow creased and he put the juice on the table. "Something else is going on, isn't it?" he said. He walked over to her again. "Talk to me."

She took a deep, shaky breath. "I love you."

"I love you, too."

She held up a hand to stop him. "I wasn't finished. I love you, but that's not enough."

He did stop. He stood in front of her, not moving, not blinking. He started to retreat, to close himself off the way he always did. Then he shut his eyes, took a deep breath, and relaxed. When he looked at her again, she saw his vulnerability, his hope.

She wanted to run to him. To hold him. To tell him that she understood what kind of victory this was. He'd called her brave, but she couldn't hold a candle to this one moment.

"Tell me what you want," he said, his voice quiet and intense.

"I want you to quit the bureau. Sam needs a father he can count on."

He crossed the distance between them, and held her by the shoulders. "What do *you* need?" Then he kissed her, hard. His fingers dug into her flesh as he crushed her lips with his own.

She brought her hand between them and pushed him back. "No," she said, as he let her go. "I need to know you'll come home at night. I can't live the rest of my life in fear."

He stared at her for a long time. When he spoke, the words came slowly. "I love you and I love Sam. But I can't quit. It's all I know."

She closed her eyes as the disappointment washed through her. Why had she let herself hope? When she looked at him again, he had turned toward the door of the kitchen. She followed his gaze. Sam was standing just inside.

"You're not coming home, are you?" he asked, staring at his father.

Mike looked back at Becky for a quick second, then turned back to face his son. "No."

The word hung in the air. Sam's face changed into an angry mask. "Then why did you come get us?" He was yelling, the hurt so raw it was like an open wound. "We were fine at home. We don't need you."

She went for him, but Mike was quicker. He grabbed Sam's arms and pulled him close. "I love you, Sam. Nothing can change that."

Sam twisted out of Mike's hands. "You don't! You love your job better." He ran past him, and she knelt to catch him.

"That's not—"

She looked up, instantly frightened at the way Mike was

staring past her to the kitchen window. He rushed past her, as her heart thudded in her chest. "What is it?"

He moved the curtain an inch to the right. Becky felt a scream building inside her.

Then he let the curtain drop and he turned toward her. "Witherspoon's snowmobile. It's parked outside. But he's not on it."

Chapter 15

Witherspoon must have ridden over on the snowmobile during the night. It was the only explanation Mike could find for not hearing the engine. Something had stopped the old man from coming to the cabin door. Something, or someone.

"Get the food," he snapped at Becky. "Sam, get upstairs. Mommy will be up in a second. Do just what she says. Be quick."

Becky still held Sam tightly. They both looked terrified. He fought back the urge to yell at them to move. That wouldn't help anything. He knelt so he could be eye-level with Sam. "It's going to be okay if we just use our heads. Becky, I want you to take the food upstairs. Sam, I want you to go up ahead of her and get inside the closet. Just like we practiced. When Mommy gets there, she'll make sure you're comfortable, and that you're not alone."

Neither of them moved. He touched Sam's cheek, brushing it with the back of his fingers. "I need you to help me, Samson. I'm counting on you to watch out for your mom while I'm down here. Can you do that?''

Sam nodded. Becky's eyes closed and Mike reached over and touched her hand. When she finally looked at him, he could see she didn't want to leave him.

"You can do this," he whispered.

She nodded, then stood. "Come on, kiddo. Let's move it."

Mike got up, too. "Don't forget the gun," he said.

Becky went to the table and picked it up. She checked the safety, then slipped it into the shoulder holster.

"The ammunition is in the closet beneath the stairs," he said. "Take a few boxes with you. Now go."

Becky grabbed the large paper bag filled with food and drink. "I'll be right behind you, honey."

Sam ran then. He darted out of the room without a look back. Mike wanted to race after him, to hold him close and tell him he'd been wrong. He didn't give a damn about his job. Only his family.

He picked up his rifle. When he turned back, Becky was already on her way out.

"I won't let him hurt you," he said.

She looked at him one last time. "I know."

He watched her go, praying this wasn't the last time he would ever see her. Dammit, why had he said he wasn't going home to them? All he wanted was for Becky and Sam to be safe, and to be with them. The bureau had lots of jobs that wouldn't put him in the line of fire. For the first time in two years, it mattered that he might die. That he might not be around to watch Sam grow up.

Forcing his mind to clear, he went back to the window above the sink and moved the curtain so he could see outside. Nothing much had changed, except the level of the snow. It was really coming down. God, the whole world would be covered with white soon. Witherspoon's snowmobile was completely blanketed now, a lump to match the other two vehicles.

Mojo could be hiding behind anything. The snowmobiles, the Bronco, a tree, the woodpile. All Mike knew for sure was that Mojo would have a plan. He wouldn't just shoot his way in, using force as his weapon. No, the man was too vain, too proud of his insights into Mike's character to do anything so gauche. Mojo would do something with a little finesse.

Mike left the kitchen after checking the lock one more time. The living room was cold and empty, but nothing had been tampered with. The dead bolt was firmly locked, the windows were all intact. He pushed the drapes aside, just enough so he could see out. Great swirling masses of snow and ice and wind flew into the glass.

No one was coming to help. He knew that. Sully might try, but he was only human. Hopefully, he'd found a snowplow, but that would take God knows how long to clear a path all the way to the cabin.

Mike heard a thump from above, and in seconds he was on the stairs, taking two at a time, racing almost as quickly as his heart.

The bedroom door was open and when he went inside, he found Becky standing outside the closet, holding the .45 in her hand.

"What happened?"

She shook her head. "I dropped this." She lifted the gun. "I'm sorry, it was clumsy of me."

"Don't worry about it." Mike went to the window and checked the lock. Mojo could climb the tree, he supposed, but it would be tough with his bum leg. He looked down, but it was a useless gesture.

He turned back to Becky. She had pushed the sliding door all the way to the right and was crawling into the closet, moving aside pillows and blankets. He caught a glimpse of Sam, sitting cross-legged with a sleeping bag on his lap.

Becky settled in, camouflaging her position with the linens. When she was through, he could see bits of her, an elbow, a knee. It wasn't perfect, but it was the best they could do. If Mojo really looked for them, he would find them.

So he wouldn't get up here. Period.

It was time to go back downstairs. He checked the closet one more time, closing it a little more. "It's going to be fine," he said. "Just stay put. No matter what. I don't want you two leaving this closet. You got that?"

He heard a muffled "Yes" from Becky. There was nothing more for him to do up here, but he hated to leave them. Out of the corner of his eye, he caught sight of Sam's computer. It was still plugged in near the bed. He went over and picked it up. It had a battery that would run for several hours. No reason Sam couldn't have it with him. He unplugged the cord and took the machine to the closet. He slid the door fully open and bent over, moving aside a pink quilt until he saw Sam's face. "I think you forgot this," he said.

Sam reached out and took the computer. The grateful look he gave Mike didn't quite hide the fear. Then the quilt fell again, and Mike couldn't see Sam's face anymore.

"Listen up, guys," he said. "When this is all over, things are gonna be different around here. No more of this every-other-weekend crap. Becky, we'll talk about the job, okay? We'll work something out. Sam, you're more important that anything, buddy. Don't you ever forget that." He quickly slid the closet door three-quarters shut and left them.

He would be back.

Becky didn't know whether to laugh or cry. She believed him. He would make changes, they both would.

There was a real chance they could be a family again. *If* they got out of here alive.

She shifted in the tight cocoon of blankets so that her hip was against Sam's. She was sitting cross-legged, like him. There was really no other choice in the cramped space. But she wanted him to feel her there next to him. To take comfort in her company. It was a small comfort, she knew that, but it was all she had available.

God, they had to get out of this. It was too cruel, too unthinkable that their future could be snatched away just when it was looking so bright.

She thought about the first night they'd spent in this cabin. How she had barely been able to talk to Mike, how trapped he'd been on his island of bitter regrets. They'd gone through a lifetime of changing in the past few days.

Mike had found his heart again, and it had given him life. He'd seen, all on his own, that his family was what really mattered. That watching Sam grow, teaching him, loving him, was the greatest gift he could ever receive.

Something else had changed. Finally, after two years of denial and misspent grief, she was able to say goodbye to Amy. Of course, her little girl would always be with her, but now, and forever more, Becky would be able to remember the good times, the sweet moments.

Sam bumped her with his elbow and she looked down at him. He'd opened his computer on his lap. While she watched, the screen came alive as his swift fingers ran across the keyboard. She moved an afghan behind her neck, which not only felt better, but let her see the screen.

She was glad Mike had thought to give the computer to Sam. It would distract him. Her, too. God knew how long they would be shut up in here.

The thought of Mike downstairs, of what he might have to face, hit her again with the force of a blow. She strained to hear him, but it was useless. The pillows, blankets and sleeping bags cut off the rest of the world. It was just the two of them, in this strange little cave.

Sam was typing again. Only he wasn't playing a game. He was writing a note. Becky put the gun in her left hand and flexed her right for a moment, then gripped it again. Only when the barrel was pointing straight out in front of her did she lean a bit to her left to see what had Sam so interested.

It was only one sentence. A simple question.

"Are we going to see Amy in heaven?"

If he was Mojo, how would he break into this house? That's the question Mike pondered as he stood by the staircase. He could see the front door from here, and the kitchen door, too.

The easiest way would be to break a window and climb through. If he was careful and patient, there wouldn't be much noise, only the crack of broken glass for a second. If Mike was in the kitchen, with this wind howling, he wouldn't hear glass break in the living room.

Okay, so which window? The living room? Too obvious. Mojo would assume Mike would be there. The kitchen? No good. He would have to climb over the sink. He wouldn't do that. The bedroom? That was a good choice. But not the best.

If he was trying to break into this cabin, he would go straight to the basement. The window was easy to get to from outside, and big enough to let a slim man slide through. The drop was an easy one, and the room itself was dark and cut off from the rest of the house.

He made the decision that fast, and went toward the kitchen. Just as he reached the door to the basement, the lights went out. He froze.

Either Mojo was in the basement already, or he was still outside near the power line. Mike looked up, as if he could see through the ceiling to where Becky and Mike sat in the closet. Did they know the electricity was gone? He tried to remember if they'd left a light on in the bedroom, but he couldn't. Maybe they didn't know. Please, God, they didn't.

He took some slow breaths, consciously slowing his rapid pulse. He listened hard, struggling to hear a shoe fall, a box being dragged, anything. But all he heard was the infernal wind.

He grabbed the doorknob with his left hand, keeping the rifle poised in his right. Slowly, patiently, he opened the door and moved toward the steps. One more second, and he could get through.

The shot shattered the doorframe an inch from his temple.

He hit the floor, his lower half still in the kitchen, his left arm braced on the second step, the only thing stopping him from taking a header down the stairs. Pain shot from his hand to his shoulder, red and blinding, but he had no time for that now. At least his question had been answered.

Mojo was in the basement.

It was dark down below. Another shot, this one slamming into the wall behind him, was only a few inches off the mark. Ambient light from the kitchen was acting like a spotlight, giving Mojo plenty of time to get his aim right. Mike had to move. Now.

He pulled his legs in, until he was hunched over in a crouch. Thankfully, the door swung shut behind him, but not before Mojo got off one more shot. This one hit the stairs, and Mike felt a sharp sting on his cheek. It had to be a splinter. How big, he had no idea. He was bleeding, but he could still see and move, so it made no difference.

Now the darkness was more even. The only gray area was a shaft of dull light from the broken window high on the other side of the room. The only thing illuminated was a barren patch of concrete floor. Mike tried to see into the shadows, to see the glint off the gun or a blur of movement. Nothing.

He had to get down the steps. Even without light, Mojo knew where he was. It was only a matter of target practice until he found the bull's-eye.

Keeping a tight grip on the rifle, Mike shifted slowly until he'd reversed his position, and his legs were below him on the steps. At least he wasn't upside down anymore. He didn't sit for long. He squeezed as tightly as he could next to the wall, and eased his butt over the edge of one stair to the next. Sam used to do this when he was learning to walk. He used to sit at the top of the stairs and ride his bottom all the way down to the ground floor.

Mike waited before he moved again. The wind was louder in here and a steady stream of billowing snow flew into the dark room. He thought it must be cold, but he didn't feel it.

Was Mojo behind the dryer? Or had he moved underneath the staircase, so he could point his gun straight up?

It was torture to be still. To hunt the dark recesses with inadequate eyes. To play this deadly game of chicken. He had to win, because if he didn't, Mojo was going to climb another set of stairs, open a closet door, and—

He couldn't think about that. Not now. He had to be smarter than the man waiting for him. More patient.

Mojo would grow tired. He would shoot again, and this time Mike would see where the shot came from. All he had to do was wait. He started counting his heartbeats and waiting for act two.

Becky bit her lower lip so hard she tasted the salt of her own blood. Sam had grabbed her arm when they'd heard the first shot. His grip had tightened, and now she heard the quivering short breaths that told her he was crying.

"It's okay, honey," she said, as loudly as she dared. "Daddy's going to come up here real soon and get us. You'll see. He's fine."

She could see the bottom half of Sam's face in the eerie blue-green light of the computer monitor. She'd thought it would go out when the electricity went off, but then she'd realized it was running on batteries. Not that he had any attention for his games now.

She had to do something to take his mind off the long stretches of silence, and the more horrifying bursts of gunfire. But how could she, when her own fear had her by the throat?

"Did I ever tell you about the day Daddy and I found out you were going to be born?"

He didn't answer her. She didn't want to let go of the gun, but she forced herself to loosen her left hand. It was stiff from squeezing so hard for so long, and she had to flex her fingers for a minute. Then she turned just a bit toward Sam and put her arm around his shoulder.

He fell against her, and she felt his trembling as if it were her own.

"It was a Tuesday. Wintertime, like now. Daddy didn't have a clue that I had such a big surprise for him. See, I'd gone to the doctor that afternoon. I'd had a hunch. Dr. Richman said I was pregnant. I couldn't wait to get home."

Sam turned his head a little more, burying his face in her side. The computer tilted, but didn't fall. Now, the light illuminated his shirt.

"I baked a cake. Vanilla with chocolate icing. And I cooked him his favorite meal. You know what it was?"

She waited, but didn't really expect him to respond. After a moment, she said, "It's your favorite meal, too. Lasagna. When we get home, I'm going to make a big pan of lasagna for my two favorite guys. Anyway, I made a big fancy dinner, with salad and garlic bread. I even bought wine. For him, you know. I couldn't drink that anymore. Not with you inside me.''

She moved her hand until she felt his soft hair beneath her fingers. She petted him, over and over, trying to calm him—and herself. There hadn't been another shot for... She had no idea how long. It could have been five minutes or two hours. They were in some kind of dark limbo, where time and space had no meaning.

''We lived in an apartment then. Off Pearl Street. Anyway, Daddy was due home in a half hour. So I went and took a shower, because I wanted to be pretty for him. When I got out, I smelled something funny. I wrapped myself in a big towel, and went into the living room. That's when I saw the smoke.''

Sam had calmed down a bit. He wasn't shaking anymore, at least not so much. His breathing was more even and steady. Oh, if he could only sleep. Perhaps that was too much to hope for.

''The whole kitchen was on fire. I got so scared. I tried to put it out, but it was already too big. So I raced into the bedroom and put on my robe. I grabbed my pillow and the photo album and I got downstairs at the same time the fire engines pulled up in front. When Daddy came home, instead of the wonderful dinner I'd planned, he saw everything we owned go up in flames. I thought I'd started the fire, you know, with the oven or something. I was crying pretty hard. Daddy took me in his arms and said he didn't care. Not one bit.''

She squeezed him tight. ''That's when I told him about you. He was so happy, he lifted me in the air and spun me around. I was in my bathrobe, with a big old fire department blanket around my shoulders, but he didn't care. He just whooped and hollered, and he gave me a big fat kiss. Then he told me that this baby, that you, were going to be lucky your whole life. Anyone who started out with this much of a ruckus was bound to be the luckiest kid in the whole world.''

She laid her head back against her makeshift pillow, remembering that day, the look in Mike's eyes. Had she ever felt more wonderful in her whole life? They had nothing. Not even clothes. But it hadn't mattered. She'd had her man next to her, and her new little baby all safe and warm deep inside her. ''Of course, when we found out a few weeks later that it wasn't my lasagna that had caused the fire, I was pretty grateful. It had something to do with the wiring in the building. Anyway, I said a prayer that night, before I went to sleep. I made a promise, too. I prayed for you to be healthy, happy and lucky. In return, I promised I would take care of you forever.''

She leaned over and kissed the top of his head. ''I'm gonna keep that promise, kiddo.''

She heard him sniff. Then, in a soft, high little voice, he said, ''Should I pray now, Mommy?''

She closed her eyes tight. ''As hard as you can.''

Mike hadn't moved a muscle. His cheek throbbed from the splinter, and he thought he'd sprained his wrist. But he hadn't budged. The wind had died down a bit, which made him strain even harder to hear. Mojo was as silent as a ghost.

Why hadn't he taken another shot? He must have some idea where Mike was on the staircase. What was he waiting for? Nightfall? No, it was already dark in the house. He was planning something, but Mike didn't know what.

A soft scrape made him freeze. He knew that sound. A shoe on concrete. He'd heard it before, two years ago, in an isolated warehouse in the middle of the night.

With infinite caution, Mike reached his hand down to his back pocket. He pulled his wallet out and held it close to his chest. Carefully opening the leather billfold, he slipped the plastic picture case from the center and put it in his breast pocket. There was a photograph of Amy he didn't want to lose. Then he braced his other hand on the rifle and tossed the wallet to the floor.

Gunfire shattered the quiet, a barrage of bullets first on the basement floor, then right over his head. A wild volley that kept on and on, the noise deafening.

All Mike saw was the red flash of gunpowder as it lit up the hands that held the weapon. He lifted his own rifle and pulled the trigger.

The raging gunfire stopped instantly. A crash, boxes toppling, glass breaking, was followed by the clatter of a gun falling to the ground.

Mike was up before the smoke settled, down the stairs, his rifle chest-level, ready to rip.

Mojo's body lay sprawled on the boxes of toys and old clothes. He was facedown, the hood of his jacket covering his hair. Mike found his gun—a semiautomatic rifle— with his next step. He kicked it again with his boot, and made sure it landed across the room. Mojo didn't move.

When he got up close to the body, Mike poked the butt of the rifle into his shoulder. No response. Mojo was dead or unconscious. Mike hoped for dead.

He reached down with his right hand, grabbed a chunk of parka, and rolled Mojo over onto his back.

Only it wasn't Mojo.

It was a woman. The nurse. He'd known she wasn't a hostage, dammit. Suddenly, it came to him. How Mojo had found out where they were. How he'd found out everything.

Mike ran faster than he'd ever run before. He took the stairs two at a time as he struggled not to panic. He threw his shoulder into the door and raced through the kitchen. He had to slow for the turn in the hall, and then he was on the steps leading to Sam's room.

"I think you'd better stop right there."

He did. It was a voice from the past, straight from hell. Images of the warehouse came back, and he saw Gordon lying in a pool of blood. Mike turned slowly to face the man who wanted him to die, too.

Mojo sat in the wing chair. The .357 Magnum resting easily on his lap pointed straight at Mike's chest.

He hadn't changed much at all. He was still too thin, with a beak of a nose and a small cruel mouth. It was too dark to see his eyes, but somehow Mike knew they were shining with pleasure.

"It's good to see you again, old friend."

"You sick bastard."

Mojo frowned. "That's not very nice. And here I came all this way, just for you."

"You didn't need to do me any favors."

"I assume my compatriot is no longer with us."

Mike nodded. "You mean Darrelyn, don't you?"

Mojo smiled. "Very good. You finally figured it out."

"How did you know Sam and I wrote to each other?"

"A little article in your local paper. It even gave the instructions for signing on to the bulletin board. After that, it was a simple matter to locate Sam and befriend him. We got to like him, actually. He's a bright kid."

"Then leave him alone."

Mojo shook his head slowly.

Mike thought about that article in the Denver paper. How Mojo had tricked him. Worse, how he'd tricked Sam. Damn it all to hell, the clues had been there. Why hadn't he made the connection? Everything Mojo knew had been in his letters to Sam. Every detail. "What do you want, Jones? Huh? What is it you expect to gain from all this?"

"You know perfectly well what I want." Mojo stood. It took him awhile to straighten up, but he never stopped staring into Mike's eyes, and he never let the gun waver. He took a step, then another, his body twisting to accommodate his misshapen hip. He moved into shadow, and then a shaft of light from upstairs hit him full in the face. He was ghostly pale and thin, and he'd combed his hair straight back. More a cadaver than a man.

"I gave you every chance," Mojo said. "I told you to pull that trigger two years ago. You didn't listen. I told you I would find you and your lovely wife. You didn't believe me."

"Why don't you just kill me and get it over with? Your quarrel is with me. No one else."

"Ah, but I made a promise. I am an honorable man, Mike. Unlike you, I keep my word."

Mike took a step toward him.

"Uh-uh." Mojo lifted his gun an inch. "Don't even try it. If you're very good, I'll kill Rebecca and Sam quickly, painlessly. If not..."

"Don't you touch them, you son of a bitch."

Mojo's smile disappeared. "It's too late to change my plans now. Did I tell you I had three operations, Mike? They left me to rot in the prison hospital for months. I have you to thank for that."

"I should have killed you that night."

"My point exactly! If anyone is to blame for this predicament, it's you, my friend."

Mike thought about shooting him, right now. It would certainly result in his own death, but wasn't that better than letting Mojo live to kill Becky and Sam?

"I think you'd best put down that rifle."

Had his thoughts been so transparent? Or did the evil little troll just know him too well?

Mike thought again of taking his best shot, letting the cards fall where they may, but then he saw that Mojo had moved closer and was now standing on the long carpet runner.

"Okay," he said. "Give me a minute." He bent his knees and went down slowly, keeping his eyes on Mojo. With exaggerated caution, he held the rifle at arm's-length in front of him. "Just don't do anything foolish. We can discuss this."

"The time for discussion is long over. I—"

Mike dropped the rifle and grabbed the edge of the carpet, yanking it with all his might.

Mojo fell. But first, he pulled the trigger.

The force of the bullet threw Mike on his back. He felt no pain, only shock. Becky, Sam... God, no.

Just before the darkness came, he heard laughter.

Becky couldn't keep the gun steady. Mike was dead or seriously wounded. She knew it. If he was all right, he would have been up here already. That last shot was much louder. Closer.

She reached forward, her forehead pressing into the pillow, until she touched the closet door. She closed it all the way, sealing their tomb. No, she couldn't think like that. She had to protect Sam. If Mojo found them, she would have to pull the trigger. Her aim had to be true. Oh, God, why couldn't she stop shaking?

"Mommy?"

"Shh. We have to be very quiet now. It'll be all right." She should be holding him. He was pressed up against her side and he'd grabbed her shirt, but it wasn't enough. But how could she aim the gun with only one hand? It was too heavy. She couldn't afford to miss on what might be her only chance.

"Where's Daddy?"

"He's downstairs, honey, but please," she whispered. "You have to be still. I know it's hard and it's scary, but you need to be brave for a little while longer."

The computer tilted a bit more and the side jabbed her knee. If there had been even an inch more room, she would have kicked the thing away. Instead, she ignored it. Maybe the tiny light from the monitor was good though. Sam would be even more terrified if it was completely dark.

Why was it so quiet? Maybe they'd killed each other, or maybe Mojo was dead and Mike was hurt and needed her help? He'd said not to leave the closet, but how long could they stay in here?

She knew one thing, Sam couldn't take much more of this.

His breathing was loud and strained. She thought he might hyperventilate soon. He needed something to do, something quiet.

"Sam," she said quietly. "I need you to do something very important." She risked taking her eyes off the closet door, and turned her head. Sam looked so scared, she nearly moaned. "I want you to go to the back of the closet. You'll need to dig behind all those pillows and blankets. Do you think you can do that?"

He shook his head, not even willing to look up at her.

"Sure you can. Put the computer on the floor. Go on."

Sam's fingers released her shirt, and he shoved the computer off his lap. The sleeping bag was in the way, though, and he started kicking his legs. She could feel his panic, and took one hand off the gun and wrapped her arm around his shoulder.

"It's okay, honey. Shhh. It's all right. Calm down."

Her hand was on his neck, and his pulse raced so fast she didn't see how he could take it. There was no choice, though. There was a hell of a good chance that Mojo would find them up here. If he did, she was going to have to kill him. But that didn't mean he wouldn't get a shot off first. So Sam couldn't be right next to her. It was too dangerous. No matter what, she didn't want Sam to see.

She checked the safety with her thumb, and satisfied that it was engaged, she put the gun down on the floor. Then, moving as quickly as her shaking hands would allow, she started to clear a path for Sam. First, the computer went on the floor. She left it open, grateful for the light. Then she lifted one layer of pillows and blankets.

"Can you move in there?"

Sam didn't do anything for a moment. Then, just as she thought she would have to abandon the plan, he scooted to the side to fill up the space she'd made.

"That's great, honey." She reached over him, and pushed some more things out of the way.

Sam took over from there. He managed to get on his knees, and soon, he had moved most of the blankets to the front of the closet, as he crawled to the back.

It was a pitiful measure, with the closet being so small, but it was something. She took one last look at him. He'd brought his knees up tight against his chest and wrapped his arms around his legs. He was as tiny as he could be, a small, helpless kid trying hard to be a brave soldier.

That bastard had no right to do this to her son. No right at all. "I love you, Sam," she said, then she let go of the blankets between them. She couldn't see him now. And he couldn't see her.

This time, when she picked up the gun, her hand was steady. She eased the safety off, and gripped the weapon tightly, tilting the barrel up, imagining the chest that would be her target.

In the darkness of that tiny womb, she knew she could pull the trigger. She could fight like a tiger. Morris Jones had picked the wrong woman to mess with.

She waited. Long, excruciating minutes went by, and she struggled to clear her mind. She could only afford to think one thing: He wasn't going to touch Sam. Then she heard it.

Someone was coming.

Mojo was coming.

He didn't walk like Mike. He dragged one foot, she could hear it clearly. He was in the room now, moving closer to the closet.

She lifted the gun higher, waiting, waiting for the closet door to slide open. Praying the killer outside would disappear.

A high-pitched beep made her jump so violently, she nearly dropped the gun. The computer! There was a red light flashing and the words *critical battery* something were in the middle of the screen, and the beeping kept on and on. It was loud, insistent, a signal for Mojo to come and find them.

She let go of the gun with her right hand, and groped until she found the top of the machine. She tried to shut it, but something was in the way. She couldn't look, she couldn't turn her gaze from the center of the closet door. Moving as quickly as she could, she found the corner of the pillowcase and yanked it free, then slammed the computer shut. Even then the beeping didn't stop. All she'd done was muffle the noise.

The footsteps came closer and she grabbed the gun again with both hands.

The door moved, but oh, God in heaven, it was the wrong side!

Chapter 16

Becky lunged for the door. She pushed against it as hard as she could trying to keep it closed, the gun now a useless obstruction in her hand. She tried to see Sam, but the damn pillows and blankets were in her face.

It was no use. The door slid open beneath her hands. Her balance was off, there was too much in the way. God, he was going to get her baby.

The door smashed into the jam on her side, as she fought for control of her gun. She still couldn't see Mojo, couldn't see Sam. There was no more time. She pointed the gun toward the center of where she thought Mojo would be and pulled the trigger.

The sound ripped through her eardrums, wood splinters flew, her hands jerked back painfully, throwing her against the cushioned wall. The ringing in her head was deafening, and for a moment, she thought she might pass out. Then she threw herself against the closet door again and it fell forward, carrying her with it. She nearly lost her balance, and had to step wide to stay upright. But she was in the loft.

She turned, expecting to see a bloodied body on the ground. Instead, she looked down the barrel of a gun.

"You shouldn't have done that." His words were muffled, as if he were speaking in a tunnel. He looked like a rat turned human. Pale and thin, with a sharp nose and black eyes, he was worse than her nightmares.

"Why are you doing this to us?" She knew she must be screaming even though her voice seemed very far away. "What do you want?"

"Justice," he said. "Vengeance." His mouth turned up in an ugly smile. "Fun."

Becky felt faint. Nothing had prepared her for this. Not Mike's warnings, not any horror story she'd ever heard. He was the essence of evil, and she knew he wouldn't hesitate to kill her, and then Sam. Behind Mojo, she saw the hole in the wall where her bullet had landed. She must have been off by just a few inches. She lifted her gun, prepared to die, but not before she killed him first.

"Think again," he said.

That's when she saw Sam. He crashed into Mojo's legs as if he were a tackling dummy. Mojo screamed, a high-pitched wail, and then bullets sprayed the room as he fell to the floor.

She pulled the trigger for the second time, but this time, she hit him. The bullet smashed into his thigh and he screamed again.

She darted forward and grabbed Sam's arm. "Come on," she yelled, pulling him behind her. The last thing she saw was the blood-splattered yellow quilt, then they were on the stairs.

Holding on to her gun with one hand and Sam's arm with the other, she tried not to fall as she ran. She looked behind her, expecting to see Mojo in the doorway, but there was nothing. She'd killed him. Maybe.

She got Sam down the stairs without hurting him. "We have to get out of here," she said, shouting to be heard against the ringing in her ears.

"Daddy!"

Sam's piercing scream stopped her cold. He pointed toward the kitchen. She turned. Mike's body lay twisted on the hardwood floor. There was blood coming from an ugly wound in his shoulder.

She didn't let go of Sam as she ran. Tears nearly blinded her as she knelt next to Mike. Shoving the gun in the holster, she freed her right hand and touched his face. It was warm. Her shaking fingers pressed his neck, but she couldn't find a pulse. "Mike, get up. Please, get up. Don't do this."

Sam stood behind her, and she heard him sob.

"Sam needs you. I need you." She grabbed his collar and pulled his head up. "You can't die, damn you!"

His eyes opened.

She moaned and cradled his head in her arms. "Oh, God, thank you. Mike—" A crash from upstairs made her practically jump out of her skin. She looked up.

Mojo was still alive.

"Get out of here."

Mike was pushing himself up with his good arm. "Go on. Get out. Now."

"I won't leave you."

"You don't have any choice. Dammit, get Sam out of here."

He looked bad. His face was white, his lips a thin line of pain. How could he fight that madman? He was barely alive. But Sam needed her protection.

She helped Mike to his feet, then turned to their son. "Get to the back door and unlock it. Wait for me there."

He didn't move. He stared at her with his mouth open.

She let go of Mike. When she was sure he wasn't going to fall, she turned to Sam and grabbed his shoulders. "Sam, you have to go. Now."

His eyes focused on her from someplace far away.

"Get your coat, then go to the back door," she said again. "We have to leave."

Sam looked up to the loft. She saw him swallow, then he looked at her again. "Okay."

She closed her eyes as relief poured through her. "Hurry." She let him go, and he raced to the closet to get his coat. In a flash, he was past them again, and in the kitchen. She turned back to Mike. He looked as though he wouldn't make it another minute. There was so much blood. "You can't stay. He'll kill you."

Mike shook his head. "No, he won't. Give me your gun. You take the rifle."

She looked upstairs again. Mojo was still making noise, but he wasn't at the door yet. She ran to the kitchen and grabbed two of the dishtowels from the sink. If she didn't stop Mike's bleeding, Mojo wouldn't have to kill him.

Mike had his arm tight against his chest. When she touched it, his face contorted into a grimace of pain. He let her move the arm down. When she lifted his shirt back, she heard a sharp intake of breath, but no sound.

The wound looked sickeningly bad. There was a lot more blood then she'd imagined. Her stomach rolled, but she didn't stop. It was tricky, tying the two dishtowels together and wrapping them tightly around his shoulder and under his arm. Finally, it was done, though, as tight as her shaking hands could make it.

"I'll be okay," Mike said. "Go on, now."

She reached over and took his good hand in hers. After she put the .45 in his palm, she leaned forward, careful not to touch him too much. She kissed him once, on the lips. "Please don't die."

He gave her a smile. It wasn't a very good one, but it gave her the courage to move.

Her coat was still in the closet. She slipped it on. Another sound from upstairs jarred her into stillness. Mojo moved something big, scraping it across the floor. There was no more time. She had to save Sam. God, she didn't want to leave Mike. But Sam . . .

Moving as quickly as she could, she took a box of ammunition from the top of the closet and stuffed it in her pocket, then she hurried over to the far wall, where Mike's rifle lay. It was very heavy.

She walked back to Mike. His gaze was fixed on the upstairs door, his gun pointing dead center. When she turned, she could see Sam still standing by the open back door, waiting for her to take him outside.

What if she stayed? What if she pointed the rifle at the door, just like Mike was doing? Together, they could kill that bastard, she knew it.

No, that wasn't true. He might kill them both, and then go after Sam. She forced herself to turn away from Mike and walk to the kitchen.

Snow from the open door flew into the house, swirling over the linoleum floor. Becky checked to make sure Sam was zipped up and his gloves were on.

Looking behind her, she could just see the bottom of the staircase. Mojo wasn't down there, yet. But with each passing second she felt their chance of escape growing narrower. "Come on," she said. "To the snowmobiles."

After one last look at her husband, she stepped outside.

The cold hit her like a fist. She gasped and felt the ice burn her throat. They would never make it out of here. She couldn't take it, and neither could Sam. She didn't even know which way to go. "Over there," she shouted, pointing to the lumps of snow that hid the snowmobiles.

Sam started toward the vehicles, moving slowly against the wind. He sank into the snow waist-deep at the end of the deck, and it was incredibly difficult to pull him free, even after she'd put the rifle aside. She was exhausted, and they hadn't even begun.

He was too small to go on. She lifted him, and his bulky arms went around her neck, his feet around her hips. She could barely see. There was no way she could carry the rifle and Sam. She left the weapon on the snow, and moved on.

The steps weren't too bad to negotiate, but when she'd cleared them the snow was up to her thighs. Moving strained all her muscles. Every step was an effort, with the wind and the cold battering her from all directions.

She hadn't put on her gloves; she'd needed her hands free to use the rifle. Now, the ice bit into her fingers with sharp teeth, and she knew frostbite was sure to set in.

She was almost there. Just another foot to go. She turned to look behind her, and saw nothing but the closed door. If she could only get them out of here, she could go to another cabin. They could hide, until the weather cleared, or until she could get help. All she needed was a few more minutes.

Closing her eyes for a second, she took another step. Her foot caught on something big, and with Sam in her arms, she couldn't compensate. She fell forward, turning to her side just in time to get Sam out of the way.

She let him go while she struggled to get up. When she looked down, she saw what it was that had tripped her.

Witherspoon.

Mike struggled to stay on his feet, to keep the dizziness from winning. Mojo had to come down those stairs, and he had to be ready.

It was hard to hold the gun straight. The pain was continuous, a throbbing counterpoint to each breath he took.

At least Becky and Sam were outside. They would get away, that's all that mattered.

Darkness threatened again, that sickening swirl of blackness from deep inside. He fought it, as hard as he'd ever fought anything in his life. He couldn't pass out now. Not yet.

Upstairs, something moved. He didn't hear it this time, he saw it. Mojo was at the doorway.

Mike lifted his gun higher and pulled back the hammer. His hand shook uncontrollably, and he cursed as he concentrated on taming his muscles.

There he was. Blood covered his bad leg—Becky must have shot him. Mojo had no trouble aiming his weapon. The big .357 pointed straight at Mike's chest.

Mike pulled the trigger.

Witherspoon lay frozen, buried in snow, except for the top of his head where she'd kicked him. Becky backed away, turning so she wouldn't see, fighting to keep from being sick.

"Mom!"

Sam's voice pulled her back, and she found him standing in waist-deep snow right next to the snowmobile.

"I'm coming." She stepped over the old man's body and kept on moving. "I'm coming."

Finally, she reached Sam, and she began brushing the snow from the snowmobile with both hands. The key was in the ignition, thank God. She hadn't even thought of that. She went to brush more snow away, and realized she hadn't put on her gloves yet. It scared her that she could barely feel her fingers. She stopped right then, and pulled the thick gloves from her pocket. It was an effort to put them on, and when she did, she hardly felt a difference.

It didn't matter. She had to get Sam out of here. What she couldn't understand is why she hadn't heard anything from inside the house. The thought of Mike wounded and bleeding, facing that man alone, made her sick to her stomach.

She threw her leg over the seat, and turned to Sam. "Grab on to me and climb up." It was still necessary to shout to be heard, but her voice didn't seem so far away now.

Bending to her left, Sam wrapped his arms around her neck and climbed in back of her. He let go, then she felt his hands on her waist. She found the key and turned it. The motor started immediately, and she wanted to cry with relief.

The handles moved, and she tried turning the one in her right hand. That was it. The snowmobile jerked forward, then stopped. She tried it again, this time without letting go. It worked. They moved forward, too quickly at first, then slowly, which was better. She felt very unsure about driving this thing, especially with Sam on the back.

Turning in a wide circle, she headed toward the front of the house and the main road. Maybe she could find Witherspoon's cabin. She could try to get help on his ham radio.

They moved in a relatively straight line, the wind making it terribly difficult to see. She squinted as they rounded the bend, then turned her head to check on Sam. "You okay?"

He nodded.

Then she heard the gunshot.

Mike fell. He landed on his shoulder, and the pain ripped him in two. He heard screaming, and for a moment he thought it was his own voice. Then he heard the thump of a body landing on the floor, and he realized it was Mojo.

He'd shot the son of a bitch. It was over. He turned his head, the pain swelling with the movement, until he could see the body.

Mojo stared at him with the same look, the same evil glare as that night in the warehouse. The bastard was still alive, still moving. Maybe he couldn't be killed.

The darkness threatened again, stronger this time. Mike fought to move, to conquer the pain. He needed one more shot. One more. He lifted his hand. The gun was lopsided, not pointing at Mojo. With every ounce of energy left in his body, he turned the .45.

Mojo smiled.

Mike blew him away.

Epilogue

Becky opened the door to Mike's hospital room. He was asleep.

His shoulder had been bad, and the surgery to repair it had been touchy. But the surgeon had been optimistic. The rehabilitation would be grueling, but Mike was a strong man, and she had no doubt he would keep at it until he was one hundred percent.

She moved toward the bed and noticed Sam's homemade Get Well card on the mattress by Mike's pillow. She put it on the side table and sat down.

The chair and the room were familiar. She'd spent so much of her life in hospitals. This time, though, it wasn't going to end in tears. Mike would come home.

"Hi."

She put her purse down and scooted closer to the bed. "I thought you were sleeping."

"Nope. Just resting."

She smiled. "Sam wants to know when you're coming home."

He lifted his good hand and she took hold of it. "How does tomorrow sound?"

"Really?"

He nodded and caught her gaze. "They don't want me around here anymore."

"I know some people who do."

"Yeah?"

She squeezed his hand. "I think we can do this, Mike. But you need to be certain it's what you want."

He pulled his hand away and found the remote control button. The sound of the bed moving was loud in the small room. When he was sitting up, he reached over and touched her cheek. "I've never been more certain of anything."

"We still have some work to do, you know. I managed to hurt you pretty badly before. I don't ever want to do it again."

"What do you suggest?"

She looked into his brown eyes, at the love and peace she saw there. This was the Mike she'd fallen in love with. The Mike she would love for the rest of her days. "The way I remember it, you asked me to marry you last time."

He grinned. "That's how I remember it, too."

"So this time, I'll ask."

"I accept."

She moved to kiss him, but stopped just short. "Would you really have quit the field, even if you hadn't been wounded?"

The smile faded from his lips. "Yes." His hand came up to her face, and he cupped her cheek. "I almost lost you. Twice. It won't happen again."

"I have something to tell you."

"Hmm?"

"I've always loved you. From the moment I first met—"

His kiss stopped her, but she didn't mind one little bit.

* * * * *

COMING NEXT MONTH

MILLION DOLLAR SWEEPSTAKES (III)

No purchase necessary. To enter, follow the directions published. Method of entry may vary. For eligibility, entries must be received no later than March 31, 1996. No liability is assumed for printing errors, lost, late or misdirected entries. Odds of winning are determined by the number of eligible entries distributed and received. Prizewinners will be determined no later than June 30, 1996.

Sweepstakes open to residents of the U.S. (except Puerto Rico), Canada, Europe and Taiwan who are 18 years of age or older. All applicable laws and regulations apply. Sweepstakes offer void wherever prohibited by law. Values of all prizes are in U.S. currency. This sweepstakes is presented by Torstar Corp., its subsidiaries and affiliates, in conjunction with book, merchandise and/or product offerings. For a copy of the Official Rules send a self-addressed, stamped envelope (WA residents need not affix return postage) to: MILLION DOLLAR SWEEPSTAKES (III) Rules, P.O. Box 4573, Blair, NE 68009, USA.

EXTRA BONUS PRIZE DRAWING

No purchase necessary. The Extra Bonus Prize will be awarded in a random drawing to be conducted no later than 5/30/96 from among all entries received. To qualify, entries must be received by 3/31/96 and comply with published directions. Drawing open to residents of the U.S. (except Puerto Rico), Canada, Europe and Taiwan who are 18 years of age or older. All applicable laws and regulations apply; offer void wherever prohibited by law. Odds of winning are dependent upon number of eligible entries received. Prize is valued in U.S. currency. The offer is presented by Torstar Corp., its subsidiaries and affiliates in conjunction with book, merchandise and/or product offering. For a copy of the Official Rules governing this sweepstakes, send a self-addressed, stamped envelope (WA residents need not affix return postage) to: Extra Bonus Prize Drawing Rules, P.O. Box 4590, Blair, NE 68009, USA.

SWP-S895

ELLEN TANNER MARSH

A FAMILY OF HER OWN
(SE #978, August 1995)

Jussy Waring had been entrusted to care for a
little girl, but her lonely heart still longed for that
special kind of family she'd only heard about. When
Sam Baker came into her and her young niece's
life, would she dare hope that her dream
could finally come true?

Don't miss A FAMILY OF HER OWN, by Ellen Tanner
Marsh, available in August 1995—only from
Silhouette Special Edition!

ETM

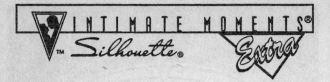

As a *Privileged Woman,*
you'll be entitled to all these *Free Benefits.*
And *Free Gifts,* too.

To thank you for buying our books, we've designed an exclusive FREE program called *PAGES & PRIVILEGES™*. You can enroll with just one Proof of Purchase, and get the kind of luxuries that, until now, you could only read about.

Big HOTEL DISCOUNTS

A privileged woman stays in the finest hotels. And so can you—at up to 60% off! Imagine standing in a hotel check-in line and watching as the guest in front of you pays $150 for the same room that's only costing you $60. Your *Pages & Privileges* discounts are good at Sheraton, Marriott, Best Western, Hyatt and thousands of other fine hotels all over the U.S., Canada and Europe.

Free DISCOUNT TRAVEL SERVICE

A privileged woman is always jetting to romantic places. When you fly, just make one phone call for the lowest published airfare at time of booking—or double the difference back! PLUS— you'll get a $25 voucher to use the first time you book a flight AND 5% cash back on every ticket you buy thereafter through the travel service!

SIM-PP4A

*F*REE GIFTS!

A privileged woman is always getting wonderful gifts.
Luxuriate in rich fragrances that will stir your senses (and his). This gift-boxed assortment of fine perfumes includes three popular scents, each in a beautiful designer bottle. <u>Truly Lace</u>...This luxurious fragrance unveils your sensuous side. <u>L'Effleur</u>...discover the romance of the Victorian era with this soft floral. <u>Muguet des bois</u>...a single note floral of singular beauty.

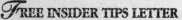

YOURS FREE!

$50 VALUE

*F*REE INSIDER TIPS LETTER

A privileged woman is always informed. And you'll be, too, with our free letter full of fascinating information and sneak previews of upcoming books.

*M*ORE GREAT GIFTS & BENEFITS TO COME

A privileged woman always has a lot to look forward to. And so will you. You get all these wonderful FREE gifts and benefits now with only one purchase...and there are no additional purchases required. However, each additional retail purchase of Harlequin and Silhouette books brings you a step closer to even more great FREE benefits like half-price movie tickets... and even more FREE gifts.

L'Effleur...This basketful of romance lets you discover L'Effleur from head to toe, heart to home.

Truly Lace...
A basket spun with the sensuous luxuries of Truly Lace, including Dusting Powder in a reusable satin and lace covered box.

Complete the Enrollment Form in the front of this book and mail it with this Proof of Purchase.

PROOF OF PURCHASE
Offer expires October 31, 1996

SIM-PP4